THE PAR

A Romantic Family Drama of the

Edward and Kathryn Parker Family

By J.W. Perry

Library and Archives, catalogue in Publications
J. W. Perry, 1942 ISBN 978-0-9914218-0-0

El Dorado Hills, California 95762
916.293.8271
1 3 5 7 9 2 4 6 8

First Printing 2015, Printed and
bound in the United States of America
Second Printing 2016 ver. 19
Cover by the author
Sandpiper Inn, Unit 21,
Holetown, Barbados B.W.I.

ACKNOWLEDGEMENTS

This book would not have been possible without the incredible encouragement and massive sum of patience from my family, especially the head of the family spear, my wife Donna. Her lance prodded my behind frequently with the sole purpose of having this project reach its conclusion, then exercised her tireless editing skills to mold the words into a readable story. My daughter, Elizabeth Laswell, and surprising input and editing from my 95-year young mother, Eva, reinforced Donna's efforts. The discerning contributions from daughter Michele Zumwalt, a published writer in her own right, proved invaluable as her wisdom always provided clarity and direction.

To those who patiently tackled its contents along the way to reform the story into acceptability from 200 to 310 pages, I salute: My friend, General John Gosdin, U.S. Army Ret., daughter-in law, Mary Elizabeth, and my favorite uncle, James P. Merriman, winner of the DFC for bravery flying the Mitchell B-25 for the Marines in the Solomon Islands during WWII.

The last bow is for Toni Seymour Bowes for her encouragement while interrupting her own published works of *Ricochet through Life*, *How to Weave Your Way Through a Brain Tumor*, sure to be a best seller, and her gifted husband Orthopedic Surgeon, Dr. Donald Seymour, for his scrutiny and guidance.

PROLOGUE

Eddie Parker was crushed. He was convinced that his devoted Kathryn was seeing another man. It seemed inconceivable, and if true, would shake the very foundation of the Parker family. After all these years, 'why? *Why now?*' While opening a folder in his email meant for Kathryn, it read like an old co-worker of hers was a lot more than that. Eddie wasn't prying, but simply opened her mail by mistake. The imagery stung, worming through his chest wall, boring through the pulmonary artery into his aorta.

Missed you so indescribably / I miss you so much / your sweet smile / need you more than ever / need you close to me / my special person /you are worth the wait / once in a lifetime!

Eddie's very special Kathryn, his life partner, walking away? Again. Really? They had been through so much together in San Diego, Honolulu, New Orleans, and even sleepy High Point, North Carolina. They had protected their marriage with such savage exclusivity. How could she do it? How long had it been going on? His eyes welled up with restless tear ducts normally reserved for weddings, funerals, graduations, and grandbabies. Eddie wasn't always perfect, but he was dependable and at times very romantic, especially for a 49-year old veteran, salesman, and father. His kids adored him, even though they felt that the sweetness was draining from his spirit, probably his love life to boot. It was an unfair state of affairs for Eddie. Maybe his feeling partly to blame for the death of his best friend became too burdensome; perhaps the letdown of nearing retirement and feeling himself only a pedestrian salesman undermined his ego and libido to the point that he quit caring. His only somewhat selfish therapy was alone time in his airplane, a contraption Kathryn dreaded, would never trust, and learned to hate. On top of this marital development, his cool little grandson, Joshua, was struggling with a mysterious blood disorder, likely to kill, disfigure, and cause him more and more unrelenting pain. Why did this have to happen now?

This guilt of his and Kathryn's bloodlines carrying the devious gene that conspired to target this innocent child, was already weighing in on him. This blame, Kathryn's stunning email, and a frightening war long forgotten, were the devious gravediggers gnawing away at this brave husband's heart. The Parker duo was definitely at cross-purposes in their marriage.

The whole family put Eddie and

Kathryn's slow destruction of what had been a perfect union on the back burner. It would have to wait. Joshua Edward Matthias was the focus now. Kathryn and Eddie were to be joined by their daughter Scarlett and son-in-law Alex, Josh's parents, and their son Michael, his wife Alicia, and daughter Annie, at the Children's Hospital of Orange County. All determined to be with little Joshua to support him through what they had hoped would be a life saving bone marrow transplant. Eddie was making his way in his private airplane to arrive in Orange County around nine in the evening to be joined by Kathryn the next morning.

It was a beautiful November night, starring a brilliant full moon that swabbed the mountain peaks protecting the Los Angeles Basin. The cool mountain air smelled like death as the sienna smeared peaks watched with sadness the rugged terrain swallowing two small airplanes into its brush, rocks and muck. Each carried a single male pilot; each with loving wives, special children and grandchildren; both proficient enough. One, a middle aged ex jet fighter pilot, the other a retired airline captain. One would become one with the earth and die, while the other's destiny murky and painful. One widow would anguish while the other would suffer a different shape of torment. Edward William Parker waffled between the serenity of the clean cool mountain air and the anxiety of an uneasy marriage about the texture of a crumble apple pie. All that became unimportant the instant his cockpit was filled with blinding cold air and bird parts. He had one of those dreaded moments most had read or heard about of their past flashing through the mind's eye just before death. Football, Kathryn, the first time, infidelity, Kathryn, Michael, Kathryn, Aimee, René, Scarlett, Kathryn, fishing, root-beer floats, Annie, Josh, blood, Kathryn, always Kathryn......*always*. The images all sped through his mind. Through his daze and confusion, Parker was helpless as his aluminum airframe now very un-airworthy, tumbled, wobbled and abruptly became one with the mountain. The crashing sounds, earthly debris, and resulting pandemonium became still, dark, and hushed. The mountain had claimed its second victim that evening.

Even so, the world continued to spin, the lights of The City of Angels below still winked with rare clarity. Los Angeles area families had late suppers served on rickety TV trays while watching their television shows, like *High Plains Drifter* with Clint Eastwood, on ABC's *Sunday Night at the Movies*. The members of one family, however, had a different schedule.

Chapter One

*"One can find women who have
never had one love affair,
but it is rare indeed
to find any who
have had only
one."*
~ ~ *Francois De La
Rochefoucauld*

November 22, 1992

It was just a few ticks shy of six o'clock Sunday evening in the Sacramento area. The sun had done its doleful job that day, ducking below the horizon in embarrassment a few minutes earlier. It was a bone cold, rainy, slightly foggy, night-like evening, definitely not an ideal time to crawl into a small airplane. The tedious November evening spun an eerie mist that meandered through the streets and spilled from the Curragh Downs' bluffs along the American River and Lake Natoma spillways without a sound. The rolling fog shrouded the streetlights as if to get warm, causing a reflected brilliance of colors showing off like a heavenly kaleidoscope. Most sensible families were either in grocery stores catching up on firewood and cider, or were tucked in their family rooms watching the early evening news accounts by plucky ABC Television Co-

Anchor Diane Sawyer, of the aftermath of the Gulf War in the Middle East.

There seemed a deafening silence between Kathryn and Eddie on the ride to the rustic Cameron Park Airport, just east of downtown Sacramento and their home in nearby Fair Oaks. The hollowed out airfield was 25 years old, principally developed with surrounding oversized lots and streets to accommodate homes with attached airplane hangers instead of garages. Eddie enjoyed the convenience of being only a few miles away, but he wasn't keen to live there. Too many of the houses were boxy and resale of the nicer homes took forever. At any rate, the convenient location to simply hangar the airplane, for the most part, suited him just fine; Kathryn, not a big fan.

As they made their way north on California's Highway 50, only the squeaky noise of the windshield wipers and the occasional splashing and bump of small potholes filled the void of stillness in the car. The blather of the Bernie Ward program on San Francisco's KGO radio station was the only conversation of significance, serving as a pitiful white noise for the maligned couple. The chill between them was icier and pricklier than the whiskers on an Arctic Seal. The intermittent oncoming headlights revealed an austere chiseled faced woman, hardened by the intimidating marrow transplant for their grandson, an unwelcome yoke to the tension that had been building between the pair over the past several months. Truth be told, the last several years had been less than idyllic for this Type-A couple. Military burdens, Father Time, and predictable divergent interests were all fueling an inevitable confrontation, almost certain to threaten the marriage.

The elephant in the back seat had been there for some time now, growing older by the year. He (or was it a she?) lumbered along behind them, from the car to the house, to the dining table, sometimes even to bed, then back to the car again; pretty much wherever they were. The exceptions were the occasional breaks Kathryn and Eddie managed when they snuck off to Barbados for a week or so. They never missed the rare opportunities to relax, reclaim their 'ideal lovers' title, and defuse most of the issues that weigh on hosts of middle-aged lovers. As therapeutic as those times were, the elephant was always at the airport to greet them when they crept back home.

The e-mail from Chris Riley that Eddie found by accident on Kathryn's computer several days ago, was a simmering menace of seismic proportions to the 25-year, otherwise near normal partnership. The concept of infidelity confused Eddie, and most unthinkable of his woman. Steadfast, loyal, ethically firm, all were woven deep into her character. Traits that drew him to her when they first met. Except for a few stumbles as a teenager, Eddie knew Kathryn to be highly decent and maintained permanent integrity, more so than anyone he knew. Her moral compass always pointed due north. No exceptions. This woman was confusing him far beyond the narrative in the book *Men are from Mars and Women from Venus*. For a long time they knew each other's thoughts, could finish each other's sentences, and rarely argued. Something about her behavior was just too off the wall. And for sure, as soon as Josh was through the worst of his procedure and recovery, she and Eddie had to realign, or they would end up in the ugly ditch of divorcees that clutter the thorny roads of matrimony. Right now, though, they had to focus on the welfare of their grandson and the family, then try to reclaim the magic that brought them together twenty-five years earlier. Kathryn tugged Eddie back into the present as she cleared her throat and murmured, "Are you sure you want to go up in this goopy weather? You can go to Orange County tomorrow morning with me on Southwest, saving us both a lot of trouble. You won't get that much more time with the kids by leaving tonight, and frankly, I think you're causing a lot of inconvenience to me and to them just to be flying that stupid airplane tonight." That, with the tone of a heart saturated in cold black coffee. Eddie thought for just a moment, even considered her offer, but replied, "No thanks. I need some time to clear my head. The transplant isn't until Tuesday afternoon, and it'll still give me plenty of time to see Scarlett and Alex as well as spend some time with Josh before his transplant."

"What do you mean to clear your head? Seriously, you need to clear *your* head? Why you silly old man. You are the one who has been acting peculiar for a long time, and I for one don't like it a bit. Even the kids have commented that you are beyond your usual cantankerous self. Go! Get out of town and let everyone around you clear *their* heads. In the meantime, you need to have a talk with yourself and find out what is making you so cranky. The way you have been acting lately is stink all over itself. No one can stand to be around your sorry butt." Strong words, but no time to argue that just now. The outburst frustrated Eddie; made him really angry. *She* has some serious explaining to do and the consequences of her behavior with Mr. Riley might take more than just a few minutes or hours to sort out. Getting to Southern California early was Eddie's only priority now.

As they pulled up to the small hangar on the east side of the runway, Eddie kissed Kathryn's frosty cheek and thanked her for the ride. She glanced at him with that quizzical look that wasn't a frown and wasn't a smile. She squeezed his hand lightly twice and then coaxed an austere smile, her way of kissing him back, indicating that everything between them was almost okay but needed a lot of work. A slightly softened Kathryn shifted in the seat to look him squarely in the face and offered, "Be careful, Eddie...okay?"

"I promise. I always am." As soon as Eddie closed the trunk of the car to remove his flight bag and small suitcase, Kathryn twisted the car around and vanished into the shroud of the early gray evening.   She left Eddie standing in the shadow of the hangar, dimly lit by a single 100 watt light bulb hanging from a long cloth cord, circa 1940's. He wondered just how long this thing between her and Chris Riley had been going on. He wondered a lot of things. He wondered hard and he worried hard. Eddie reached deep into his psyche and memory to see what would compel Kathryn to risk 25 years of marriage. Things often got testy between them every now and then, but an affair? It is the greatest humiliation a marriage partner could suffer. It was, in fact, a public notice that one or both had failed in a contract so easy to promise, but one or both found too difficult to honor. Eddie folded his arms over his musty leather jacket, leaned back on the front of the airplane's right wing, and thought back.... way, way back.

October 1960 At the University of Texas in Austin, Kathryn was being rushed by the Tri Delts and the Kappas, the cream of the crop of all the ladies sororities at T. U. Some would say they were the best, always near the top in academics, a reputation that Kathryn valued the most. Both sororities had the most beauties, cheerleaders, athletes, and student government officers. I was running for the President of the Freshman Class and enjoyed a baseball scholarship when we met. At the time, I was being rushed by the Sigma Chi and Phi Kappa Tau fraternities, but still unsure about the whole fraternity thing. I was determined to keep my focus on academics, at least for the first year. Taking the time to pledge any fraternity would be hard, especially in the spring when so much time was spent in baseball practice. We had already been working out on the sly, making the best of the Longhorn Phys. Ed. gym by using rubber coated baseballs.

While scanning the barely lit room of a late autumn Phi Kappa Tau mixer with the Kappas, I spotted her. Our eyes ricocheted, lightly flirted with curiosity, then connected. Her eyes instantly shifted to those nearby in her circle of friends, as the electricity ran from my finger-tips to my toes, and hormonal sensitive places in between. She filled the room with her smile and soft manner. Her shiny chestnut accented auburn hair was the perfect compliment to her amethyst tinted blue eyes. I had never before seen eyes that color, nor have I since. They were so alive. Her lips and nose were perfectly proportioned, making her even more striking. The porcelain skin painted her small high cheekbones that enhanced her flawless widow's peak. Her very thick burnished hair covered the top of her ears and disappeared behind her into a twisted curl ponytail that teased the top of her shoulders. She wore a simple knee length pleated skirt and snug V-neck baby blue sweater. The overall package revealed the character of a strong, yet soft young woman. Her slender perfectly shaped fingers longed to be held by a worthy partner and I wanted it to be me, and soon. I was a goner the moment I saw her. Toasted in the purest sense.

Kathryn commanded the room that night, moving politely from person to person, always smiling, always graceful. Her movements were planned and with purpose. She was not skinny, but slight; ample breasts, but not large, statistics that the campus male catalogued. Her neck was elegant as a swan's, milky white and perfect in length. Neither of us had serious previous relationships, not even in high school. In my case it was my shyness, and in her case academics, that earned her Summa Cum Laude honors at Abilene High School.

Kathryn and I were both juggling the business of education while tempting social involvement as we sped from our teens to young adults.

I wasn't sure, but I could swear that I saw her looking my way as she was whispering to one of her girl friends. With more than a little encouragement from my 'babe' savvy pals, I edged her way, chatting here and there so as not to be too obvious. I got so carried away by this stealthy diversion, that I backed into her and knocked the drink right out of her hand and all over both of us. Now that alone was embarrassing enough, but everyone, it seemed, turned to watch me grovel around on the floor trying to sop up the mess with my handkerchief. It was like time froze. The lights were bright, and I felt as if every eye in the room was staring at me - then the muffled laughter. Like one of those slow motion scenes from a zombie movie, all the faces were exaggerated; twisted with echoing voices grotesque that were low and slow.

Kathryn knelt down near me, and whispered, "Don't worry about it, Mr. Parker. Let me give you a hand." Her sweet floral perfume descended on me, attacked, overwhelmed, and caused me a cryptic corporal harm of the worst sort. God in Heaven, I was helpless. "I probably just turned at the wrong time." With that amazing smile of hers, she continued in a clear loud voice that ended the slow motion movie. "At least I know now that I'm not the clumsiest person in the freshman class. Ha!" Noting that she had sufficient interest to know my name, I was encouraged that I might have a chance with this remarkable young lady. With her silly unselfish comment, it was over. The room was neutralized. Everyone's voices returned to their normal cadence and tone to chatter on about the business of trying to impress each other. Unnoticed, Kathryn and I adjourned to the quiet of the small backyard gazebo, and got acquainted.

"Hi, my name's Kathryn Whitmore, and yours must be *the* Eddie Parker." Yep, I was that guy, and a near speechless guy at that. She was folksy, yet clearly intelligent, and in my opinion, the most naturally beautiful girl I had seen and actually had a conversation with. Without being aware of the change, I became relaxed and conversant enough to get through that first night without scaring her off. One topic led to another, and somehow I mustered enough courage to ask her out, even though I was keenly aware of the lack of intellectual and social parity between the two of us. Although I might have been school smart, I was in fact, boy stupid, as most of us guys were at that age.

I wasn't really anxious to go to the mixer that night. School had just started and I was buried under the 18 classroom hours I had chewed off. My parents were stretched financially, so unless a rich uncle died, I wouldn't be joining any sorority, at least this year. Nonetheless, it was a chance to meet some groovy kids, and on that pleasant Austin night, I did just that. The Kappa mixer was with the Phi Kappa Taus, one of the top five of Fraternities on campus; so I thought, 'what the heck.' It was just a short walk from the nearby parking lot just south of the Campus, so I could call it a night after making as good an impression as possible in thirty to forty five minutes. Afterwards, I could be safely tucked in by eleven, and get a good night's rest before my 6:00 A.M. study ritual. I changed into a warmer sweater and pleated skirt that my mom had made; simple, but typical of her perfect sewing skills.

I never complained of my financial circumstances, and thanks to the creativity of my mom and dad, my friends never suspected that we lived on the edge of poverty. They made up with my lack of cashmere sweaters and expensive jewelry with their overwhelming love and support. I would not trade places with any of the other girls on campus who had the fancy cars, finer clothes, and trips to Europe. What I had, money could never buy - unlimited love and intense devotion from my parents.

A simple choker pearl necklace, a hand-me-down graduation gift from my great aunt and a splash of Jungle Gardenia and I was ready to go. I didn't have time to do my nails, but they were always a bit of a mess, so it wouldn't have mattered anyway. My hair was so thick it was what it was; just wavy enough to hang loosely over my shoulders. Thank heavens I washed it yesterday, or it would have been a nightmare to manage on short notice. Tonight it would have to be a wavy ponytail, the easiest. I met up with one of my Abilene girlfriends, then we walked arm in arm down Nueces Street along Fraternity Row to the Phi Kappa Tau House.

As we chatted and giggled along, the evening was still and the leaves on the sidewalk crackled curtly like Rice Krispies when doused with the expectant dose of milk. After only a few more lighthearted minutes, we skipped up the few wide wooden steps and entered the oversized door. An older Phi Tau escorted us to the main ballroom, a room that was crammed with first year men and women, all moonstruck over the prospect of being rushed by their favorite sorority or fraternity. The large cavernous ballroom was still intimate, probably because it was purposely under lit and overcrowded. A not too discrete spotlight, half hidden in the corner behind a well-worn couch, illuminated an oversized rotating crystal ball. Scanning the room revealed the same group of frat 'rushees' at previous parties. Some cocky, some shy, some handsome, and most were just plain.

For reasons I cannot explain to this day, I was drawn to a guy tucked in the shadows of the far corner of the hazy room. I swear that he had a soft spotlight shining from his head to his knees that only I could see. The way he carried himself was like an open book; sure of himself, nice looking, a permanent smile of confidence, and a nice fanny (most girls our age catalogue those things, you know.) I thought he might have glanced my way; I couldn't be quite sure.

I had to check this young man out and satisfy a tingling curiosity. As I started his way, he had begun to worm his way in my general direction.

I caught him glancing at me, even if just for a second, pleasing my puritanical ego. A few minutes passed as I shook hands with several guys, and fellow sorority rushees, while edging further along in his general direction. One girl that I knew from Freshman English, pointed to "that guy", knew his name, and mentioned that he was an All-State baseball player in high school and anointed future quarterback for the Longhorns. In my estimation he didn't look the part, not quite six feet tall and at the most maybe 175 pounds soaking wet. His upper frame was tapered, even through his blue blazer you could imagine a strong build; I think. He HAS to have some muscles if he is a football player. My nasty mind's eye of his fleeting image just out of the shower flustered and embarrassed me. (What is the matter with me?)

    After a few more minutes of small talk, I turned to see where this intriguing man was, then we smacked into each other, firm enough to splatter my Dr. Pepper down my sweater and all over his coat and pants. In an instant, he was on the tile floor trying to wipe the puddle with his pocket-handkerchief while muttering an apology. I suddenly felt his embarrassment more than my own, then realized an unexpected connection. I said the accident was all mine and quickly knelt to help and offered a few comments that seemed to get the party back to normal, giving us a chance to talk. He started to help brush the coke off my sweater, then caught himself, and blushed again; so much his crimson face was visible in the near darkness of the ballroom.

Eddie Parker was uncommonly natural and easy to read. There was ruggedness about him, softened with a silky refinement. He liked me, and me him, at least a little. He asked about me and actually knew a few of my friends from Abilene, probably through sports. Most young men his age wanted to talk about themselves, but Eddie Cross examined me like a witness in a murder trial. I coaxed him enough to know that he liked airplanes, athletics, and unexpectedly, enjoyed classical music. He was taking piano lessons but had to stop because of an injury to his thumb. This hunk of a guy was almost a renaissance man. After I shared the story of my parents, he ducked the details of his parents and skipped to his great aunt, who I could tell he adored.

There was something about his gray/green eyes that held mine. They were piercing and with purpose. He wasn't glancing around the room like the others, but rather his eyes were glued to mine. They pierced through my cornea, retina, and powered on through into my core. The effect was disarming and attracting me more than I wanted or was prepared for. I *quickly said okay to a coke date, and that was the end of my lack of serious interest in a boy. I was smitten and couldn't wait to know more about this understated Adonis. I was surprised that he didn't have a 'steady' and immediately agreed to see him when he asked me out. It started as a date to the local A&W root beer drive-in for an innocent banana split. There I could share my own piano playing lessons and other ditties I held secret. My diary would record the experience as one of the most memorable dates in my young life. I agreed to go out with him, and promised myself not to get too serious. Although, we DID seriously hold hands that night, for when Eddie reached for my hand, he touched my heart. For the life of me, I couldn't figure what was getting into me. It was all so very odd and unfamiliar.*

It began simply as a coke date. The A&W root beer drive-in on 6th street had the most spectacular banana splits, the fancy dinner that I volunteered for our first date in the rowdy town of Austin, Texas, that winter night in 1960. We never left my mustard yellow '57 Chevy that night, and for several nights thereafter. There was much to know about each other, and it served as a suitable hangout to explore each other in the ways of 18-year-olds. We mostly talked and laughed and talked and laughed some more.

On the third date, she surprised me with a soft natural kiss to Roy Orbison's, *Only the Lonely*. That kiss was a perfect kiss. I didn't have an impressive 'curriculum vitae' of experience in that area, but what I felt while in her arms rewired my body's circuits forever. I had moisture on my upper lip, under my arms, and my hormones celebrated in ways never imagined. My brain ceased to function, just as my runaway heart began searching for guidance needed to make her mine. My vital organs were not helping when I needed them most. I never knew what softness meant until then, nor did I really understand the meaning of chemical dependency. Her perfume rendered me defenseless, a sensation I totally and gladly surrendered to. God knew what he was doing when he made Kathryn, and I thanked him a lot, and more than once.

The world she took me to was an unimagined universe. Her smells were more exciting than the smell of a freshly oiled baseball glove and her soft voice more resonate than the roar of 30,000 high school football fans. The gratification of making and hearing the velvety ripple of her laugh was the highest reward I could ever imagine. I could not have her out of my thoughts for more than one minute. When I got up each day, I wondered if she would approve of my wardrobe, and when driving by myself, I felt her void next to me. For the first time I let my imagination pry underneath her blouse and skirt. It was all too much. I was overwhelmed and overmatched. She switched my ego from me to her, and that was okay with me.

As time crept on, a day wasn't worthwhile if we weren't together. She and I became the perfect couple. I knew it was a flawless love, because the way we said each other's names was always special; we knew our mutual feelings were protected in the vault of each other's cloistered heart. I loved her quick mind, her kindness, her feet, and her very soul. My bonus was her wonderful sense of humor. She laughed from way down deep and made me laugh more than I thought possible. Together we indemnified the sanctity of respect and humor, cornerstones that we built our relationship on.

Over time, I learned to appreciate the rich connection she had with her parents Vera and Edgar Whitmore. Having been adopted at birth, she grew up as a child in one bedroom apartments, had most of her clothes made by her mom, and would have qualified for food stamps had the Whitmore's chosen to apply. They were not designed or inclined that way, and made the small income from Mr. Whitmore's modest work pay the bills. Kathryn's whole extended family was of the same mold. They all created fun out of simple pleasures, whether it was a Sunday afternoon surrounding a used piano made to pound out their favorite gospel tunes, or the gathering of vegetables from their modest weed splotched backyard gardens in August. They had more pure joy grilling hamburgers on a Sunday afternoon than my parents ever had on any single day that I could recall.

Her mom added a few bucks to the coffee can by taking in ironing and doing some custom sewing. Kathryn always sparkled like a bandbox, excelling in school because of her loving parents and her own marvelous instincts. She and her parents had a bond and trust I had never seen before. Ever.

Kathryn and her folks moved into a small little rent house in Austin earlier that summer. Kathryn lived with her parents rather than on campus to help conserve their meager resources. Their lack of extra money also prevented her from joining and becoming a rising leader of the women's sorority world. Her dad was a butcher at Piggly Wiggly, enjoying the perks of taking home dated pork chops and pale hamburger meat. When we went out and planned to stay late, Kathryn would casually tell her mom she would be home around one or two. Her mom would matter-of-factly answer, "Have a nice time dear, and tell Eddie, he better take care of my baby. If it's not way too late, tell him to stop in for a glass of milk and a piece of pie." About midnight, Kathryn would find a pay phone, no matter where we were or what we were doing, and tell her mom she was fine and that she would be home soon.

When I did take her to the door at awful hours and peek in, the smell of something from the stove always lured me in, like an ant to sugar. Pre-planned for sure. Kathryn's mom and I had the most fun talks at two in the morning. I nibbled on whatever she mixed with the shredded day old meat Mr. Whitmore had scored and mostly listened to her insight on life, revealing how easily Kathryn became so grounded. Usually, the more disciplined Kathryn smartly retreated to her bedroom to catch up on her sleep, while her mom, dressed in her favorite blue gingham housecoat and I, talked and laughed into the wee hours. I loved her mom from the beginning, as she spun stories not only of Kathryn, but also of her aunts, uncles, and scurrilous in-laws. From all that debris of humanity, it was clear why Kathryn was strong, sure, clear thinking, and adventurous. This bond with her mom and dad became the cement of her moral foundation.

At times, Kathryn's mom would go to the drive-in theater with us, a curious situation as she really enjoyed the movies, but especially the popcorn. She would sit in the front seat while we made the best of the back seat. One winter night, she said, "You 'youngins' quit smooching so much; you are foggin' up my windshield. Hand me that blanket, my legs are getting cold." She knew exactly what she was doing and exactly what we were doing. In her charming crafty way, she was able to put a wet shroud around our enthusiastic petting; for the most part, that is.

We were inseparable that year, making all the parties, football and basketball games; saving every spare minute for ourselves. I loved our bowling dates, but for her it was the ice skating rink. She spent most of the time gliding around me in a circle, laughing at me on my backside, perfectly parallel to the ice. It was a little deserved humility for the only freshman with a full Longhorn Baseball scholarship. My favorite times were when we were studying or lying quietly snuggled together, allowing me to smell her mild floral perfume and be close to her soft flowing hair. Our intimacy and commitment to each other grew strongly, as we became the perfect college couple. Marriage was discussed, but not seriously until the spring semester. As soon as the lilac, mauve, yellow and white flowers of the Crocus yawned up from the earth, we did have that talk. It did not go as expected. That summer at the end of the freshman year, I found a job rough-necking in the oil fields of Western Oklahoma and panhandle of West Texas. A friend of my mom and dad owned a small mobile drilling company that had just won a government core drilling contract, to determine possible suitable sites for underground missile launch pads. Kathryn had planned to work at a local department store, as well as co-presiding over a three-day conference of Young Texas Men and Young Texas Women Leaders. The two organizations were collaborating to find ways to engage and encourage more industries to offer more employment opportunities for young graduates with high grade point averages. Then my thoughts curdled, snapping my attention back to the Mooney™ and the trip to Orange County. I promised myself to focus my thinking on the discipline of flying, and try to forget the next chapter of the mysterious Kathryn Whitmore.

Chapter Two

You never take a love
affair for granted.
~ ~ Robert Frost

Sunday 6 P.M.

As soon as Eddie finished checking his fuel tanks, oil level, and exterior systems of his airplane, he tucked himself into the cockpit of the intimate Mooney. At the same time, 400 miles to the south in Orange County as the sun was dialing back its celestial rheostat, his stepson Michael and his wife Alicia with daughter Annie, turned off Newport Avenue, winding their way through Trabuco Hills to join Eddie's Daughter Scarlett, her husband Alex, and son Joshua. In the backseat, Annie was swinging her high-spirited feet, anticipating playing with her favorite cousin, Joshua. The quaint township of Tustin was nestled in the heart of Orange County, not far from Michael and Alicia's home in Lake Forest, chartered in 1991 from the township of El Toro, a quaint village rooted in the late 1880s. Michael and Alicia purchased their home in 1985 while Scarlett and Alex followed in '89 just before the real estate bubble popped in 1990. As Michael crunched through the crushed seashell driveway and slowed to a stop in front of Scarlett's house, Alicia asked, "When is Scarlett going to pick up your dad tonight?"

"Mom told me that Dad would probably get to the Fullerton Airport around nine o'clock. After he gets the plane parked and tied down, it'll be 9:30 or so. He likes to get in before nine while the controllers are still in the tower. Sometimes the foggy marine layer settles in really fast, lowering the visibility to nearly zero. As good a pilot as he is, the tower is good insurance against hitting that radio tower just west of the airport. When the wind is from the east, the landing pattern takes the airplanes awfully close to the tower. Truth is, the Mooney is getting old, and he doesn't have the newer fancy GPS equipment with a moving map that all his buddies had. Plus he just enjoys talking to his pals in the tower. Anyway, Scarlett will leave here about eight or eight fifteen. That'll give us time to visit with little Josh and family before he goes in tomorrow to finish his prep-work."

Alicia listened patiently. "Why don't you go with Scarlett to meet your dad? He would really like that and you always enjoy watching him come in. Annie and I will even go with you if you want. You know how she likes to see Pops come dropping out of the sky, then running to him on the tarmac to crawl up and onto the wing."

"Any other time Honey, but tonight is a school night and you know how hard it is to get Annie out of bed when she doesn't get a full night's sleep. We need to get an early start tomorrow to get to St. Jo's by eight. Besides, Dad is famous to fart around on the way in and seems to always be fashionably late. Next time for sure, though. You know, Honey, Annie has never been up with Dad, and as soon as we get through Joshua's transplant, I'll bet she would love a short hop over to Catalina. Which reminds me; he keeps promising that he'll teach me to fly, but we just haven't been able to make it happen. In fact, we haven't hooked-up on a lot of loose end plans here lately. Let's go on in before they think we got lost."

Alicia heard the lingering edge to Michael's voice and put her arm on his as the other reached for the door. "Hang on a sec Hon. What's going on with you two? You are crazy about your dad, but you don't sound that way. Talk to me." "It's nothing really, Sugar. But you are right about me being crazy about my dad, but here lately I seem to struggle for his time, and for some reason we never connect. When he does call, it's usually on short notice when I can't get away, so maybe he has given up. He's almost retired; pretty much his own boss now. With his large chunks of free time, we should be able to fix the problem. It's all-good though, Lis. Everything is going to be okay. I promise. As soon as we help Scarlett and Alex get Joshua on the mend, I'll have a talk with him and things will get back to normal. We can plan a fishing trip and capture the magic we had when I was a kid. Just think. If it hadn't been for him, the family would still be struggling to find a bone marrow match for Joshua. Dad's terrific and I just want more time with him, that's all."

Satisfied, Alicia, with her disarming smile, patted Michael's hand and whispered, "I love you. Grab Annie and let's go on in." They climbed the three steps to the porch and watched the motion sensor turn the outside lights on. Guests needed the light to see and bang the old-fashioned doorknocker Eddie had bought in Hong Kong as a wedding gift. When Kathryn and Eddie left North Carolina, it had been consigned to an unpacked box, but when mounted on Scarlet's house, it gave the whole Parker gang nostalgic memories of kinder times in the 70's and 80's.

"Hey, hey. Come on in and have a seat you guys. What took you so long?" Scarlett ushered them in, hugging Michael and Alicia as if they hadn't seen each other for ages. This was always the routine of these two close families, always glad to see each other. Annie and Joshua, even though three years apart, managed to have fun playing together, mostly with dolls or action figures. Annie had always been protective of Josh, and sensed that he was in danger, even as careful as the family had been not to discuss little Josh's medical issues in front of her.

After Alex put Annie down, she headed straight for Joshua's bedroom. The little cousins were closer than most natural siblings and could play happily and quietly for hours. In her sweet tone, Scarlett held out her hands. "Thanks for coming, really; Joshua always likes seeing you guys. Alex and I really treasure your support during this situation." Almost in unison Michael and Alicia said, "No problem, glad to help."

"Toddy anyone? Scarlett found some new Cream of Limóncello at Trader Joes and it's really *yummy.*" Alex with that exotic European taste of his had her buy a full case. "Anybody?" Michael and Alicia held up their hands, him with both thumbs up. As Alex made his way to the built-in bar, Joshua came around the corner, a bottle in one hand and a blanket in the other, with Annie bringing up the rear. Seeing his Uncle Mike and Aunt Alicia, he broke into a stumbled run. He didn't know which to target first, as he was crazy about both. Michael had longer outstretched arms, so he got to the little guy first and had him tossed three feet into the air all in the same motion. Encouraged by Joshua's squealing feedback, Michael could have continued the human ball-toss for hours. Alicia cut in and had her five minutes of hugs and blowing slobber onto his little neck as his infectious little laughter was rewarded with still another slippery kiss. Pretty soon Scarlett turned party pooper, as she scooped Josh in her arms. "Come on Junior, you have a couple of big days ahead of you; it's time for nighty night."

Joshua didn't know much about the first part, but he did recognize the nighty night part. With only a fake whimper, he and Scarlett disappeared down the hall that echoed a soft lullaby soft enough to put an incurable insomniac dead asleep. Annie, without her little cousin, shuffled her way through the big people and found the familiar warm spot in Alicia's lap. She curled up like a baby kitten and was made peacefully content and protected by the laughter of her favorite people. She would steal a few winks as the chatter faded into a dream about puppies and bubbles.

They all nursed their Limóncello for a few more minutes, then relaxed a while before getting topped off. Michael took advantage of the opportune pause of chitchat, and asked, "Does any one here besides me have a feeling that Dad is getting more and more isolated? Lately he has become harder than a New York Times Crossword to figure out."

The unexpected break in the mood was met with shuffling feet, stillness, and nodding heads. Michael continued, "Maybe it's just me, but I feel like he's holed up in some kind of an agitated state? We all recall that for several years after Vietnam, he was bummed out over Mr. Thibadeau's death, but Mom told me that he had gotten over it. We all know the stories of Dad's strong bond with Rene´, not only as a bombardier and navigator, but also as his best friend. None of us has had to endure a loss like that, so who knows? As kids, Scarlett and I had lots of good times, especially in the early years. But to me, he's been drifting more and more into himself these past few years, and most frequently this past couple of weeks. Not that long ago when he took me to watch the Tom Cruise movie, *Top Gun*, he seemed uncomfortable, especially during the scenes of the Goose character getting killed. In the movie, the pilot, Maverick, took a long time to get over the loss of his co-pilot, also his best friend. I am wondering if that might have triggered some buried feelings that he hasn't been able to shake? What do you think, Sis?"

"I am glad you brought it up, Michael honey, since it's been on my mind a lot here lately. I had planned to talk with you and Alicia, but this mess with Josh has had me tied up in enough knots, so I thought it would wait a bit. Alex and I have both noticed a change, just as you mentioned. I think the most noticeable difference for me, started just before we all moved out of the house in High Point, about the same time period you are talking about. I talked just briefly with Mom only the other day, but she always seems to squirm away from the subject. I do know she hasn't been as happy as usual. You know Mom, always up, but she's just not as spunky as her usual self. I don't know how to approach Dad, but sooner or later, at least the four of us, will have to have a 'sit down'. There might be something we can do, even just talking about it might rid whatever is troubling Dad."

Alex Matthias, Eddie's son-in-law, gave his two cents worth, echoing most of what had been said. Alex mentioned that since his ancestry was from the region of Europe that carried the Cooley's Disease, Eddie might have partially blamed him for Josh's sickness. Eddie was a gentleman and wouldn't say anything, but it worried Alex. To a person, they assured Alex this was not true, even though Eddie's side of the family had equal blame for the genetics of the disorder.

Alex had the floor now, and began to talk quietly. "I need to share with you things about Eddie that you may not be aware of. As you all remember and know, I grew up as a child in a Catholic orphanage in Kumanovo, a Yugoslavian town about 150 miles west of Thessalonica, in Greece. You know that my city of roughly 100,000 has a wanderer's identity, somewhat Turkish and somewhat Albanian. At times I am anxious from this lack of identity, as Scarlett can tell you. As kids, our only real fun times were when the nuns took us kids to the annual Days of Comedy Festival, and later in our early teens, to the world famous Kumanovo Jazz Festival. Luckily, I had strong guidance to study and made high enough marks on the National Level Exams while at Goce Delcev High School, to earn a scholarship to Aristotle University of Thessaloniki, where I met Scarlett. What you also may not know is that from the very beginning, Mr. Parker took me aside and spoke with me about confidence and self-esteem, that the power of the soul was ours to enjoy and for our use to empower others along the way. Those simple words, and others from time to time, energized my very outlook on life. Knowing of my shyness, he told me that if his daughter, whom he loved more than his own life, fell in love with me, that I must be a very special person.

"He gave me his unequivocal blessing, knowing very little about my background. Even though he told me that I shouldn't feel guilty about my family genes, partly being responsible for Josh's disease, I still do. He helped me not let it interfere with my day-to-day outlook on life. My point is that whatever Mr. Parker's troubles or behavior might be, please remember that he was and is a good man. He fought for his country and loves you all more than you know. Be patient with him and remember that his resolve should be measured in Mach, not miles per hour, and his character in fathoms, not feet. I think him to be beyond profound and he deserves our kind understanding to try and rescue him from whatever is causing his torment. I can assure you all, that I promise to do whatever is necessary to make him whole and happy."

His last words drifted into a hushed whisper as they became tangled in his thickening vocal cords. They were answered with stillness and a few tears. A minute that seemed like an hour passed before anyone spoke. Scarlett and Alicia sniffed and reached for the tissue box on the coffee table. Michael nodded and Alicia was the first to speak.

Alicia didn't know Eddie as well as the others, but was crazy about him, especially so when she saw the affection for his stepson Michael and her husband Alex as absolute as his love for his natural daughter Scarlett. She saw only the good in Eddie, but did admit that perhaps he was going through some sort of 'mid life crisis'. What did she know? The laughter that Eddie might have aging issues broke the mood and ushered in another round of Limóncello. Alicia was a book smart genius, but sometimes an unpredictable jester whose naivety the family thoroughly adored. She was always full of energy and sparkled like a shiny new dime. Not long after Annie crawled into her mom's lap, she began to make a rattled purr. "We gotta scoot, guys.

This one needs to be in her own bed." Alicia pulled her up into her arms and after some one armed hugs and good byes, made her way to the door, with Michael bringing up the rear adorned with her over-sized purse.

After Michael, Alicia, and Annie piled into their Lexus LS 400, they crunched their way out of the driveway to the streets of Tustin and back to their Lake Forest home. Scarlett locked the front door and plopped down on the couch close to Alex and asked, "What do you think?" Alex slipped his arm around Scarlett and offered, "I dunno Honey, it just seems like there's been a negative aura around Eddie lately, and I find it hard to pinpoint the cause. But like I said before, and as Michael summarized so well, we should give him some time and the benefit of the doubt. His personal and close up involvement of René's death could haunt a man for many lifetimes and may have more to do with his recent funk than we know."

"Good enough; that may be easy enough for us since we don't have to live with him, but I think that's the best way to approach the situation. I'll talk with Mom in the morning and start the ball rolling from her end." He agreed that any resolution should wait until Josh was on the mend. That was both their overriding concerns for the moment. Scarlett smiled, and then pinched in closer to snuggle. With her head on his chest, she teased the tuft of chest hair peeking over the top button on Alex's blue oxford button-down shirt that was hiding the promise of a full clump underneath; the bushy hair that she loved to feel on her own bare chest. While sliding her hand over the pointed end of his breast, she whispered that they might slip into something more comfortable, like nothing. Hand in hand they headed to the bedroom, knowing it might be several days before the mood and circumstance would give them the opportunity they had that night. They would make good use of the few minutes they had before Scarlett would head for the Fullerton airport to pick up her dad.

Chapter Three

*"You have screwed yourselves
into this mess, now
screw yourselves out.
~ ~ Gramps Parker*

Sunday Evening

I reached through the pilot's window and flipped on the master switch to do my routine preflight of the airplane; checking the fuel and oil levels, the stall warning horn, the control surfaces, a warm pitot heat probe, and bright exterior strobe lights including the rotating beacon secured to the belly of the airplane. I attached the tow rod to the nose wheel assembly, then tugged the reluctant 2,000-pound airplane out of its cozy hangar into the light drizzle, and locked the hangar door. The cockpit of the older model 201 Mooney was snug; a bit smaller than the front seats of a '63 Volkswagen Beetle, only 43 inches across and less room front to back. I hopped onto the low wing and opened the only access door to the cockpit. I removed the grey weathered leather flight gloves from my old navy flight jacket, threw them into the passenger's seat, and carefully placed the jacket into the back seat. Both the gloves and jacket were distant reminders of a different sort of flying during a more dangerous and odious time. I squeezed into the seat-belt-harness assembly and closed the aluminum door. Then I turned the starter until the engine reluctantly coughed to life, then was rewarded by its welcome and familiar drone; the Mooney saying, 'okay, I'm running now, so let's get movin'. I flipped, twisted, and pushed switches to bathe the cockpit with a glow of red light and flipped on the landing lights to illuminate the taxiway and runway. I did my takeoff checklist to ensure that I had proper oil pressure, fuel level indications, and full movement of the control surfaces. After hearing the scratchy hiss of the radios and seeing a familiar reading on the GPS, I nudged the throttle forward and coaxed the airplane toward the blue lights of the taxiway. I aligned the gyroscope compass to 130 degrees, the runway heading, and the general direction of my destination to the southeast.

I loved flying, and knew even as a kid, that flying was the life for me. No fireman, doctor, or movie star was in my horizon, just some kind of pilot. As a nine-year-old kid, I clutched the porcelain coated wooden mane of the fiercest looking horse on the carousel at the summer carnival. I felt the rising and falling sensations as I plowed through the skies of 1917 France astride my Spad Bi-Plane in search of German Fokkers. As I grew older, I pedaled my wobbly old Monarch bike, equipped with playing cards attached on the frame near the spokes and made sounds like a motor to the airfield just east of town. I loved watching the reckless crop dusters zoom out of nowhere to land near the end runway, then taxi to the local base storage tanks for more insecticides and fuel. I marveled at multi-engine airplanes as they lumbered into some sort of a landing pattern and screech onto the runway and stop just in time at the far end. In high school, I was jealous of the group of guys that were cadets in the Civil Air Patrol. Even as student pilots, they could participate in searches of missing airplanes. At lunch I would sit close enough to them to overhear tales of their flying lessons and descriptions of the tail dragger airplanes they flew. Our parents didn't have the money for me to join the program, but I always knew that I wanted to be a part of this daring and envied fraternity.

Winter of 1960 - '62 During my freshman year at The University, I took out a $625 student loan and spent the money on flying lessons. My instructor was a gruff old veteran of WWII who reminisced of flying ' The Hump ' in the Himalayas. His air group and squadron dropped desperately needed supplies to the Chinese fighting in Burma at the northern edge of India, as they battled valiantly against the Imperial Army of Japan from 1937 until the war's end in 1945.

He taught me the basics in an old Cessna 150, the usual two-seater used by most neophyte airmen like me that could cruise at a zippy 110 miles per hour. We flew down cotton rows at 90-degree intervals to learn the effects of wind. We did touch and go approaches required to make precise landings a routine event. Finally, on a windy day at Mueller Field just a few miles from Austin, in 1962, my instructor got out of the airplane and stood by the side of the windy runway. No warning.

All alone in my rented little blue and white Cessna, I heard the tower say, "Cessna 5556 Echo, cleared for take off." Just as my instructor was closing the door on the airplane he said, "You are on your own now, Eddie. Good luck and just relax. This will be fun for you." That would be the first of many solos I would make in airplanes that grew in size, complexity and purpose.

Right now, thirty years later, it would be a four-place airplane built in Kerrville, Texas, built not too many years after I soloed as a college student.

Sunday Evening After bouncing the Mooney down Cameron Park's severely weathered taxiway to the north end of the 4,100-foot runway, I pressed on the brakes to a full stop. Then gently throttled up to do a quick check of the magnetos and recycle the prop to get warm oil into the variable pitched propeller. Satisfied, I throttled back, changed the radio to frequency 123.05, and pushed the mike button on the yoke to announce to any evening traffic, "Mooney Two Zero One Tango, departing Cameron Park on runway one three." It was no surprise that no other pilot in the near vicinity replied at that hour, so I urged the throttle forward to the full position, pressed slightly on the right rudder pedal, and with the red glow of the instrument panel as my guide, accelerated into the darkness to my destination in Fullerton. After clearing the airfield, I gained sufficient altitude above the runway to avoid the surrounding foothills, and adjusted my heading slightly a few degrees to the right. I changed my radio to the frequency 128.6 and radioed Northern California Departure Control.

"Norcal departure, Mooney Two Zero One Tango, departing Cameron Park runway one three at two thousand feet, southeast heading, destination Fullerton, one four five degrees, altitude niner point five, requesting radar service, over."

"Roger, Zero One Tango, squawk 4263 and I-dent." I dialed the numbers into my transponder and punched the 'ident' button.

"Mooney Zero One Tango, radar contact. Do you request radar service?" "Affirmative, for One Tango."

"Roger, Zero One Tango. Proceed VFR to Fullerton via El Monte and contact Oakland Center 132.95." I did as instructed, doubled checked my heading, and continued my climb to 9,500 feet. The Oakland controllers could now see my 'blip', a unique shape with altitude and direction information appearing as white letters near the blip image. My blip would remain the same as I would be passed along to controllers from Stockton, to Fresno, to Bakersfield and on into the Los Angeles basin. The climb was slow but reassuring, and at 3,000 feet, the Mooney and I broke through the clouds to a moonlit, star filled sky. The towns below were like fluorescent mushrooms hiding below the haze along California's old State Highway 99, the original asphalt artery between Northern and Southern California.

The slippery Texas built Mooney airplane, the legacy of Al Mooney and pride of Roy LoPresti, was reliable, fun to fly, and even a little sexy. It was built to carry four people and a few pounds of baggage that could be stuffed behind the rear seat. The low wing airplane on this night cradled just me, a 50 year-old veteran of an almost forgotten Vietnam War, father of two great kids, and two precious grandchildren. The evening grew reassuringly crystal clear at my approved altitude, an altitude designed to give me 1,000 feet of separation above and below northbound oncoming traffic. That altitude of nearly two miles high would also keep me clear of the Tehachapi Mountains just North of the Los Angeles basin, in case visibility should suddenly drop. The Tehachapis had their own wilderness spirit, claiming the lives of scores of careless pilots since the beginning of flying machines. Caution was always critical here. Tonight however, the world was tilted on its exact correct axis, the barometric pressure was just right to showcase a beautiful indigo painted evening, pierced only by a chartreuse neon lit moon; it's task for the night yet to be completed. Level and on my true course, my 9,500 feet felt like 95,000 and the moon my new best friend of the night.

The drone of the sturdy Lycoming IO-360 engine humming at 2500 RPM, would nudge the power of my 200 horses by cleverly mixing the perfect blend of fuel mist with oxygen available at my altitude, about 16 inches of barometric pressure in the carburetor's manifold. The cacophony of the Williamsport, Pa., engine was a virtuoso of steel, high-octane aviation gasoline, and shell lubricant. I felt as one with the Mooney, conjoined at the brain, knitted skin to skin, and each of us tamed beasts unsure of when the next adrenalin rush would come.

From time to time, the growing rift with Kathryn spoiled these comforting sounds and airborne pleasures, but for at least the next two hours my world would be at peace. But still, I really needed to talk to Kathryn, and quit tiptoeing around like a nine-year- old ballerina and quiz her about this Christopher Riley guy's e-mail.

I talked with Flight Service through Stockton, Lemoore Naval Air Station, Fresno, and Bakersfield, anticipating the hand off ultimately to Southern California Approach Control. I was now only about thirty or forty minutes or so from landing at the Fullerton airfield, 25 miles southeast of Los Angeles, only a stone's throw from Disneyland in Anaheim. With the outside cool air being directed gently into my face, I drifted back to better days with Kathryn.

Summer 1961 When Kathryn learned that I would be out of town most of that summer at the end of our freshman year, and she would be 'left alone' as she put it, she spoke often of how we should get married; find part time work, and still have a reasonable social life. I didn't see it that way, but I nonetheless couldn't visualize not being with her the rest of our lives. The difference of opinion had caused her to be unusually quiet during our frequent long distance phone conversations. She volunteered little and responded less; the same person only weeks ago that could talk faster than a Texas livestock auctioneer.

During a rare time that we were able to see each other in mid-July as we parked at our favorite A&W root beer hangout, scarfing down our usual banana split, Kathryn continued to be remote. Not cold, but distant, not warm but detached. It was a mood I couldn't quite define and had not ever seen before. She was resting with her back against the Chevy door and the back of the seat with her head down, eyes hidden by the shadow of the drive-in awning. Busy with her banana split, she suggested that we go to my house and watch TV. Ben Casey, the show about a doctor, was her favorite. What was on TV was of no matter to me, since I envisioned more intimate matters.

"Mmmm, I'm not sure that's is such a good idea, since Mom and Dad are out of town, and you know how they feel about us being there alone, and besides, I don't trust us, especially me. It's just too risky and I think we should skip the idea." She didn't say anything for a long time, then, "I still would like to go." Then that, 'pleeese;' her special petition that I could never refuse.

"All right, Kath, we'll go, but I am still not persuaded that this is a good idea." I flicked my headlights for our roller skate server to notice that we were ready to vamoose. After she removed the tray from our car window that had been rolled down halfway, I cranked up the Chevy and headed to my house. Along the way, as Kathryn snuggled next to me, inching the heel of her hand up my inner thigh; my heart started pumping extra hard and other parts of my anatomy were now on full alert. Once we were inside the front door, we managed our way back to the den. We kicked off our shoes and snuggled up on the oversized sofa with our only light the luminosity of the TV. That was more than enough light to guide lips, hands, and legs.

When the phone rang, we must have jumped a foot, and my heart nearly leapt out of my body. It scared the be-Jesus out of me, and Kathryn was so shook up she had the expression of a jailed shoplifter. "Hello. Mom? Oh, nothing, just watching TV. Okay, hang on a second and I'll check." I went to the oversized desk in their bedroom and retrieved their checkbook. "It says the balance as of yesterday was $1876.01." She thanked me, seeming frustrated that she left it at home. Apparently, she had 'treed' a diamond ring at the wholesale jewelry mart in Houston, and wanted to be sure they could cover the check. Dad carried his checkbook, but Mom paid the bills and kept up with the balance as the family bookkeeper.

"You're welcome, Mom. Are you having a good time?" She went on about how muggy it was in South Texas and that a large bag of Texas Ruby Red grapefruit cost only a dollar. My dad was being given an award for his service in the *Scupper Society*, a fraternal organization for retired navy servicemen. He had served on a transport carrier that was attacked by the Japanese in the Solomon Islands during World War II. I always wondered why they waited to give it to him, but then I really didn't care. I think he was a cook or something, and just surviving, to me, wasn't particularly valiant. He and I weren't particularly close, so he in fact, strengthened my resolve not to make that same mistake with my children and have a secure relationship with them no matter what.

"I love you too, Mom. I'll see you Sunday night, and good luck with the ring. Can't wait to see it. Bye now."

"So they are really out of town and the house is ours?" "Yeah, but I don't feel right about moving into the bedroom." My upper lip was now very moist. "Me neither. Now where were we?" It didn't take long for the mood to return, especially with me. As things progressed and at the point we usually stop just short of home plate, Kathryn continued, urging me on and on. I pulled away a bit, reminding her of our vow to give our virginity to each other as our mutual gift after we got married. She pulled my face to hers, and whispered, "I love you more than anything else, and I will not regret making love to you. I mean that." Her eyes had softened and seemed a little moist. The smile was there. "Eddie dearest, based on our little talks, and your determination to wait until we graduate to get married, that may be a while. We have both talked about graduate school, then what? I have just finished my period, so there is no worry about getting pregnant. So, what do you say?"

I wasn't able to overcome the devil that night, and nodded just enough for her to know the answer. We had been intimate for a long time, stopping just short countless times. We were not strangers to each other by any means, but the process of talking about it, the real thing, had me very aroused and disoriented, I couldn't think straight enough to shoot a kid's bow and arrow three feet in front of me. I often thought about how great that moment would be; how complete a commitment it would finally mean. I was beyond talking and could only just hold her tighter. Our young bodies were very prepared for this moment, having been known to each other for so long, would move by their own laws. While the expectancy was exhilarating and full of wonder, I was anxious of embarrassment, clumsiness, and possible regret.

We turned the TV off and were lit only by a bit of reflected light peeking through the curtains of a nearby streetlight. We undressed and grabbed a large quilt my grandmother had made, and covered up. We lay there, together, in the shadow of morality and all that we had been taught about sex. As soon as flesh met flesh, the anxiety turned to anticipation and eagerness. Soon the Wise Creator fit our parts together, as He intended. At least we told ourselves so. The unexpected intensity of pleasure cannot be explained, nor is intended to be, and can never be. You just have to be there.

We were fused together as never before, bound by one purpose and one promise. Our young bodies strained and strained against every principled value we had both been taught, until the relaxing peace that followed. We would have not made a very good adult movie that night, as the replay would only show a shifting quilt that suggested a peaceful couple slowly worming their way into one figure, at peace and without guilt. The recorded sounds would reflect a few strained murmurs, rushed breath, and painful pleasure. The film would have been brief; all too short, for me at least. When our heart rates dropped from their celestial pounding to a rhythmic tranquility, we became still and fell asleep.

I thought after it was over, that this date would be as important as our anniversary or either of our birthdays. She was wonderful, tender, and at times smiling. I wasn't a pro at this sort of thing by any means, and always thought the female wiring was mysterious, as it began to reveal itself during this special time. We clung to each other for a very very, long time, and as for me, I didn't want to ever let her go. Ever. Being tangled up in her hair and stuck to her with dried perspiration all over my face and shoulders was like being in the womb of life itself. The smooth surface from Kathryn's lower buttocks to her lower back was the inspiration of Michelangelo, I was certain of it. I was sure I didn't injure her, but just before we parted that night, she revealed that her amazing amethyst blue eyes were covered with a vaporous mist. A tear even... a tiny tear, maybe. I tugged her face closer to mine. "From happiness, Dear Eddie, from pure happiness." Christmas came early for me that night; a wonderful tattoo that was inked to the inner chamber of my heart.

When Time Stood Still The following day, we both went back to our summer responsibilities, she to another Leadership Conference in Nacogdoches, and work at Yaring's Department Store when in Austin; and me back to the panhandle of Oklahoma and the grimy work of my Failing Mobile drilling duties. A few weeks later, as we were enjoying our usual weekend call, the earth began to liquefy beneath my size ten work boots. I began suffocating from the inside out. Kathryn had met someone at one of her conferences, and she became attracted with the male presiding leader from Stephen F.

Austin College, a Jared Penrose. He fell for her like I did, and being more anxious to get married than I, won her hand, at least for a while. My heart felt like a giant fist had found its way around it, squeezing harder than I could bear. My spirit had just been seriously flogged. I was gravely flattened, especially after us sharing that special night only a few weeks earlier. I wondered why she was not secure enough with her decision to tell me in person? I wondered if she had known this when we were making love? There was more but I couldn't put my finger on what was going on in her mind. Had I inadvertently done something? Or said something? Christ, what was happening to me? To us?

As time crawled by that summer, I stayed in denial, and commiserated with her mom, as she just as dumbfounded as I was, if not more so. I lost 20 pounds from not eating and the unrelenting grind of 12-hour days rough-necking. Her dad wasn't a happy camper either. It wasn't too much later that I learned that she was pregnant. Another blow below the belt, so very unbecoming of this baffling young woman. I still couldn't believe what was happening to me. It was so surreal. My trust system had been compromised; shattered like a crystal vase dropped from a ten-story building. I guess I wasn't a man after all, since I was told real men didn't cry.

She and her new husband moved to

the sleepy town of Nacogdoches that fall semester to continue their studies at Stephen F. Austin. This quaint piney woods town of East Texas, would be the birthplace of their new son, Michael. Boy, she didn't waste any time in that department. It allowed me to get fuming mad at her, though not easing my wounded and slowly scabbing heart.

Occasionally, Kathryn's mom would babysit my younger brother and sister while I was grinding through the last weeks and months at The University. As the semesters passed by, she described a slow deterioration of Kathryn's young marriage. Her mom didn't go into a lot of detail, as Kathryn would not have wanted her to, and I sure didn't care to know. I felt helpless and deeply saddened. Conflicted that I might imagine her free again, and then again, so what; she deserved it all. Deep down, however, I knew no one deserved to be mistreated or abused, especially someone like Kathryn who grew up in a world of kindness and gentleness. I dated around, but Kathryn was always the standard that none of the other beauty queens or class leaders could quite match. She was on my mind, seemingly, all the time.

Summer 1961 *As a child I always had my way and was pretty much in control of what I did and where I* went; that is until I met Eddie. The guy disrupted my college and social life in a most unexpected way. As the summer of '61 unfolded, I envisioned a small but tasteful wedding with a few friends and family. We would find a small apartment near the campus and both get part time jobs. We wouldn't have much time for activities, but that was okay; we had each other. For some reason, Eddie didn't see it that way. According to him, we had plenty of time, and we could both pursue a full college experience, each living at home with our parents. We would be together for sure, but just not like I envisioned. Not fully enough, though.

While moderating a Student leadership seminar in Austin in late July, I met my male counterpart who would not leave my side. I liked the attention, but it gradually moved in another direction. He wanted to be my steady and actually proposed to me. "Love at first sight", he said. Why I didn't mention Eddie to him is still a mystery to me. The urge to settle down and be a student wife was more powerful than my love for Eddie. That was my rationale and explanation for being stupid. I was going to have control, and this guy was my ticket. His family had money and I could have the things that the other girls had. My selfish person was rising faster than a loaf of yeast bread. So .... I agreed to follow him to Stephen F. Austin University in East Texas to be his wife.

The control I expected was just the opposite. I became a prisoner to a freakish family, suffering in silence, but determined not to crawl back to Eddie. He wouldn't have me for sure, and at least if I could stick it out for four years, I would have a degree and could get back on my feet.

Still I owed Eddie. He taught me deep affection, tender love, and unselfish devotion. When I sat in the car at the A&W drive-in where we had our first date, I felt a strange notion of making love to Eddie. Thinking maybe for him to be the first, maybe for him to change my mind, and maybe just to have his baby. That would be the best outcome, since he would have no other choice but to marry me. Another mistake. A promise broken, a mistake I would never repeat.

September 1964 After I graduated from Texas at end of the summer with an engineering degree, I headed to Pensacola, Florida, to begin living my dream of flying on and off aircraft carriers for Uncle Sam's Navy. I wasn't discouraged that over 30 percent that entered the program would washout because of medical screening, mostly for not having 20/20 vision; and a few just not up to the Navy's rigorous standards of flying skills. There was always the specter of 'washing out'; pressure that some couldn't cope with and thus became the victims of their own fate. My modest bit of flying in the little Cessna came in handy, giving me a little edge at the start of the program. It was pure fun for me, and very energizing just to be part of these elite fliers.

As the weeks drifted by, I began to enjoy some of the benefits of Florida panhandle living; especially traveling nearly every other weekend to New Orleans to enjoy a small three room apartment on Dauphine Street in the French Quarter. Two other squadron friends and I rented the apartment for $120 a month, so the monthly 40 bucks was a cheap weekend, a great alternative to the expensive Roosevelt Hotel on Canal Street, or the Conti Hotel in the Quarter. Since the others seldom took advantage of their share of their available weekends, it was like having my private getaway, allowing me to govern the French Quarter till the early morning hours, spending lots of cozy time with the gal who helped me find the apartment. The three-hour drive from Pensacola through Mobile, Pascagoula and Gulfport was plenty of time to be reminded of Kathryn, especially when I heard our favorite songs like Roy Orbison's *"Only the Lonely"* and Buddy Holly's *"True Love Ways."* The nagging memory of better days with Kathryn continued to haunt me off and on, and at the most unexpected times. The waft of Jungle Gardenia perfume from a pedestrian on Bourbon Street, a female shape from behind that was like Kathryn's, the Texas fight song, or a movie plot where the girl does the guy dirty. I tried to write her a time or two through her mom, but as my Sheaffer fountain pen dug deeper and deeper into the paper, I just couldn't. There was still too much rage, plus the inappropriateness of the whole idea in the first place.

I often wonder what Eddie is doing now? Probably chasing beautiful rich girls in bikinis from Austin to Pensacola Beach or wherever... When I talked to Mom the other night she said as much, and frankly, bully for him. At least one of us will be happy. If he could only see me now. In a trailer house ironing my snotty husband's shirts, with a two-year old child on one hip while burning pork chops that smelled up our place like a fumigation treatment. The worst part is taking crap from not only him but his weird family, too. Why didn't I see all of this dysfunction coming? I am carrying 18 hours and going year round to graduate as soon as humanly possible, so I can get away from this dreadful place. I've lost at least 10 pounds or more, and even hate the thought of eating, probably the reason for my new crop of facial acne that is stubbornly unfazed by any and all lotions, even prescribed ones. I felt desperately ugly. Darn, here the creep comes now, chubby little Jared, a proper toad now, probably to give me the forty dollars allowance to buy groceries and baby food. This always provokes a scene, as he doesn't have a clue how much just the formula and baby food cost. I get another five, then finally ten dollars that still is shy a sack of hamburgers once a week. After the 'discussion,' he will go to his precious church meeting while I do his and my homework. He resents my 4.0 GPA against his 3.2, a full point higher than he could do on his own. Oh Eddie, I miss you and just wish we could somehow; somehow start over. It is so unfair to hear the songs we cuddled to at the drive-ins, and unfair to smell your favorite cologne on some other guy in one of my classes. UNFAIR!

February 1965 Aimee Brion was a Cajun through and through. Jet-black hair and clear olive skin with a figure one only sees in Playboy Magazine. It didn't sink in until later, but she was absolutely striking, stunning, out of this world, a ten plus, untouchable; all still not even close to describing her beauty. If she were auditioning for a movie part, I could imagine her demeanor and strong body language signaling to a would be producer; "don't talk to me about the casting couch buster, or I will park this high heel a mile up your saggy cheeks."

We met in a musty bar along Highway 98 about halfway between Pensacola and Ft. Walton Beach, just before Valentine's Day late one Sunday evening. Wintertime was tough on the local bars, with just enough traffic to pay the rent. Patrons were mostly from the disenfranchised that otherwise wouldn't be allowed in during the busy summer months. The lights were not real bright in the smelly near deserted bar, but the gal I offered to buy the Whisky Sour was soft on the eyes, even in near dark. I was pretty sure she would survive the coyote test; little did I know...

She was visiting her stepfather for a few days, then was going to head back to New Orleans the next day where she lived. The jukebox was plowing through its cache of 45-RPM Rhythm and Blues records, as were most of the bars along the miracle mile of beaches along the Florida Panhandle. Aimee and I hit if off, neither trying to impress the other, just curious and restless. Both of us were dumped by our not-so-significant-others; just drifting and burning time with the faceless thinly numbered patrons listening to Wilson Pickett and James Brown. We danced to the slow songs punctuated by the sound of clicking billiard balls and shuffleboard pucks. We were immediately drawn to one another by our circumstances and the kismet of the dance floor. She made me laugh again and I suddenly felt confident that I could probably get interested in another. Before we parted, she bumped and rubbed my belly with hers, them smiled for me to know that it wasn't an accident. Her soft parting kiss felt like a tsunami; wet and as powerful as a solar flare. It wasn't hard to connect the dots, as my personal parts jumped smartly to the ready. Kathryn Who?

I had to go to work the next day, as she was heading west, back to graduate school at Tulane. When I mentioned my apartment in the French Quarter, she knew immediately where it was, only blocks from her own pad. I got her phone number and promised to call the next week, just as soon as I knew my flight schedule. With the lousy weather that time of the year, we had lots and lots of time together.

Only days later, we were propped on our elbows facing each other on the bed in my apartment. After an energetic two-hours of non-stop love making, we finally talked. She was toying with my ear, tracing it like it was the first time she had ever seen one. With her bangs stuck to her beautiful forehead and her top breast areola peeking out of the sheets still anxious and ready, she smiled and whispered, "Eddie, tell me about your Ex." I lifted my eyes to hers. "You tell me about yours." "You first." "Well, Aimee, she was my first real girl friend. Her name was, um, I mean is Kathryn."

"The first time is always the worst, Eddie. What else?" "You're telling *me*. Well, I think she wanted to get married sooner than I, and she just found a guy at a convention in Austin and that was that. The crappy thing she did was to let me make love to her only weeks before they were engaged. It was like a brick to the side of the head; totally emasculating. I was crazy about her, and I thought she loved me just as much. I still feel like a schmuck." "You got to be shitting me."

"Now what about you? What's your story?" "Mine is a little like yours. I was a cheerleader at Tulane and my guy was a basketball player. Not a star, but he was the cutest and endowed like a mu ..... well you know." That made her blush and hide her head under her arm for a minute. We both laughed as I looked under my sheet and shrugged. 'Oh well, you can't be perfect,' I thought. I got a little flushed at my own 'little Eddie's' humble proportions, but she seemed not at all disappointed with our recent erogenous circus, so I fell back into the conversation.

"Problem was, Eddie, that's all we had. Just sex. While we had little in common, I learned he had no interest in a serious relationship, so we just coasted for a while. Over time, I let myself get too attached. Then he moved on, bored maybe, or just the type that liked variety. It still hurt though. It hurt a lot. What about you? You the type that chases variety or are you a one woman man?"

That caught me by surprise and I had to think. I really didn't have an answer. I thought about her. She was easy to be with, and so damned gorgeous, not to mention the sex. "You know, Aimee, I am not sure, but I think I might be a one woman man. I think it'll take a while for me to really know for sure. Let me ask you the same question. You a one man woman?" It got quiet for what seemed like a long time. She looked away and said she wasn't sure either. "I really like you Eddie, and like the whole navy bit. Sometimes I wish I were a guy so I could do the same thing. Athletics not so much, but flying those fast assed jets and landing on a carrier sounds like the top of the mountain for fun. For us, maybe we should just enjoy the moment and see where it leads. Right now, let's concentrate on another round. But I have to tell you. I like you a lot, Honey. Really a lot." "I'm up for that Aimee, well kinda. You gotta give me a few minutes, you know to catch my breath." With a smile as wide as the Mississippi River, she shifted my way and kissed me and at the same time challenged, "Okay Flyboy, but don't keep a girl waiting." Her amazing kiss got me back in the mood faster than either of us had expected. We laughed, then got down to business. Nice and slow, knowing deep down it might have to last us both a long long time. We dated for several months, both of us happy as pet rabbits and busy as wild minks.

Then I met René Thibadeau. That changed my life, Aimee's life, and for certain, René's life forever. In addition to the pleasures of the Crescent City, there was plenty to do during my free time in and around Pensacola. I played on the Pensacola Naval Air Station Goshawks football team as a quarterback and punter. We were composed mostly of other aviation trainees, while our coaches were Naval Aviators with college football backgrounds. We even had our own private squadron, flying in the morning and practicing or playing football games in the afternoon or evening. Between flying and playing football, I still managed to find other activities to round out my fun. Once we had to evacuate as many of our airplanes as possible from the Naval Air Stations in Pensacola and nearby Brewton, Alabama, to Tallahassee, as a precaution from the damaging winds of hurricane Betsy. The co-eds at Florida State University must have had a spy in Pensacola as we were met at the Officer's Club by two girls for every aviator, the same ratio of women to men at the school. Parteee time. Then there were the dingy Tiki Bars sprinkled along the sugary white beaches from Pensacola to Panama City loaded with wives of Aviators who were out of town or overseas. My roommate was selected to serve as an escort for one of the finalists of the Miss America contest in Atlantic City, an assignment I just missed.

Then there was the New Orleans apartment, a place to rest and relax...sorta. The lifestyle was sooo good. I even thought that I might have been wrong about being a one-woman man. As such, the invigorating lifestyle was putting a healthy distance between my fun and the less frequent memories of Kathryn. I felt liberated and was having a ball as an Ensign in the U.S. Navy learning to fly really cool airplanes with the unbelievable perks of Northwest Florida.

November 1965 This wonderful lifestyle began its surrender when Mrs. Whitmore called and mentioned that Kathryn wanted to see me during the Thanksgiving holidays. She and Michael had moved back to

Austin with her folks after having been physically abused by her husband. Apparently, she had been verbally abused regularly, but a smack in the face was the last straw. It only took Kathryn a day to drive to the courthouse and file for divorce. After the last Goshawks football game of the season, we got a break in our flight schedule for the Thanksgiving holidays. The 14 hour drive to Austin went by quickly by as I flipped back and forth between aggravation and anticipation. I tried to imagine what she looked like. Older? Puffy? Skinny? Was her hair long or short? Maybe dried out and like straw? As beautiful as I remembered her? Why should I care how she looks? How would she explain being intimate with me, then breaking my heart? Why did she really want to see me? I stopped only to pee and refuel the entire drive back, grabbing only a tube of summer sausage, a box of crackers, and two bottles of Delaware Punch soda for sustenance. For hours and hours, I wrestled with all the possibilities. Would I take her back? Would she be whiny and easy to leave for good, or what? The pain was returning, echoing the feeling of five years ago when she casually told me she had fallen in love with another guy. What a mess. What a mess indeed

Chapter Four

"As for women & affairs during
their lunch hour, I've never
met a woman in my
life who would
give up lunch
for sex."
~ ~ *Erma Bombeck*

Thanksgiving 1965

After catching up on my sleep at Mom and Dad's, I shaved my humble twenty four year old stubble and took a long shower. I moved slowly into the morning, not at all anxious to have this get- together with Kathryn. Late that afternoon, after watching the Detroit Lions upset the Baltimore Colts, broadcast for the first time in color, I rolled into the downtown parking lot not far from the Varsity Theater, a familiar hangout for us both. There were lots of memories in that theater, good ones. I spotted the car, her mom's old '56 Buick parked in the back corner of the lot with no other cars nearby. I approached from the opposite direction and when about 10 feet away eased to a stop. She was slumped down in the seat with the collar of her tweed wool coat pulled up to her ears. She ever so slowly turned my way as I turned off my engine. Even though it was overcast a nd near dusk, she managed to have on a pair of Lana Turner sunglasses to hide what I might see of her face. This was very mysterious for Kathryn, usually straightforward and direct, no matter the situation. Kathryn had mentioned that she wanted to stay in our cars and speak through the car windows so we 'couldn't touch'.

She went first. "I don't trust myself to be any closer than this, and maybe you can't be trusted either, she sobbed." She tucked some hair behind her right ear, and continued. "Eddie please hear me out and let me finish before you say anything. First of all, thanks for coming. I know you must be furious. I would not blame you if you were. I was in such a rush to get married... I made a stupid foolish mistake, and really paid for it. I should probably thank Jared for being so manipulative and cruel or I probably would have stuck it out. You know me, always determined to 'do the right thing.' I knew that before you and I made love that night, I would probably marry this guy, but I wanted our intimacy to be remembered as my first time. You deserved that much. I did care about you, loved you dearly, but somehow waiting years to get married was overwhelming. I never quit loving you. I accepted the treatment and evil I got from Jared as my daily punishment for being such a dope."

She blew her nose, wiped away most of

the tears, let her mascara wash below those dumb sunglasses, and went on. "My impulsiveness was so contrary to the way I always had conducted myself. The way I was taught and the way I will want my children to live their lives is not the way I behaved. I was foolish and naïve. How my thinking overcame my love for you is a mystery and is still a puzzle to me. Someone once said that 'sometimes the bright lights of love are so intense that it blinds the eyes of good judgment'. I am living proof that this is so. My love for you was and is that intense. It is not only blinding, but like a magnet that draws me to you, no matter how hard I try to resist. Remember, I am still married, but here I am. I have just left and am divorcing my husband, and I would understand if you can't forgive me or don't care about me." The word husband stung hard.

"When my divorce becomes final I would like to see you again. I do still have a small shred of decency in me, but it is only for respect of the vows, not him, that would have me wait. The deceitful part of me wants to get out of this car right now and crawl into yours, and into you, never to come out again. Can you still love me, Ed, someday maybe?"

With all the time on that drive to Texas, I thought about what I would say in this situation. But now, when it mattered, I was mute as if someone had ripped out my voice box. I was caught off guard with her honesty, but still hammered with the notion that she had spent all this time with someone other than me and to have just had a baby with someone else. I just didn't know... She looked so pretty, even though she was ten feet away in a parked car. Her eyes never really connected with mine, but then I knew she wouldn't look me in the eye, because those amethyst tinted blue eyes always betrayed her heart. So what was really going on with that spirit of hers?

She dropped her chin on the bottom of the car door window frame and finally peeled away those piteous sunglasses. "Say something, Eddie, just anything." I was looking down at my steering wheel and noticed that my hands were so tightly wound around it, my knuckles were as white as Central Texas cotton. I managed to at least relax my hands and think for a second before I answered. "I can't deny that it is great seeing you, Kathryn, but a lot..... a lot has happened. I've changed a bit. I really need more time to think about it all." By now I felt that fist around my heart again, and it began to squeeze hard enough to coax a few tears of my own from their manly hideout. By now I was blowing *my* nose, clearing *my* throat, and wiping *my* forehead, all with the same hankie. After taking a minute to regroup, I managed to try to sound as normal as possible, and replied across the pavement to her.

"Right now, at this moment, I am having such a conflict of feelings spinning around inside of me, that I can't define it as love. My insides are as twisted up as they were when you told me you were going to marry someone else, then promptly have a baby. For a very long time, I woke every day feeling the disappointment and betrayal. I cried real tears more than once. My soul cried every day for a long time, Kathryn. Until this very day, I haven't been able to find finality or peace. Over time I managed to heal a bit. I finished UT with good grades, and right now I am having a great experience learning to be proficient in really fast airplanes. Even while dating some pretty neat girls at Texas and in Pensacola and New Orleans, you were always the standard by which they were judged. Now this. All this is a bit much to get my arms around. Part of me wonders if you really care, but maybe you just want a 'bounce back guy' to marry, once your divorce is final. My left-brain is screaming for me to run like hell, while the right is highly attracted to the idea of getting back together. I just don't know."

"It's fair what you feel, Eddie, but there's no rebound with me. I have always loved you. Every day I thought of you and wondered why I was so stupid. I don't know why I didn't trust my heart, a disgusting mistake I regret and one I will not make again, with you or anyone else. That's a promise. Jared's love was controlling, demanding and sometimes cruel. For all the wrong reasons, I tried to stick it out. He never ever knew love, especially a love like ours. The only good from all this is my precious little Michael, who is the source of any strength I have left. He has been my rock through this horrible mess and gets me through each day. Eddie, I can only hope you can forgive me and that you will see me once more before you have to go back to Pensacola. Come over and see Mom and Dad. They have their hearts set on seeing you, and you must meet Michael. Please, please? Tomorrow afternoon, okay?"

Those riveting and determined eyes started misting again. It just wasn't fair. My brain was screaming one thing and the heart another. Was it love or hurt that was hammering my soul? Sweat was worming down the back of my neck into my shirt like I was in the Sahara Desert with a long sleeved wool turtleneck.

My first inclination was 'no way, not on your life'. To see the result of another guy's sex with Kathryn flew all over me. The thought of reconnecting with Kathryn meant I would see this child as a reminder of Jared for the rest of my life. I didn't feel grown up enough for it. I didn't have a clue of what to do. Then the heart took over. Somehow I got just enough air to brush my vocal cords for a weak, "okay".

"Great." That's all she said as she started the car and drove away, looking back at me only once. She might have correctly assumed that if she lingered, I might have changed my mind. Her unsure use of the stick shift and resulting jerky departure made me chuckle a bit inside.

I didn't dare tell my folks where I had been, or where I was going that next afternoon, for that matter. They would have been furious with me had they known. As ambivalent as they were to most of my college and navy social activities, they were really hard on Kathryn when she left me. Nonetheless, I drove to and sat in front of the modest Whitmore house and gathered all my courage to peel out of the car and shuffle up the short sidewalk to the front door; more courage than to climb into those loud jets loaded with bombs and 6,000 pounds of flammable jet fuel. That was easy compared to all this.

I rang the doorbell of the small two-bedroom house in the 3700 block of old but quaint Kerbey Lane, a house that had been all too familiar with me only a few years earlier. The little house was framed between West 38th Street and Jefferson, modest like all the others in the area. All were small and accented with very old shrubs and trees; most lacked care. Lawns were worn to mostly dirt and the sidewalks cracked and unfit for bicycles or roller skates.

Kathryn floated to the door and hugged me like nothing had happened. She still had that signature smile, but that evening I saw crow's feet embracing her eyes. The softness of those lips brushing my cheek and sneaky perfume that I had always hated to adore, caught me flat footed. At that point I was convinced that my gray matter had vaporized into a pea soup colored jellyfish and my mind was joining my emotions to become a whirlpool of conflicted senses. I was silly putty, but didn't bounce. I just made a splat. She sported a knee length navy blue pleated skirt with a matching thin polyester three quarter length sleeve, and a powder blue sweater that sagged a bit over her collarbones. I wasn't quite prepared for all that, but then I seemed never to be prepared for her, and now, all this emotional Ping-Pong. She nudged me into a small room where her family was huddled. Her mom and dad were perched on the side of a small bed, hollow eyed and pale. The house was, for me, way too warm, but I am sure they thought it just right. The bare windows were smothered with the moisture of condensation, dribbling down to the sill below to mingle with the summer's dust. Maybe it was just me. I am sure it was me. No, it was very warm. It could have been a hundred degrees, but in their present state of mind, they wouldn't have noticed.

Seeing Vera and Mr. Whitmore felt good though; natural like. After shedding my heavy wool Navy Pea Coat, they greeted me like I was somehow magical; able to return the peace that had been stolen over the past four years. Their grim smiles reflected hope and comfort. I had to remind myself that they too had become victims, watching their pride and joy suffer so, as they themselves felt Kathryn's pain each and every day.

My eyes reconnected naturally with Kathryn's mom. Her hair, usually coiffed to perfection, was a quick set French Twist, the hurry up style she preferred for family and friends. I answered her faint smile with my own. "Mrs. Witt, you look ornery as usual, and how I have missed your sweet potato pie and fried okra. And Mr. Whitmore, I have still not mastered hand carving of the ball inside of a cage you tried to show me. In fact, I can't even carve just the ball. You know me; all thumbs. Hopeless as can be. It's great to see you both. I wish I hadn't just eaten, or I would have to raid those leftover Thanksgiving goodies I can still smell." I fibbed a little, for I could not have eaten even one bite of her magical sweet potato pie. My insides were just too overcome with hordes of oversized moths and other ill-tempered bugs.

The aging Whitmores were gracious and seemed maybe a bit more relaxed after a few words were exchanged. One then the other wanted to know all about the Navy, about the airplanes I was flying, and all about Florida. They envisioned beaches and cheap orange juice, with the truth that my first winter in Pensacola had the awful aroma of paper mills, and more often than not, cold and rainy, unlike the postcards that spun around the drug store carousels in Austin. They expressed concerns for my safety, but buoyant that nothing had happened to me, 'big strong Eddie'. I gave Vera a reassuring hug, her return hug I thought I might not be able to recover from, and a warm two-handed handshake from Mr. Whitmore. His father taught him to squeeze the hardest as he always had done, but on this night, it was just right, signaling that we were equal men with equal burdens. His eyes were those of a dad with his only daughter in distress, and no way to help her.

We made more small talk as the Whitmores extended me the courtesy of not bringing up Kathryn's unfortunate situation. We discussed their kinfolks, my parents, TV shows, the weather, and even Buckles, their prune faced Pug, who delighted over being confused with the more famous bulldogs.

They all had been crying. Everyone's eyes suffered with the flushed hue of highly sensitive people allergic to the dust of torment. I am not sure what they expected from me, as I felt that same helplessness. I always knew that they were the gentle and generous people of all the brigades before them that carved out humble livings and spawned the great legion of leaders and workers of our generation. They were such good people, and didn't deserve their pain.

In the somber haze of their weakly lit home, Kathryn looked tired and gaunt. The circles that surrounded her eyes were offsetting. I could only imagine how unhappy she must have been. She appeared at least twenty pounds lighter than I remembered. She looked more like a thirty something year old woman that worked in a soup factory, than a vibrant 23-year-old college student and mother. Her nails were worn and ragged, unlike the perfectly manicured nails that I caressed many months ago. Still radiant enough to make me take a deep breath though, especially after she gave me that brush of a kiss on the cheek.

I felt more upside down than ever. Across the room was a picture of Kathryn with Jared and the baby, the only one of the three with a smile. Then there he was, little Michael, tucked in his comfort blanket with his thumb deep in his mouth and his forefinger resting just below his eye. Wow, he was small for his age, slight of build for lack of hearty foods that I am sure the Whitmores were already working on. I'd lay odds on the little guy getting fat as a pig and would fill out to fit his three and a half years in very short order. He had Kathryn's auburn hair, pointed chin, and high cheekbones. Thankfully, he didn't have any striking features that favored his dad, only the small dimple in the middle of his chin. Maybe the resemblance would develop over time, who knows? Oh, me. What to do?

He was in the corner taking us all in, not three feet tall. I turned and pointed his way, then he came to me on his little bowed but steady legs. He was cautious, but seemed to want to get closer. I leaned down to him with my elbows on my knees and hands outstretched. He climbed the couch to get up close, then plopped his head in the crook of my shoulder and played with my shirt buttons.

I could see out of the corner of my eye, Kathryn leaning against the wall with her head slightly tilted, watching ever so intently, holding her breath as she watched the two of us. When Michael looked up at me, he just grinned, then plopped his head back down on my chest. He was so light, like a feather. I was shocked for him to feel good, really good. Over the past few years, I learned to cry without tears, and had to recall that skill again when the little guy and I stuck together.

I felt ambushed on so many fronts, but that night it didn't feel all that bad. I might even learn to get fond of Michael. Kathryn wiped away a tear, but this time not in fear, but of hope.

After a few minutes more of talk about the bad navy food, and other subjects that drifted further and further from my memory and interest, Kathryn and I retired to the front room and talked a while, as Michael and the Whitmores busied themselves in the back bedroom. We sat opposite each other on matching love seats, sizing each other up. I can't remember exactly what was said, mostly of the training I was involved with, and very little about the miscreant she had married. We concentrated more on the positive such as the good times we had enjoyed not long ago and the fun she had with Michael; how his personality glowed above the darkness of her marriage. In spite of her dreadful experience, Kathryn still managed to make straight A's and work part time, all the while doing most of the duties required of raising Michael.

I kept thinking how gaunt she looked, like someone just released from incarceration, or worse. Her teeth were uneven and seemed over sized, pulling away from her gums that had been shrinking from malnourishment. I pitied this, and tried not to let it affect my feelings. I ignored her current state, replacing it with the picture of her before we split, vibrant and alive with fun and energetically looking forward, only forward. I was so attracted to her, it was hard to think straight. She repeated that she still loved me, always loved me, and just made a terrible mistake. I might have told her that I loved her, I don't know for sure.

Overwhelmed and out of my league in the realm of love, I thought it best to move on. It was getting late, as I could hear little Michael getting fretful, probably needing to be in his pajamas and put into in his little twin bed. I stood, and apologized that I should get going. She agreed. As she retrieved my coat from the closet, I noticed Kathryn's familiar Bible she had received as a gift when she graduated from high school. It was open to the book of Hebrews, chapter eleven, where verse one was underlined in red. It was clear that she was leaning on her faith; hope anointed with confidence. She was a tough one, and with or without me, would survive her situation stronger and wiser. I wrestled with the contradiction of her decision making; devout to a higher power, but still capable of such an impulsive act to marry this guy she knew for only a short time.

We agreed to stay in touch just by phone, until she was legally divorced. Only as friends, which we did. I crawled into that oversized coat, wriggled my unsure fingers into my fur lined leather gloves, told everyone good-bye, and promised the Whitmore's that I would call from time to time; which I did. As I drove away, I noticed the curtains of the living room were parted slightly, as someone watched me disappear into the darkness. It was little Michael, and I could swear he was giving me a tiny thumbs up.

Summer of '66 As winter sped through springtime, Kathryn and I talked more and more frequently. She wanted to know about each training flight and when I would call again. We talked mostly after eleven in the evening to take advantage of the cheaper long distance rates, talking into the early morning hours. After each call, she sounded more and more alive and stronger, as her cheerfulness was vastly uplifting. It was a real kick when she answered the phone with her cheery, 'Oh, *hi.*' I was so naïve, it never occurred to me that by talking with her as I did, it drew me closer and closer to her, as I seemed to her. She told me about the funny things Michael did, and of the goings on in and around Austin. I learned that the great All-American footballer at Texas, Tommy Corbett had visited Austin on a recruiting trip and had bumped into her in one of the department stores. She mentioned me, and he had actually heard of me. He must have remembered the nice piece the Austin American Statesman did when I was accepted into flight school. I wished I could have played a few downs against him. Go figure. She told me that she shared with her folks the essence of our calls, as they were anxious to hear all about me and what I was doing. Our late night calls gradually dismissed every reason of us not getting back together. We laughed at silly things, an early habit we enjoyed when we first fell in love. As the months wore on, I realized there was just no way I was going to let her go, and thoughts of marrying her crept into my thinking. I was never surer, and never more scared at the same time. One thing led to another, and I finally asked her to marry me when her divorce was final. At first she was quiet, causing me to think maybe I had misjudged us. Finally, I heard a whispered 'yes', then a firm 'yes'. She had been 'crying with happiness'.

We set the date for early July, just weeks before I was to get my wings, and tastefully a few weeks after her divorce was final. We would reconnect; this time for life, and made the ultimate contract, the vows of marriage. Serious promises. My folks thought we were nuts, while the Whitmores thought we should have done it a long time ago. But then, what about Michael? It all makes one ponder about the Grand Puppeteer and the way He creates such a unique patchwork of events to His purpose. Maybe time will reveal His ever-increasing interest in our little

Parker family.

She flew to Kingsville with a chaperone, an old friend from High School and college, who just happened to be a Justice of the Peace and Baptist minister. We had dinner together, he bunked with me, while Kathryn stayed at the Peddlers Inn just outside of town, all fine and proper; her idea. Kathryn had begun to put on some weight, and looked finer than ever, driving me crazy to be with her, in the biblical sense.

We married in the Navy Chapel on the Kingsville Naval Air Station Base, while Michael spent a week with Kathryn's parents, fatter and filled out just as predicted. Our honeymoon was a two-day weekend on Padre Island, near Corpus Christi. The Beachcomber Motel was a cheesy little 22-room strip motel just a short walk to the beach. It would not have been any more meaningful had it been the Ritz in Paris, as it was all about us, and only us. We dipped our souls into a mutual pool of an aromatic bonding cement. We added another vow almost hourly; promises never to break. It felt so natural to wake up with her nearby. The lovemaking was just perfect. It was all about loving and pleasing each other. It was about being as intimate as possible and never letting go. I couldn't imagine being away from her ever again. She made me feel so perfect. I was confident that I made the right decision to marry this girl, who evolved into my lovely auburn haired queen. We were bound together as if wrapped with invisible piano wire. My take on the night was summarized by one of Frankie Valli's recent hits.

'Oh, What a Night; Hypnotizin, mesmerizing me. She was everything I dreamed she'd be. Sweet surrender, what a night! I felt a rush like a rolling bolt of thunder spinnin' my head around and taking my body under. Oh, what a night!'

We lived a short while in a smallish teepee shaped A-frame apartment near Kingsville costing a tidy 110 bucks a month that included ten dollars extra for Michael. I guess they thought he would poop on the floor or use a lot of water, I dunno. A child discrimination lawsuit if I ever did see one. It featured a small cottage sized spiral staircase leading to our small loft bedroom and a diminutive swimming pool Kathryn took advantage of nearly every day, transforming her gaunt girlish looks into a tanned beautiful woman. Ten pounds heavier and no circles around the eyes. Just perfect, even better than before and she was mine.

The quaint little apartment was so small that I had to sleep on the stair side of the bed, as Kathryn preferred that I be the one to tumble down the stairs in case of an episode of sleepwalking. We had no air conditioning up there, but who noticed.

Downstairs, an old-fashioned swamp cooler soothed Michael, sleeping quietly in our little bungalow just below the window, the best place in the apartment. It was here he discovered the sinful habit of raiding a refrigerator in the night. We were always short of fruit, cheese and hot dog weenies. He would make a fine Dagwood in that area.

On a rare Saturday day off from flying the Navy's sleek F-11 Tiger, Kathryn and I were laying on our backs sun bathing together on a large beach towel in front of our humble abode and hand built swimming pool. The tube-style bathing suit, with her in it, did not resemble a tube. It was more like an hourglass. I scooted up close to her and put my head in the nape of her neck. I immediately felt her hand come up and comb my hair with her nails, which felt so divine. She turned us on our side facing each other and she had big tears in her eyes and was shaking. "Honey, I have been so scared, you don't even know."

"You are safe now, Sugar. He or any part of his family will not hurt you any more. Ever. You can take that to the bank."

"Oh, Eddie, that's not the fear. I can handle them, no problem. They're just a bunch of intellectually and socially challenged redneck bullies. My horror is that you wouldn't take me back. I still have nightmares over that. Have had for years. I still can't believe that we are here, together and happy. It's almost too much." With that she finally smiled. "And by the way, Eddie Boy, you had better be careful in those dumb airplanes or I will *kill* you."

"Baby, somehow I always thought we would be together, especially when your mom told me that all was not roses in East Texas. I never let myself have a serious relationship, mostly because no one even came close to you. I am with you because I love you, and just so you know, it is endless. I took our vows seriously, especially the 'until death do us part,' part. You can take that to the bank." From that day forward, she didn't have any more nightmares. We turned back over to get more of the afternoon sun. While Kathryn had a pretty good tan going, I was white as a bed sheet, as the hot Texas sun swathed my exposed body with the color of a new fire engine by day's end. Putting on my flight suit and other skin tight gear had special challenges for a few days after that. As July gave way to August and August threatened September, the United States Navy concluded that I might be useful as a Naval Aviator. On August 25th, the Commanding Officer of Training Squadron 26, awarded me my coveted Navy Wings of Gold. With that achieved and with Kathryn and Michael at my side, I felt like the luckiest guy on earth. At that moment in time, I was indeed that guy.

While sitting in the parking lot waiting for Eddie, the thought of seeing him after an eternity would be super scary. Anyway, I was getting a divorce and going to have my wonderful Michael, regardless of what had happened with Lieutenant Junior Grade Eddie Parker. I never thought he would agree to see me, much less come by the house. To think I could dream of this guy every day of my married life argued with reason and respectability. I suppose that the heart has its own agenda, and I hoped Eddie's heart would have the same as mine. I had done some selling at Neiman-Marcus to mostly older vanity starved women, but that night meeting Eddie I needed to sell my butt off.

I could only see him from his chest up through the car window, but he looked like Steve McQueen, even better actually. He was so handsome, so DAMNED handsome. My insides exploded to see him, especially when he gave me a little smile. My brain was screaming for me to run to him, get in his car, make passionate love to him, plead his forgiveness and never leave his side again. At least, after pouring my heart out, he agreed to come by to the house and say 'Hi' to Mom and Dad. When he agreed, I was a basket case. Michael was messy from playing in his favorite dirt pile; still frail from the last few weeks of frenzied East Texas divorce drama that he endured with me.

The house was stuffy, poorly lit, and probably smelled like fried pork chops and tomato soup macaroni. When he wiped his feet and came in, I couldn't stop my self and pushed my luck with an innocent promise kiss. At that moment in another time and place, I would have ravaged his body and never let him out of my sight. I was such a mess; my brain and heart were traveling around the world at the speed of light in opposite directions for a head on collision. The heart was saying 'now. Now.' And the brain 'wait. Wait.' I was totally out of control. The Super Collider in Waxahachie had nothing on me.

Eddie was so sweet with Mom and Dad. So polite and so sincere. He toyed with Michael, and I had hoped so much, that they looked at least somewhat alike. It was so damn dark, I just couldn't tell. God he was so handsome and strong. What was I thinking? His voice was deeper and he had grown his hair a little longer, just long enough to sport a small curl that rested just above the right eye. Like Clark Kent, but a better version in my opinion. His beard was not fuzzy anymore, and that had an arousing effect. Well, hell, everything about him was an erotic pistol pointed straight at me. I was still a mess.

Before Eddie gathered his coat and gloves, I felt a slight connection just before he left, enough for him to agree to phone from time to time over the next few months and see what might develop. When we talked, usually late at night, I couldn't get enough of his airplane stuff, and suffered with him when a squadron mate was killed or kicked out of the program. He wanted to hear all about my late night job at the newspaper, shuffling copy back and forth between the reporters, editors and the copy room. Each phone call was always upbeat and positive. My mood stayed positive, buoyed by the fewer and fewer calls from Jared, and then only to hand the phone to Michael. The little guy really didn't understand much of Jared's short conversations; he just looked at me or looked all around as if bored to death. After a while he quit calling altogether, which suited me and made my life so much cheerier.

As much as Eddie loved flying, the briefing, flying, and debriefing every single day became a grind. He reminded me that once in the fleet, that would be the job, whether flying mail to and from bases or aircraft carriers or even combat. Although a grind, Eddie wanted no less. I wanted what he wanted. I mainly just wanted him.

Our conversations became more and more personal, and it wasn't long before we realized that we were meant to be. The icing on the cake was his strong interest in Michael; his behavior, his likes and dislikes and all about his motor skills and bathroom habits. Without really trying, I think Michael sealed the deal at Mom and Dad's old house last November when Eddie came by. I was amazed and profoundly affected by this man that agreed to marry me with a four year old from another marriage. I was so impressed with his love and overpowering devotion, I vowed to never leave or quit on him, no matter what. I was the luckiest girl on earth. I *promised myself not to trip up; ever!*

Spring 1967 After an all too short of a honeymoon, we collected Michael and made our way to San Diego for my training in a replacement air group squadron, flying the dominant F-4 Phantom. A few weeks later I was assigned to Fighter Squadron 154 attached to the USS *America*, an attack Aircraft Carrier of the Seventh Fleet. We trained in and around the Miramar Naval Air Station just north of San Diego for several months of ordinance training, close formation-flying, night bombing techniques, as well as re-qualifying for carrier operations, night and day. It was here I was reacquainted with my Radar Intercept Operator and back cockpit companion, René Thibadeau, my old friend from flight school. René's night vision had deteriorated to below Navy Pilot standards, so he had to bow out of the flying part of the Navy, but qualified as a rear seat navigator and bombardier. His role was just as important as mine, just different. With him behind me, we would grow closer than if he had his own airplane, plus I could do a better job of looking after him. Seeing him again was like finding a long lost friend, a kindred spirit through and through.

He and his new wife and my old 'friend' Aimee Brion, now a Thibadeau, became permanent fixtures for Kathryn and me. As best friends, we spent every free day possible with each other. I told Kathryn all about 'us', and she totally understood. She confessed she would have done the same if she had been in my shoes. René and Aimee were fun and full of life, and like us, optimistically happy. They were their own perfect couple, just like the two of us. We talked for hours about how we were always going to be friends and do everything in our power to live close to each other. We four couldn't have been happier or closer those months of 1967 and early '68.

Kathryn and I had fully discussed this very dicey profession. She was aware of my love and passion for flying, my need to be part of a patriotic responsibility, and my understanding of her fear as a loving wife. I promised to be careful, and she promised to be brave. I got the better end of the discussion, but still nervous of the inevitable fear she would endure for months on end. My own fears would be infrequent, but on occasion, they would be of absolute terror making minutes feel like an eternity. My boy stupid logic decided that the fear in both of us averaged out.

In late 1967, René and I hauled our few personal belongings to the aircraft carrier USS *America* for our first tour of combat duty. Before we shoved off to the Gulf of Tonkin, Kathryn and I were blessed with our beautiful daughter Scarlett, under the watchful and protective eye of five year-old Michael. He was so proud of his sister, impatient to hold her as much as Kathryn would allow. When he did, he patted her head gently, radiating an unconditional love from such a young little guy. I was so proud of him. I suddenly was an instant family man, headed into harm's way to begin a journey I could never have imagined.

The *U.S.S America* was wrapped with red, white, and blue bunting around the flight deck, as men and officers formed a line behind the decorated deck. Most of our seventy plus A-7 Corsairs, F-8 Crusaders, and F-4 Phantom airplanes, were squirreled down below in the hangar decks. On the carrier's deck, though, a handful of each model was neatly grouped; showcased for the families and dignitaries to serve as a reminder of the grim work that lay ahead. As the time to shove off neared, the 500 officers and 4500 enlisted men were saying their good-byes. The married were strewn along San Diego's pier 12, embracing for the last time until the ship's scheduled return nine months later. Some nose to nose, some just wrapped together as close as possible, a few in prayer and some in intimate conversation affirming that he or she would return home soon. Sailors and pilots vowing to their loved one, that as much as they loved their country, they would do everything humanly possible to return in one piece. In spite of the entire Navy enlisted and officers' assurances, with the rousing Navy Band blaring patriotic music as the ship pulled away, some of the wives would be widowed, and others consigned to being a partner of a wounded spouse needing frustrating and burdensome rehabilitation for months or years. Planes shot out of the Vietnamese skies, shipboard fires, and accidents on the dangerous flight decks would claim scores of lives; leaving parents, wives, siblings, and children adrift in an uncharted ocean of life without the buoyancy of their loved one. It was my intent, not to be among that group.

The most wretched day of my life had to be watching MY husband and love, Lieutenant Edward William Parker, climb the long switchback gangplank onto the America's flight deck. I stood on the pier squeezing Aimee's hand so tight I am sure she had to be in torment. She too, was a mess, and crazy in love with her soul mate, René. I knew it was part of the guys' dream to be going, but it was our nightmare to watch.

Eddie's daily training flights were

dangerous enough, but now he was going to be shot at. He was a very good pilot and all things being equal, he should be okay, but being shot at made the playing field very uneven. I could only hope and pray that God would be merciful, and return him home to me; whole of body and sound of mind. Our relationship had a rocky start, but we had such a perfect outlook if not for this wicked war. I couldn't stomach the thought of losing him or having him seriously hurt. I pleaded to the Author Of Life to please, please keep him safe. I made every promise known to man for God to protect him. My tears joined the tears of hundreds of other wives and loved ones on the San Diego pier, splashing in harmony with the same hopes, as the ship slid away from the pier then became smaller and smaller until it disappeared into the Western Pacific. I wonder what he was thinking just now?

Chapter Five

"Great love affairs start with
Champagne and end
with tisane."
~ ~ Balzac

Sunday Evening '92

When the evening clouds released the moon's light, the brilliant lunar reflection did the Moonwalk on the nose and along the wing of the airplane. A minute later I was abruptly summoned back from nature's splendor, with a call from Bakersfield Flight Service instructing me to contact Southern California Control.

"Bakersfield, Zero One Tango, leaving your frequency now for one thirty four point two. Thanks for the service." I punched the frequency stored in the audio panel and checked in. "Zero One Tango with you at niner point five and one four five compass for Fullerton." The new controller gave me a new electronic transponder code that identified me. As I left the flat San Joaquin Valley behind, the moonlight sketched the charcoal outline of the Tehachapi Mountains that surrounded the Los Angeles basin.

I radioed Flight Service requesting a 360-degree turn for a speed check. After having me 'standby' for a few minutes, they radioed back that my request had been approved, but to expedite the turns due to descending airline traffic in the Burbank vicinity. I was pleased and acknowledged compliance. By then I had passed over the first ridge of mountains just southeast of Bakersfield. I had just installed a new Garmin GPS that gave airspeed far more accurate that my old equipment. I hadn't told Kathryn about the $3,000 goodie, just yet. As soon as I do tell her, she will likely head straight to Nordstrom's, and in a nanosecond, charge up to the St. John Knit's on the second floor.

My speed check turns would be at 90-degree intervals, with one minute on each heading. After each turn, the speeds would be noted and averaged to remove the effect of the wind, and reveal the true ground speed at that altitude and power setting. I really didn't need to do all this with the accuracy of the new GPS, but it's an old-fashioned habit and fun to do. I was in no hurry, with plenty of time to get into Fullerton in time to 'howdy' the controllers. Already on a southeasterly course, I turned to the South to record the speed for the first minute. As the Mooney eased to the right and leveled off on a heading of 180 degrees, the full moon was just above my nose and right in the middle of my windshield. It was bright to say the least, really bright. After jotting the speed on my kneeboard, and just as I was getting ready for my next 90-degree turn to the left, I noticed what appeared to be an irregular shaped blot emerging from the center of the moon. Before there was enough time to say, 'Rorschach Test', the image got very, *very* big. Too big!

8:45 P.M. It happened so fast. Bird Strike! Usually, a bird would normally only crack the canopy glass, rarely making it into the cockpit. This night, the large bird crashed completely through the Mooney's 3/8's inch thick Plexiglas™ and into the cockpit. Before I could get my arm up to shield the blow, my eyeglasses were twisted off; my headphones just vanished, while my entire face was plastered with guts, bones, and feathers. I was dazed and temporarily blinded long enough for the airplane to continue a wobbly descending spiral, finally skidding into the side of the Tehachapi Mountains. Thankfully, at my altitude, I wasn't that high from Mother Earth. Another thousand feet and the Mooney would have bored into the mountain like a 400 pound Maverick missile and likely exploded or crushed like a 7-up can. Even so, the Mooney tore through dense rough brush with small trees, finally coming to an abrupt stop, fairly level, nose down at a 30-degree angle. When the awful noise and thrashing in the now smaller twisted cockpit finally ended, I wondered if I was going to burn to death, bleed out, or slowly freeze to death.

My left wing was mangled, having absorbed most of the impact. I was deliriously happy to be alive, although I was squeezed even more so in this reshaped enclosure, more confined than ever. The root of that left wing had punched into the side of the airplane, pining my left foot under the rudder pedal. There was no way I was going to get out of this mess without help. I fumbled into the elastic pouch mounted just below my side window to retrieve my small, but bright penlight. The master switch was still on, confirmed by the whine of the gyro that was still spinning. For a minute, I thought I could get my left arm high enough to flip the switch to the off position. I was so squished up, no matter how hard I tried, I just couldn't quite reach it. Maybe in a few minutes when I could take better stock of my situation, I'd try again. I really needed to get that switch off to preserve the battery. I needed power to use the radios and transponder; however, I mostly needed some time to clear my head. I felt like I had just survived ten rounds with an angry Mike Tyson. The GPS would also come in handy, giving me exact coordinates to relay to whomever I could make contact with, that is, as long as the battery had life. My knee-board was still intact, so I had all the frequencies needed to broadcast specific emergency calls in addition to the 'May Day' calls I could make with my transponder. But for now, what a mess. Then my stomach dropped. My family. Kathryn. I promised to be careful, and now look at me. She is gonna kill me for sure now. After Vietnam, I thought nothing could ever hurt me. Really wrong.

There was not a lot to see out of the left window, but brush, a dirt wall, and airplane parts. I pulled another brighter penlight from my left shirt pocket, pointing it to my right revealing a jagged hole where the Plexiglas window had been and a buckled right wing. In the distance, I could make out a faint glow of lights, probably a small town. My view straight ahead was the jagged hole where the turkey-sized bird had made its entrance into my face and lap with only heavy brushwood beyond. The canopy was now more crowded with mangled parts of a disfigured conifer bush, and the remains of that big assed bird. Thankfully, it stopped just at the top of my instrument panel, but on the other hand, it would have been nice to see what was ahead. The full moon did cast a modest glow that was just a whisper of filtered light, but not enough to really help. There was just too much debris for much light to get through to me.

The first sound other than the slowing whine of the gyroscope was one reminiscent of my great-grandfather when he was trying to scare me with his false teeth. In this case the teeth were my own, which were clattering like dancing dominoes. I was as cold as the proverbial witches teat, uncontrollably shivering as proof. Smart me, with a blanket and my leather jacket in the back seat that was for now, going to be a challenge to retrieve. I never thought myself to be claustrophobic, but I was nearly there. This was scary, and I was helpless, hurting, and dependent on the FAA's air control system to find me. But then could they see me tucked discretely under the bushes of the Tehachapi Mountains?

The unwelcome menagerie of odors in my new little world was just wrong, like the familiar scents of the ocean air and the unwelcome stench of rotten shellfish. I wasn't sure if I my nose was stuck in a pile of weeds, or up the backside of a soggy bear's behind. The answer was a heap of mud and plant debris all around me, adorned with black feathers and miscellaneous bird parts. Most likely a very large condor or nearsighted eagle. Whatever it was, it made a nasty mess. It would probably be just my luck to be arrested for defacing a natural forest and killing a protected national bird. I wiped my face the best I could, but I was hopelessly stuck with the stench and the goop.

The taste of blood was my own, I believe. The slick, salty taste was coming from my scalp, dripping slowly down my forehead like the sap from a New England maple tree in the winter. As hard as I tried to size up my situation, I was still as unsteady as a college freshman suffering through his first hangover. Even to heaving a couple of times. My left hip, noggin, lower back, neck, left ankle and ribs hurt like hell, and I couldn't move much. I must have banged my head against the steering yoke. So much for all the seat belt and harness protection. The moon was *not* my friend.

It was cold, really cold. Just as I would move in and out of a fuzzy dream, I would have to pee, and then the new cold damp crotch would keep me from drifting off again; another cockpit odor to join the brush, the eviscerated bird and the mud. As hard as I tried, even with my willy out, I still found a way to get wet. Good thing I had a light lunch and no supper, or I would have been in a real stink, literally. I was weak as the scalp kept bleeding, not heavy, but the trickle a nuisance nonetheless. Not in great shape. I was wedged in the now smaller cockpit, halfway between my back and side, tangled in the steel tubing and aluminum that held the airplane together. I was one with Mother Nature's finest fauna and flora. I had some optimism with the reflection of the moon on what was left of the Mooney's silver wing, my view from out of the small window to my right. It might help any search efforts, if there were any.

The Mooney felt pretty steady as I tried to rock back and forth to test its stability. I had one small comfort of not smelling gasoline. Surely the Emergency Locator Transmitter would be activated and send the radio distress signal to overhead flight traffic as it was meant to send. I was concerned that the jolt wasn't severe enough to flip its switch, as the Mooney more or less made a controlled slide. My thinking was so goofy, I couldn't remember if the ELT battery had been changed recently. Another bite of worry to join the others in my growing worries satchel. I would find out sooner or later, hopefully sooner. Getting my memory on track was a struggle. Is there anybody in the back of the plane? Whose plane is it? Where was I going? Where had I been? Who am?

I could almost hear a helicopter, or was it a lawn mower? I thought maybe I heard what might have been an airliner in the not too distant skies. Descending even. Maybe there was an airport nearby. I wondered if I had ever flown one of those. The engines were getting louder, but morphing into reciprocal engines, like the old DC-3s that still worm through the skies of South America and the Caribbean. I needed to sleep.

October 1964 I could hear the sounds more clearly now, and it was for sure the propeller driven engine of a Beechcraft built, T-34 Mentor that the Navy had used in the 60's to train neophyte Naval Aviators. My mind was at least in familiar territory. I knew the cockpit of that airplane, blindfolded; it was no trick to recall it now. Altimeter, airspeed indicator, directional gyro, vertical speed indicator, artificial horizon, turn bank indicator, gear warning light, radio navigation instruments, engine instruments, and that flippin' fuel boost pump switch. I would somehow always forget it on take off and landing, and was smacked on the helmet by my instructor's kneeboard from his perch in the rear of the airplane. He was from Texas and I liked him, but I didn't like being popped in the back of head every day. I think I might have been from Texas? My mind is just floating around, not sure where to go or where not to go. Right now I feel like a voyeur, looking down through billowy clouds on a young Ensign Eddie Parker, bouncing through navy basic and advanced flight training. This is very weird and I am really cold.

After the Saufley field Naval Air Station and the T-34 stint, I knew that I wanted to fly the T-2A Buckeye jet trainer at the Naval Air Station, only a few miles north of Meridian, Mississippi. With an unpredictable quota system dependent on how many planes we were losing in Vietnam, the Navy needed only a handful of jet pilots the week I graduated from Saufley. I ended up at Whiting Field in nearby Brewton, Alabama, flying the propeller driven North American T-28C Trojan, destined for multi-engine training nine months later. I still wanted to fly jets, and was determined to make that dream a reality.

Spring-Summer 1965 While scheming of how to get into the jet fighter pipeline, I fully experienced the T-28 Trojan, a big loud single engine airplane that was a hoot to fly. It was noisy, oily, and deadly when flown carelessly. It was much like riding on top of a locomotive that pulled through the southern Alabama air with its powerful General Electric 1425 horsepower radial engine. I ached when two very good friends were killed there, and can still see their faces. Freddy Knopp and Willie Durpo who collided during a formation exercise. Freddy owed me money for some scuba gear I had sold him a few weeks earlier and Willie from poker night. I vividly remember going to visit my friend's widow, whom I had met a couple of times in the parking lot of one of the squadron hangars.

Talking with her while she rocked back and forth with her 18-month old daughter was tough. How does a young widow face the future without her lover and provider? How does a daughter deal with never knowing her birth father? It was the first of several tragedies when close friends were killed, always difficult to handle. Always. Why do I remember them, but how about me? Why can't I remember more of my family or who I am? I am stuck in the past. Often my memory was like trying to see through fast moving fog. A glimpse of someone, or something, then blank.

At last now, I can see my wife, standing near a runway of all places. But too not clearly; then gone. Like a car rental commercial, I feel my body floating down into the cockpit of my F-9F Cougar, to be strapped in by my crew chief. What would I be doing in a jet? He helped with my G-Suit that was plugged into the airplane's pneumatic sensor so that it would pump air into my suit and keep me from passing out on high G force maneuvers. He double checked the wiring connections for my radios, as well as the knee-board strapped to my thigh used for listing of radio frequencies, tower instructions, as well as a place to write instrument departure and arrival directives.

Finally. I could see her; a little blurry, but clearly enough. I could tell she was very pretty and that I was crazy about her. I was melting into another trainer, another jet this time. The F-11F Tiger cockpit was like a sauna, hot and steamy; had to be July or August. Our small squadron was preparing for simulated carrier practice using portable arresting gear equipment. For some unexplained reason, the Squadron C.O. was letting the wives near the arresting gear on the runway where we touched down. It was arranged so that the communications between the airplanes and landing signal officer on the ground near the runway was on a loud speaker so the wives could follow her guy. I felt like a big shot when I would say for all within earshot of the speaker to hear, two zero niner, "I got the ball". Just that, and sometimes simply "Roger." My mind shifted to Kathryn as a spectator of this exercise or sunning by the pool near our tiny A-Frame apartment. She was a very good memory. Yum. Getting home to her would be an even a *better* memory.

The instant we were herded near the practice runway to watch our husbands do carrier-landing practice, I knew that I had made another mistake. It was so bloody loud, hot, and scary as hell. My armpits were growing stickier by the minute and forget the mascara. We were told to dress casual. But me; I had to wear wool pants and a sweater. They could have at least told us the 'surprise' was outside. The Naval Officer in charge had loud speakers set up so we could hear the limited radio transmissions between himself and the pilot. As the extremely loud jet approached and it was Edie's turn to land, I could hear his garbled but confident voice mention that 'he had the ball', whatever the heck that meant. How a person could fly any kind of accurate approach to an aircraft carrier bobbing around in the ocean was beyond me. He tried to explain that night about the system of mirrors on the ship and lights in the cockpit, none of which made any sense to me. It was one of the most annoying yet amazing experiences I had ever encountered; a small peep into the world of my new hubby. This could be dangerous business.

Chapter Six

*"Those who could foresee affairs
three days in advance
would be rich for
many lifetimes."*
~ ~ *Thomas Carlyle*

Late 1969

My simple Mooney instrument panel suddenly got way more complicated than before. It was morphing into the panel of an F-4J Phantom?? Criminy, I must be a wacko. My dreams were getting worse; depression, hallucinations, flashbacks. Once I seemed to be floating in water that had filled the cockpit; but could still breathe. My arms flailed around, my hair lifted, and all the trash in the cockpit was bumping against the roof. I just closed my eyes hoping for some peace.

I turned away from my instruments, looked out to my right hoping to see the moonlight reflection, but instead saw the moon reflecting off the deck of an aircraft carrier. I found myself sitting on the port bow catapult of the attack carrier, USS *America*, in the middle of the night no less. My butt was getting really sore now, so I must have been there for quite a while. The steam whooshing up from the vents of the catapults deep in the belly of the carrier, made a star effect from the red flashlights of the deck crew as they directed traffic for departing fighters.

The supersonic jets of the Black Knights Fighter Squadron 154 could be outfitted with Sparrow and Sidewinder air to air missiles, as well as air to ground missiles called *Bullpups*. The Phantom also had one fuselage centerline bomb rack and four pylon bomb racks capable of carrying 12,500 pounds of general-purpose bombs. Tonight we were armed with just the sleek *Bullpups* and bombs, all armed and ready to fire.

I'm there. On the deck of the *America* in the Gulf of Tonkin; just sittin,' fauchin,' waitin,' engines screaming. Unexpectedly, the Air Boss crackles good hunting sentiments, reminds me not to take chances, and to be careful. The low level mission was going to be extra tricky. The Launch Officer was moving around the carrier's flight deck like a purposeful ballerina, waving his red-coned flashlights right and left, up and down, and in circles. He has one eye on me, the other on the catapult officer, and somehow stays aware of activities on the forward deck. Engines are screaming with an even higher pitch now, half flaps, chaff doors cycled, stabilizer set, head back, heels tucked under the seat, harness tight, throttle grip up and grabbed, tailpipe temp good, power stabilized, after burner lit.

"Popeye Zero Six standby for launch."

Wonder why I picked Popeye as a call sign? Must have been drunk or liked spinach, probably the latter. When the Catapult Officer was satisfied with the steam pressure in the catapult cylinders, the pitch of my engines, and is satisfied that he has a clear deck, he's ready. When he saw my final thumbs up and head back, he dropped his brightly illuminated red baton, signaling the "shooter" in the deck pod to push the red catapult plunger. The next instant, our twin-engine exhaust blast hammered the jet blast deflector behind us, as the catapult did its job, slinging us from a standstill into the night at 155 knots in less than two seconds.

This was one of those sticky and rare low-level solo missions I hated. The A-6 Intruders from squadron VA-165 usually handled these missions, but every now and then, we got one. Since it was a night mission, we would not have the company of our wingmen, Wally Allen and Aaron Feldman. Our two airplanes and eight eyes were unbeatable, winning every hassle contest that we encountered. Our J model Phantom carried such a variety of hateful ordinance preparing us for any eventuality. Air to air, air to ground, daylight, night, high altitude bombing, low level strafing, and with the large fuel tanks, my radar operator/bombardier and I could stay airborne for a very long time. Alone tonight, we were protected with *Bullpup* missiles designed to detect enemy ground radar launching surface to air missiles, we cynically called *Sams*. Our offensive power featured 12,000 pounds of 500 pound and 1,000-pound bombs, all non-guided and free falling. Tonight we would not be armed with the four AIM-7 sparrow missiles we usually carried, in case Charlie wanted an air-to-air dispute; unlikely at night. If needed, we could do combat at 54,000 feet above the earth, and could travel a total of over 400 miles to and from the target, a distance from Los Angeles to San Francisco at speeds of over 1500 miles per hour if needed. Our specific objective this evening was a firing line of anti-aircraft guns that were surrounded by protective nest of *Sam* located about 30 miles east of Hanoi near Chi Linh. They were playing hell with our B-52s and it was imperative they be neutralized. "Hey, Lieutenant", from the intercom. "René, is that you, my Creole pal back there?" René resided in a partitioned cockpit just behind mine and had the responsibility of navigating and lining up our missiles, guns, or bombs over the target. He was also an expert at reading our AWG-10 radar system, vital for our situational awareness.

"Oh yea, tiz moi, who else?" My French friend and backseat RIO teammate was from the Metairie district of New Orleans, and a true card carrying French Creole Cajun with a bloodline of pure French-Acadians. He was a freckled faced one man party with the personality somewhere between a Mardi Gras Krew Master, nightclub bouncer, itinerant preacher, and a Bourbon Street pimp. He was strong as an ox with a physique as imposing as his will. René Thibadeau grew up in a modest camelback, or shotgun house in the mid-city district bayou neighborhood of St. John, with a reputation of wrestling alligators for relaxation. René's wife and my old girlfriend, Aimee, was a direct descendant of a long line of fiery French Buccaneers from Saint Domingue in the East Indies. He loved her name as Aimee with one less 'E' at the end meant, 'I love you' in French. And he *did* love that woman.

René and I were reacquainted at the transition replacement Squadron in San Diego, where I introduced him to Aimee. She and I had dated some and were very close, but I knew that she and René were meant to be together. When Aimee and Kathryn met shortly after Kathryn and I married, they were best friends almost immediately. They hit it off like they had known each other from birth. René and Aimee shopped together, swam against each other, and threw the most fun house parties ever. They were soul mates; no one doubted that they would make it until the day one attended the funeral of the other.

René and I clicked as friends, because we were in the fraternity of married Naval Aviators that took our wedding vows seriously and didn't carouse late at night looking for a one-night stand. We four talked about trying to be stationed together until our tour of duty was up, and to always stay close, no matter what; a noble plan that didn't quite work out.

René had the most colorful way of announcing our arrival in hostile territory. He would shout through the intercom mike the all too familiar, 'Laissez le bon temp rouler', or 'let the good times roll.' It was his colorful preamble to the usual, "Be careful Pappy; there is more than one of us in this three million dollar rocket. I don't swim well, and I do *not* like the idea of having a political discussion with the Viet Cong tonight. Those flambeaux babies down below are designed to do us serious harm. Keep us safe Mr. Parker."

"Count on it, Mr. Thibadeau. Let's run our combat check list and get ready for the fireworks." We went through the familiar routine of checking our bomb and missile switches as well as our electronic countermeasure systems. After half an hour of relative quiet, we neared our assigned objective. "We are 'five by five' with the Hawkeye early warning and surveillance airplane on frequency three twenty four point four. Standby for descent to initial bombing altitude of 500."

"Roger, Mr. Thibadeau." Two minutes later, René directed my control of the Phantom. "Mr. Parker, sir, give me three degrees of nose down and maintain power." I complied, "roger, three down." Then our conversation became negligible the next few minutes, interrupted only by different ping tones of enemy search radar trying to find our oncoming Phantom and the whooshing of the powerful twin jet engines pushing us along with 20,000 pounds of thrust. Being stuffed into this rocket loaded with explosives approaching the speed of sound was not quite as romantic as a pre-historic loin clad warrior riding a mythological Roc waving his sword. Images like that are for fuselage painting, but René and I had real fear painted on our real human hearts. Fear, too, of disappointing our wives by not returning as promised.

In a few minutes René confirms to the Hawkeye recon circling safely thousands of feet above, that we are 'feet dry' over the coast of North Vietnam, just 60 miles from our target and only seven minutes away at our speed. They wish us good hunting; René clicked his microphone button twice for our response.

We tightened our harnesses expecting a bumpy ride from the low altitude concussion of enemy anti-aircraft explosions. We were two black-hearted warriors this menacing night, dedicated to piercing the communist soldiers with our deadly stingers. For sure we were not welcome; we never were. Bright lights flickered below, like giant glowing malignant hornets waiting to attack. There were also plenty of intense lights above us, resembling roman candles exploding into tiny iridescent fragments. When they exploded, our cockpits lit up as if splashed by searchlights, temporarily wiping out our night vision. For sure it's not love from those bastard Gooks with their aircraft flak and the bonus of their surface to air missiles we called *Sams,* for us to dodge. In the daytime, they weren't so bad. When our radar alerted us that they had been launched our way, we could see them and easily move out of their way. They lumbered into the sky and were like dodging king sized hot water heaters. I'm trying to remain positive, reminding myself that we have done this before, and made it back each time. Maybe a bit shot up, but always in one piece.

Screaming low to the deck 200 feet over the Vietnam rice paddies and along the treetops, we dropped our first dose of bombs, over half of our 500 and 1,000 pounders, racing back to higher altitudes after each run, outrunning their unfriendly, but thankfully, much slower missiles. We were pretty confident that our bombs cleared out a few of the anti-aircraft guns that had caused so much trouble with our Guam based B-52 heavy bombers on their nightly bombing missions. The radar systems from below answered by our own, created a virtuoso of my evasive flying and René's retaliating ordinance. Every time René would yell, 'Missile', the ECM would drop our chaff flares that were decoys for the *Sams* to chase, then we reintroduced them to the *Bullpups*, and finally dropped a few more of 500 or 1,000 pounders for good measure. For a while it was fun. Our little team was ahead 70-0, and we had another quarter to play. Each of our four passes over the target seemed like an eternity, but we took care of business, and then headed for the heavens and to the safety of the carrier.

We had just enough ordinance left for targets of opportunity, a perfect chance to do some payback. Our options were roads, waterways, trucks; anything to slow the march of soldiers and supplies to the battlefront in the south. René and I voted, and unanimously elected Kep Field and a few of its Russian MiG 21's parked on the tarmac, as well as the barracks where the pilots slept. We saw how close Kep was to Chi Linh and Hanoi, and decided beforehand just what we wanted. Earlier in the year, the carrier Kitty Hawk lost Lt. Cam Quisenbury from VF-213, one of its F-4 pilots during a low-level target damage assessment run. This was just settling the score. Quisenbury was a friend of

René's and mine from Saufley, who left a beautiful wife and three-year-old son in rural West Texas with a certain hardtack future. Kep Field was also rumored to be near a large ammunition dump, unconfirmed by radar, but a collateral hit on this arsenal would be really helpful to the grunts on the ground. This was personal now, as our visceral urges were more than fortified with determination. With René's keen provoked eyes and deft bomb release fingers, we prayed our last few powerful bombs would soak the Vietnamese Communist souls with their own blood. Just briefly, I chuckled to myself that René's one-ounce finger and his one-inch round plastic red button had the power to blast the North Vietnamese soldiers into small harmless pieces.

After emptying our bomb racks on and around Kep Field, we made a steep climbing turn back towards the *America*. "Nice and easy now René, we're just a 45 minute hop back to Yankee Station and our floating palace where we'll be nice and safe." Just as we were congratulating each other on our flying and bombing skills, we were interrupted by the unexpected but not unfamiliar jolt that was much rougher than usual. I knew we had been hit harder than ever before; hard enough to throw my head against the cockpit panel, give me a busted lip, and put a nasty gash in my forehead. It felt like we hit a speed bump at 450 knots as the Phantom shuddered at this unwelcome disturbance. Then it got quiet. The F-4 wobbled again, then started yawing left and right and wouldn't answer the stick properly. The engine gauges spun and blinked, then returned normal. All except for the hydraulic pressure, that is, where the needle began to drop; not a good sign.

"You OK, René?" Nothing. "C'mon Thibadeau, say something." "Don't get your bowels in an uproar, Mr. Parker. We have been hit by an isolated dumbass lucky SAM, probably from just off the coast near Dong Hoi. The impact felt like it hit back here, in the rear of the airplane mostly."

"René, I didn't hear the radar warning receiver, did you?" "No sir, and that is a pisser. We have to put that on the yellow gripe sheet when we get back." "And how about your Threat Display Panel?" "Nothing. The shrapnel must have severed some of the wires in the aft electrical harness. Can you still fly this bucket of bolts?"

"Affirmative, René; its just my left arm. Hurts like a bitch but it's not serious. I also got little pieces of the Cong junkyard in my back and neck, and even my ass, but I'll live. I can still move around. You okay?"

"I think so boss. I got some junk too, but I can manage. My left leg is kinda numb, and right arm not much use, but I can still use foot mike to give you a hard time. A little lightheaded, but other than that okay. Got some shrapnel under my arm and I think it's bleeding. I'll try not to go "doe-doe" on you."

"You better not go to sleep on me big boy; you owe me a hundred bucks from our last poker game, and I want you to pay me in front everyone in the squadron. Can you take the stick for a jiff? I have some blood inside my left glove and it's slippery. I need to do a quickie wrap job and it'll only take a minute. Call the boat and give them a head's up."

"No problem man, just get us home." René squeezed the mike button on the control stick and in his unmistakable Cajun accent, summarized our situation, then requested a 'straight in' approach.

The *America* came back asking our fuel state and condition. Before René could get back on the radio, I spoke to him on the intercom mike. "I'll take it from here, René." It wasn't the time for any confusion from my charming René."

"*America*, Popeye Zero Six, fuel state bingo at two point five hundred pounds, zero bullets, two souls, with probable starboard horizontal stabilizer damage. Lateral control sloppy. Hydraulics dropping with Hydraulic Power Control One and Two disabled, but holding 2300 pounds from utility pump. Pilot and RO wounded but capable, over."

"Popeye Zero Six, advise medical

condition for trap, over." "Zero Six, about fifty/fifty." "Popeye, your call. Let us know your thinking, Zero Six." "*America*, standby."

"What do you think, René?" René's speech was getting more slurred now and hard to decipher. "You're the boss, Pops. If you want to try, I know you care more about you're sorry ass, than mine, so I'll take my chances. Maybe get in the pattern and see how she handles." Then he tailed off slurring something about 'hurrying up'. I looked in the cockpit rearview mirror and noticed his head was wagging back and forth like a rag doll. Not a good sign at all.

"*America*, Popeye..." Whoa Nellie, this sucker is really wobbling around. Easy does it.... "*America*, Popeye Zero Six, requesting straight in approach. Normal pattern break not possible at this time; auto landing system disabled. Inform the LSO that if we look too unstable on final, to wave us off. Recommend the choppers to get extra close, mostly aft and to starboard. If we have to abort, I'll try to eject both of us as close to the boat as possible. RO is hurt and can't last very long in those night swells for long, and for sure won't float long. The choppers will have to be right on top of him... There just won't be much time... It'll happen really fast."

"Roger, Popeye Zero Six, standby." In the *America's* superstructure, Air Boss, Commander Scott Sensenbaugh, called down to the Captain. "Skipper, we have an F-4 from 154 that's been damaged. It's Parker and Thibadeau and they're both hurt. Not serious for Parker, but Thibadeau is unconscious. They have probable damage to the horizontal stabilizer, losing hydraulics, and need a straight in. You might want to come up to the bridge."

The anxious Captain Huddleson scrambled up the stairwells and hustled onto the bridge of the superstructure, the control tower and brains of the carrier. Parker, on his second tour of duty, was the first name called when trouble closed ranks. With over 180 missions to his credit, he took all of the crap assignments like this one, didn't complain, and most of the time came back without incident. He was every bit as accomplished as more noted aviators like Willy Driscoll and Duke Cunningham on the USS *Constellation*. Had Parker the opportunities, he easily could have been the third naval ace of the Vietnam War.

This time the captain was anxious. He loved Eddie, as did all the men in his circle and he sorely wanted him back in one piece. Huddleson knew his younger aggressive aviators could sweep enemy strongholds effectively, but the veteran Parker used whiskbroom strategy to get into every corner and bunker. He was simply the best. He was a special talent, invaluable for morale and battle efficiency; a great inspiration and model for the newer aviators. He was the go to 'button man' for the Seventh Fleet of the United States Navy. Earlier in the evening, Huddleson had second thoughts about the mission and tried to scrub just after Parker and Thibadeau had launched. According to the air boss, the Phantom reported radio trouble, then did not respond to any transmissions until they were halfway into the mission. From his own young carrier days in Korea, he knew better. Parker knew the importance of the mission and he wasn't about to abort.

Clearly a take charge Skipper, and in a clear voice, he responded to the air boss. "Thanks for the heads up, Scott. You know the drill. Get the flight deck clear, and have any returning birds prepared to initiate a 'Charlie' holding pattern for three thousand to Ten. Stack the pattern with the low fuel state aircraft on the bottom, and get two more rescue choppers in the air. Line 'em up 1,000 feet apart between one, two, and three points abaft the starboard beam. Instruct the choppers to get those swimmers into the water as soon as they see the chutes of either man or hear our order to eject. Signal the Furse (destroyer stationed a mile in front of the carrier), to pull back from her normal escort position and pull even with the stern with 300 yards separation. They will do more good there than serving as a beacon. Parker knows where the ship is. *Believe* it. We aren't sure of either man's physical condition so treat both as disabled. We'll confirm the ejection with flares if we have to, so be alert. Get the high intensity floodlights lit as they approach the boat, all hands watching for deck level chutes. Tell the Officer of the Deck I want heading 150 degrees and instruct the engine room to give me full speed ahead when on course. We will need as much wind across the deck as possible for these men."

Sensenbaugh had anticipated the orders and had done most of the prep work beforehand. "Aye, aye, sir." "Officer of the Deck, call sickbay and get the doctors alerted, with the operating rooms and critical units on standby. We may have a real mess on our hands before this night is over. Getting the damage Phantom aboard with a mangled tail aboard isn't impossible, but it is very improbable. Parker is one of the few that can get it done and that's why I am giving him one shot. If it gets too hairy or if he doesn't get aboard on the first pass, I'll have to put them in the water. We can't afford to have our inbound pilots putting their expensive planes in the drink over one cripple. This will happen fast, so everybody on their toes. Deck Boss, get some extra lights on the arresting gear, and get Lieutenant McCrae on the Landing Signal Officer's platform." Another smart,

"Aye, Aye." The America's anxious Approach Controller with more bad memories than good in situations like this, was already changing into his LSO flight gear.

Back in the crippled Phantom, Parker was getting his final instructions. "Popeye Zero Six, make your vector heading one two zero, descend and maintain three thousand five hundred, and intercept *America* Nav Signal eight miles, then heading one five zero for final approach. Your wind four one knots across the deck, sky partially obscure, ten foot sea swells, and set your altimeter as two niner five one. If you can't get aboard on the first pass, be prepared to eject immediately for an expedited rescue. We will make the call with flares on the missed approach if there is radio failure. Remain this frequency until LSO instructs." "Roger *America*, turning one two zero to intercept TACAN eight miles, then heading one five zero on final, descending to angels three point five, barometer two niner five one."

"Hang on René. We're in luck. Ha! Seas are rough and visibility only fair and we have an airplane thrashing around like an old bi-wing Stearman. Get your harness locked and your feet back under your seat just in case we have to leave in a hurry." Still no response and his head was still limp, but at least I could pretend he was okay. My butt is not numb anymore, but wet; like grease or something, and the left hip on fire now. Sorry ass luck; Gooks put some shrapnel right in my butt. Toes cold. Shit, rudder is slippery as hell. No worries.

"René, you okay? What's going on back there? "René, "René! *Gotta call the boat.* "*America*, Popeye Zero Six, turning heading one five zero final eight miles, level at three point five. Gear down, hook down, harness locked and armament locked. Not sure about slats. RO not responsive." Parker wondered why the slat handle in the J model of the F-4 was inexplicably positioned in the back seat to be managed by the RO. Go figure. 'I wish had one of those aeronautical engineers with me now.'

"Popeye Zero Six, contact LSO on three two one point five." I readied my finger on preset button six on the Radio Set Control panel.

"Roger, *America*, leaving for three two one point five." After pressing the preset frequency with my right hand, I heard a familiar voice. "Popeye Zero Six, LSO with you. We'll get through this together." I recognized my good friend from Saufley, Dave McCrae, with no doubt he'd bring us aboard alive if anyone could. He wasn't only a very good friend, he was a very experienced combat aviator, and knew the handling characteristics of a beat up F-4J from his own share of hairy close calls on the *Kitty*

Hawk. I tightened my harness as best I could, then touched the small heart shaped locket in my sleeve pocket with the picture of a smiling Kathryn taken during our honeymoon.

The prayer was directed to his wife, with a copy to God. 'My dearest Kathy, I love you more than the depth of this ocean beneath me, and if I don't survive this circus, hopefully I'll meet you at the Gates of Heaven where I know you will be. I apologize for putting René and me in this mess, and for the torment in store for you and Aimee if we don't make it. I have no regrets in this life, our life. If I had married you first as I should have, we wouldn't have Michael, who I have learned to adore and cherish. May our Merciful Creator be with us both.' The Phantom shuddered, preempting his amen.

The Same Time In San Diego *I just finished my BLT and iced tea for lunch and had started a load of laundry. I don't know what came over me, but I felt a warming, like when Eddie was around. Oh, Eddie, Eddie, Eddie? I knew something was the matter; a sudden wave of nausea took my wind away. I couldn't breathe and everything was out of focus. I felt sweat flowing* *from my forehead to my chin in a flood. Something bad was happening. I just know it. "Dear Lord please make him safe. Please, oh please." The room spun too fast; then I found myself face down on the linoleum floor.*

"Zero Six, reduce speed to one five zero knots and hold two thousand until four miles, then standard rate of descent until you have the bal. Review landing checklist and don't forget landing lights. Zero Six, jettison the Buddy Fuel Tanks, and disengage the automatic flight control system." "Zero Six, Roger."

"Disengage auto pitch control, but engage the Approach Power Control. That will stabilize airspeed so you can concentrate on directional management. After reporting visual on the meatball, no more transmissions will be necessary unless I wave you off. After wave off, commence pre-dual ejection procedures as earlier directed." "Roger, One five zero knots at two thousand until the ball. Check list complete."

"Hang on René." I knew if we could just get aboard, this night would be a memory for the ages. Little did I know it would be years of a reoccurring bad dream. I dimmed the cockpit lights and radioed the LSO.

I slowly drifted into the three and a half degree glide slope to the aircraft carrier below, where my rate of descent would drop me the distance of a 70 story building every minute. "*America*, I have the ball." The Fresnel Lens Optical Landing Aid seemed to be moving all over the place. How in the hell am I supposed to get this inebriated thing down? It's bad enough under normal conditions, but at night with my tail all crapped up, I dunno. The F-4 finally settled down using left stick and right rudder that created some sense of stability and lateral control. The cockpit was a little fuzzy, but we've done this a hundred times, "right René? René?" 'God I hope he's okay.' The F-4, usually a stable flying machine, was bucking like a DC-3 trying to land in Kansas City during a winter thunderstorm. I had the 'ball,' looking good; then I was a little high, then a little low.

"Get the nose down, Zero Six." Jesus, I have to stabilize this bad boy, or we are going swimming. "Popeye Zero Six, get the nose down a bit more and give me one four five knots. You're drifting to starboard badly. Zero Six, use just the rudder and the stick for speed." 'No shit, Sugarfoot!'

"Zero Six, steer one four seven degrees. I have your gear, slats, hook, and lights. Speed looks good, Zero Six, prepare to land slightly hot and deploy speed brakes on my call immediately after the datum lights flash green." 'Oh this is great. He wants me to rub my tummy and pat my head at the same time.'

"Zero Six, give me full flaps." 'My flaps were showing full down. The utility hydraulics must be pooping out. Too late to worry about that now, gotta take off some power.'

"Zero Six, now ease right to one five zero, and hold it. Override the Approach Power Control and give me a little power Zero Six. More... More. Nose up a bit, now hold it....Hold it there. Speed brakes *now*."

I dropped the speed brakes and jerked the throttle back just as the F-4 hit the deck with a jarring force that only a 20 ton war plane at 155 knots can deliver. By the grace of The Creator, the tail hook grabbed the last of the four cables and stopped as suddenly as it had been launched over an hour and a half ago. Ensuring that the throttle was all the way back, I got on the brakes as soon as my rearward pull from the ship's arresting gear had diminished, obeying the signals from the Aircraft Handling Officer in his blue jersey. I was guided to taxi off to the hangar deck elevator to the right, out of the way of other returning traffic, and shut down the engine. I whispered silently to myself, 'Thanks Lord. I won't forget this. I owe you.' Now to find and thank Dave.

The medical team and my crew chief

were on us like freshmen storming Andrews Hall at a Longhorn panty raid. As I was being lifted out my seat and onto the deck below, I tried to see the team of medics and crewmen helping René. "Be careful, please make him okay. Be careful. Watch his head, watch his head dammit!" He didn't look great, and then I suddenly hurt all over.

I can't remember what happened to him. Darn memory. Somehow, I halfway woke up, thinking what a bad dream, then the butt, hip, back, and left arm reminded me otherwise. "You're aboard Parker, great job. Number four wire, but after looking at your tail section, both stabilizers and port wing control surfaces, it's a miracle you made it aboard in one piece. If you don't go to church, you need to and hit your knees twice a day and thank the good Lord for His hand in your safety. He must have some special plan for you, Eddie." The voice faded off and the lights in my brain turned off. 'Who's that, a nurse? Not even close, just 'the old man', Captain Huddleson.

"At ease Old Timer, you are in sick bay now. Try to relax and take it easy. You just saved the Navy a lot of money and brought René home. If you had tried to eject him, he might have drowned, or worse, sunk to the bottom of the South China Sea. I'm sure you knew that he wouldn't have survived being punched out in his critical condition. He took a big chunk of shrapnel under the arm and thigh, and lost a ton of blood. He's in grave condition in the critical care ward with other problems as well, but our doctors are going to do everything humanly possible to make him healthy again. We'll get him to Guam as soon as he is fit to travel where he can get the very best doctors and equipment.

"As for you, your butt is going to hurt every time you get cold, or when it is going to rain, or when you take a crap, but you will make it fine. It will be a reminder that you were one of the lucky ones. Lieutenant Commander, the skill you exercised to get back to the boat was some unbelievable flying. The big story of the night is that our intelligence from the ground troops reported secondary explosions on the gun line you hit. Thibadeau must have nailed a significant ammunition dump, which will earn him a DFC, to go with yours. Eddie, with a few days of rehab and R&R in Hawaii, you can look forward to more of this nonsense." From a puzzled Eddie, "Lieutenant Commander? DFC?"

"Yeah, I forgot to tell you. Your wife already knows about the promotion by now, so congratulations. By the way, the DFC is for the *Damn Fool Coconut* award for being the most stubborn and hardheaded aviator in the Navy." Heard barely above the noise of the last few fighters returning from their own odysseys, I ignored the promotion thing and pleaded, "Skipper, can I see René? I need to see him. Just got to."

"Later Eddie, later. It's just not possible as the doctors are working on him as we speak. For now we need to sew *you* up a bit and run some more tests to see if you have any more shrapnel to dig out, and be sure that knot on your head isn't serious. Your job is to rest so we can get you out of here on the next carrier mail run. You need to forget about this place for a while, Mr. Parker. The war will still be here, and Mr. Thibadeau is getting the best care in the world." Before I could object, the thought of being with Kathryn again flooded me with a rowdy eagerness and silenced any further protests as I let the morphine have me.

A few days later just before I crawled into the Grumman C-2A Greyhound, for my trip to Guam, the captain okayed me to peek in on René. The Critical Care Ward was dimly lit, save the surgical light, bathing René in an ethereal glow. The ward, thick with medical musk, had a unique tranquility and the personality of a sarcophagus. The beeping of René's monitoring equipment kept cadence with the hiss of his respirator, and with my own anxious heartbeat. I didn't know if it was the ship or me, but the scene had me unsteady on my feet. His right arm and torso were in a cast all the way to his waist and his left leg in a sling of sorts, also in a cast. I wasn't a doctor, but I could read the monitor. Blood pressure 78 over 42 and heart rate 109. The blood oxygen saturation was no good either, below 90 and heading south. That explained the intubation for the ventilator that was moving pressurized oxygen into Rene's lungs. I was told they would keep him in a drug-induced coma until they could learn more about his injuries and get his vitals stronger.

He looked peaceful, almost dead to be honest. The ship with its gentle rocking motion and monitor's peeps and swooshes, served as a surrogate womb of sorts. Gentle, soft, and warm, and I hoped not too late to heal this exceptional human being. I felt helpless and ridden with guilt. I squeezed his good arm and left the ward. I couldn't stand it a minute longer. I leaned back against the bulkhead in the passageway and sobbed like a five-year-old kid. I watched one of my tears scatter the dust from the toe of my brown shoe into muddy droplets. This special man was so important to me, so very important. The war would indeed be waiting for me, but now all I could think of was seeing Kathryn. I couldn't wait to get off the ship.

After a few days for me to heal, they flew me to Guam for a one-night stay, then on to Hawaii. René had already been evacuated to the Naval Hospital there, but I was never able to see him. He was still in Intensive Care in another building. I learned that he was still struggling to get well, so for now, I had to focus on seeing Kathryn.

They wouldn't let her meet me at Barber's Point, so I waited at the bar in the lobby of the hotel. Man, was it great to see her push through the front door and race into my arms. I'll never forget that moment. Ever.

From our beachfront hotel room in Honolulu, I watched the news early one morning, with Kathryn snuggled under my arm and tangled with my legs, the story of my squadron mate Ron Nash splashing a Russian built MiG-21 Fishbed near Vinh. I also learned the regrettable news that my own Black Knights had lost another pilot and RO, two of ten aviators killed or taken prisoner by the Viet Cong from our air group that week. For the moment, though, I was safe; getting lots and lots of TLC from the only one that mattered.

Chapter Seven

*"I have certainly had my
share of long distance
love affairs."*
~ ~ Drew Barrymore

Saturday November 22

After three days of blissful, balmy days in Honolulu with Kathryn, I answered what I thought was our room service meal. Instead it was a telegram. A telegram from my Captain Dick Huddleson through the Commander-in-Chief of the Pacific Fleet. It was a telegram that I will never forget; one that would change the course of my marriage, my self-respect and my confidence. Except for my special Kathryn, I would have died.

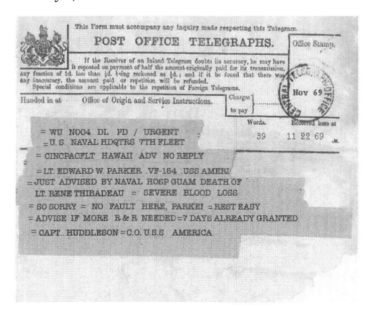

Sunday   November   23rd   1969
Kathryn and I both cried that day and for days after. We tried to call Aimee that next morning, but her phone must have been left or taken off the hook. They would have called her before they sent the telegram, so maybe she just didn't want to talk with anyone right now. I finally managed to communicate through the Naval Air Station at Barbers Point to learn that René had more than just loss of blood. Apparently, a small shrapnel fragment penetrated the base of his skull just under his helmet to make a tiny bleeder that ruptured in the brain that eventually was the cause of his death. We spent another three listless days trying not to think too much of our times with René and Aimee. Up and down the beach, at dinner, or just watching television there was always a reminder. Someone would look like him or sound like her; have his accent, or her laugh. We couldn't get them out of our minds.

Between Johnny Carson and the late night movies, we devoured the news late in the evening, always seeming to be preoccupied with our air losses. Strike Fighter Squadron 143, nicknamed the *Pukin' Dogs*, from the carrier *Constellation*, lost an F-4J Phantom (same as mine) over Laos. My friend "Wheels" Beddington ejected, narrowly escaping capture, while his backseat RIO didn't make it out of the airplane. It happened on the exact date of our telegram. There just wasn't any escape from the evil that I had come from and ultimately had to re-confront. The memories of our last mission turned into that acidic cockpit filled with blood and hideous images of René in tormented expressions. Then more vivid nightmares enhanced by intensely fearful sounds and smells. Kathryn became so alarmed and anxious about my safety that her lovemaking became frantic as if it were going to be her last. Mine, too, at times. My dreams would follow me to the carrier where they would become my companions for years long after the Navy. As the Vietnam War embossed many with its cursed images, it so stamped me.

A very pregnant Aimee and I held hands at the pier with the other wives and girlfriends, while we waved to our handsome guys shoving off to Westpac on the U.S.S America. We were like a small family, all six of us. We had such fun memories. Aimee, René, Eddie and I spared little effort to make the most of the precious free time the guys had before this dreaded day. The men flew during the day, and together we flew at night and weekends, to music, fine food, movies, and Disneyland for curious Michael and energetic baby Scarlett. We exhausted the San Diego Zoo, Balboa Park, and day trip fishing for Blue Marlin from old H&H Landing. As the weeks wore on, Aimee and I suffered through every news story about casualties from the air war in Viet Nam. We stayed in close touch with the Casualty Assistance officer from the Commander's office of the Seventh Fleet's Headquarters in San Diego, getting daily updates on casualties. Some days there would be none, some day there would be a few or several, and occasionally there would be one from our ship of interest, the America.

As the days wore on, with reports of only spotty casualties from the fleet, Aimee and I got less and less worried about Eddie and René. The week before Thanksgiving of 1969, the phone rang in the early morning hours. It would have startled me no less than if it had been a gunshot. It scared Michael and Scarlett as they screamed their lungs out, unnerving me even more." Mrs. Parker, over." The sound quality was poor and filled with static.

"Yes. Who is this please?" "This is Captain Huddleson from the America, Mrs. Parker. We are being patched through short wave radio. Can you hear me okay, over?"

"Pretty good, sir. Has anything happened to my husband, uhh, over?" "Your husband, Lieutenant Commander Parker and Mr. Thibadeau ran into some trouble last evening on a night mission over North Vietnam, over." I quit breathing and the floodgates of tears crashed open like the spillways of Hoover Dam. "Mrs. Parker are you still there, over?" I choked a weak, "Yessir, over." "Mrs. Parker, your husband sustained some nasty but minor injuries, and he should be just fine in a few weeks. In fact we are flying him to meet with you in Honolulu for a week of R&R, maybe longer depending on how quickly he mends. His friend and backseat radar bombardier René Thibadeau wasn't quite so lucky. He suffered shrapnel injuries under his arm and leg that caused a great deal of blood loss. He is still in intensive care and is in guarded condition. As soon as he is well enough to travel, we are airlifting him to Guam where he will get the care he deserves. We are trying to be optimistic but it could go either way. We are in the process of attempting to reach his wife as we speak. By the way Mrs. Parker, your husband is being recommended for the Distinguished Flying Cross and has been promoted to Lieutenant Commander. Is there anything else we can do for you before you start packing? Anything at all, over?"

"No, Captain Huddleson. Not at

this time. Thank your for your call. It means a lot to me." I couldn't think of anything, and barely started to breathe again. "Thanks... thanks a lot for calling. Bye, and tell Eddie I love him and can't wait to see him. Bye again. Over and out, or, whatever." I immediately tried to call Aimee, but there was no answer. Maybe she was on her way to Guam? Anyway, I could catch up with her after I got to Hawaii.

When I met Eddie in Honolulu, he was at the bar in the Hilton Hawaiian Village Lagoon lobby. For security purposes, I was told I couldn't meet him at the Naval Air Station at Barber's Point, but to go directly to the hotel. They flew Eddie from the carrier to Guam, to NAS Barber's Point just west of Honolulu, and immediately by chopper to the Ala Wai Heliport near the hotel. With Michael and Scarlett safely in the hands of a friend and neighbor back in San Diego, all I could think was of Eddie. My hair must have been a mess and I didn't even have time to shave my legs. With the unexpected heat and just the short time it took to get to the hotel, the roll on deodorant has already begun to 'roll-off.' My dated summer dress with the spaghetti straps was the only lightweight cotton sundress I could get my hands on on such short notice. The bathing suit was a one piece job that I bought before I was pregnant with Scarlett. It'll probably fit like a sausage casing.

At least I won't be mistaken for a hooker, except that my lipstick is probably smeared like an old madam. He'll think me a slob and probably won't be excited as I. I don't care though, because I am seeing my man. He must have seen me in the large mirror at the bar as he turned just in time to catch me full on. I ignored his "ouch" and pressed as hard as a woman could to her man with clothes on. My carry-on makeup box hit the floor and probably made a great cartoon to the main attraction of two reunited lovers oblivious to the audience.

"Oh God, Eddie, you scared the life out of me. Don't you ever do that to me again," sobbing the whole time. His own tears were no less salty than hers, but tasted heavenly. "No worries Dearest, no worries. As soon as this mess is over, I am coming home to stay. Jesus in heaven, I have missed you and the kids so much." They joined the hand full of guests trying to gather Kathryn's make-up that had scattered onto the barroom floor like mice trying to escape a herd of cats. Her make-up compact scampered like a runaway wheel and headed for the door of the hotel and beyond. After thanks all around and a lot of laughs, they adjourned to their room for a much-needed rest and catching up on more carnal matters.

Kathryn didn't even notice his limp until later in the night. 'Wow', she thought. He had fresh scars on his lower back, neck, and buttocks of all places, but the wounds didn't seem to interfere with his lovemaking. He held on to her like a vise grip, afraid to let her go for fear he would awaken in that cursed cockpit again. Several times, she wiped his silent tears as they rolled down each side of his nose onto her breasts. In addition to Eddie's battered hip, he was drawn and hollow-eyed. How the Navy treated their finest was a mystery to his Kathryn. Only later did she realize how lucky he had been, and how lucky he must have been every day that he crawled into that horrible airplane. It was all a nightmare, but they were together for now, and that is all that mattered.

When they got that dreadful telegram that René did not survive, Kathryn quickly noticed that it shredded something in Eddie. He tossed and turned that night and on the third night, he began those cruel nightmares. They were always of the mission with René. When he finally returned to the carrier and Kathryn back to California, at least she had memories of his soft chest and strong clean smell that she missed so. Those memories would have to last as Eddie was flown back to the aircraft carrier somewhere in the Western Pacific only a few days later, to crawl back into that monstrous airplane that caused her own desperate dreams.

I worried about my husband when he left me in Hawaii more than at any other time, because the Eddie Parker they sent to me was not the man I returned to them. I prayed for him; I prayed for me. I prayed for René. I prayed for Aimee. I prayed for the both of us extra hard. There were no promises this time, for we both knew Eddie's odds of coming home in one piece faded the longer he stayed on the USS America.

Monday morning November 24 Aimee had just returned from the Miramar Naval Air Station Commissary to get some odds and ends for Thanksgiving. Soft cranberry sauce, a few yams, and a ready-made pumpkin pie would do. Next to Christmas, it was the most lonesome of lonesome holidays with René so far away. She even thought the holidays would be a little better this year, because he would be home soon afterwards. Besides Kathryn, she really had very little company, save the near daily letters from René. It took a week or ten days to get one, but she read them over and over and over. He and Eddie had only two more months, and then they would be home. Finally, home. After this second tour, they could be home at least six months, maybe forever. For the meantime, she would wile the days away reading Michael Crichton's *Andromeda Strain* and Robert Wilder's *An Affair of Honor. Portnoy's Complaint* was too weird and even though *The Godfather* was at the top of the New York Times best-seller list, she would wait on the movie. If not, she and René could read it together.

She was changing clothes to run one more errand, a visit to the Navy's Balboa Hospital in San Diego. They had a great OBGYN and maternity department, and now that she was eight months along, she wanted only the best of care for René junior. She squeezed into her new purple 'floaty' tunic top and spandex pants just as the doorbell rang. 'Who in the devil could that be?' She peeked through the small modesty window and could see only the hats of two Naval Officers.

She froze and stood as quietly and still as possible. She breathed through her mouth real slow so they for sure couldn't hear her. She knew they weren't there for a quick cup of coffee. After several minutes, Aimee heard one of them say, "Mrs. Thibadeau, we know you are home. We watched you walk from the car with a sack of groceries just a few minutes ago. We really need to speak with you and can't leave until we do."

"Go away please and come back later. I don't feel well and it might upset the baby." "We can't do that Mrs. Thibadeau. We aren't allowed to leave until we speak with you." She knew that, but still wanted them gone. When she finally did crack open the door, the blood ran from her body to her feet. She had to steady herself and just hope she was wrong. René was supposed to be getting well in

Guam, so maybe there has been a change in his condition? "Hello, can I help you?" There were two, but she directed her question to the Navy Commander with the gold Leaves on the bill of his cap and the three gold stripes on his blue coat sleeves.

"May we come in, Mrs. Thibadeau?" She waddled from side to side, opened the half torn screen door and stepped aside for them to enter. They removed their hats and stood politely in the tiny foyer.

"Have a seat, please. May I get you something to drink?" "No thanks, Ma'am, but thanks for the offer. My name is Commander Peter Gosdin from the Commander in Chief of the Pacific's office and this is Lieutenant Commander Chester Lovins from the Chaplain's group at NAS Miramar." Gracefully dispensing with the usual 'We regret to inform you', "Mrs. Thibadeau, your husband suffered fatal wounds during a mission flown several days ago." As he drew a breath to continue, Aimee broke down. Completely.

She became lightheaded, exhausted, and succumbed to the numbness in her limbs. Seeing her washed stare and very pregnant, Lovins managed to break her fall as she slid to her side on the slippery linoleum floor. The Commander managed to get Aimee to take a sip of water, then she slowly settled into a pitiful groan and sob.

"Why, oh why? My God, it's just not

fair. There must be a mistake? They called a few days ago and said he was resting comfortably and might be able to travel in a few days." She turned up to the Commander with a pitiful expectant expression hoping he might agree. He took off his hat and jacket and knelt down beside her, as she sniffed and struggled to catch her breath.

"Mrs. Thibadeau, I wish I could give you some shred of hope, but your husband passed away last Friday. Let me help you up and I can tell you more of the details that might give you some peace." After a long minute, Aimee, with the help of both men, settled onto the couch where she and René had made love on so often and not so very long ago. With a new box of tissues, she let out a long breath and blew her nose. Only then could she halfway listen to the officers who hated their roles, often finding their own peace in their own wives' arms as they silently shed their own tears. They didn't volunteer for the job, but like many others, they did a lot of duties they never thought they were capable of. This was the toughest.

The Chaplain spoke this time. "Mrs. Thibadeau, as you know, your husband was wounded on a night mission over North Vietnam suffering several shrapnel wounds. He lost a lot of blood on the way back to the carrier, and seemed somewhat stabilized enough to be flown to Guam a few days later.

The blood loss was the main concern, and he really did rally and looked like he might make it. He died last Friday and as the doctors determined that a tiny piece of jagged steel the size of a small BB had penetrated the brain at the base of the skull, ultimately causing your husband's death. It was so small, it was easily overlooked and caused the blood vessels to rupture quite suddenly." The words hung horribly in Aimee's consciousness, just hanging there. "His body will be flown to Travis Air Force Base in Northern California for mortuary services awaiting your instructions for burial. Mrs. Thibadeau, Commander Gosdin and I are determined to be with you throughout this process and after. Please let us know of anything we might do for you." Aimee seemed to be in another realm as they spoke. "Do you know anything about Mr. Parker, the pilot? Was he wounded or anything like that?"

"We only know that he suffered several wounds, but none life threatening. He is being directed to Hawaii for a few days rest with his wife. We also know that he and your husband were recommended for the Distinguished Flying Cross; your husband for pinpointing bombs on an important ammunition dump and airfield and Lieutenant Commander Parker was decorated for bringing the badly shot up airplane safely back to the ship after suffering his own wounds. Their original mission completed, both men's' wounds were suffered after their targets of opportunity had been struck. Those secondary targets they destroyed turned out to be the most important in deterring the Vietnamese from their movement of troops and materials from the north to the south. They saved the lives of a lot of servicemen that night, Mrs. Thibadeau."

It shook Aimee to her bones when she heard this. Some of René 's letters, even though somewhat censored, made some vague references to some of their extracurricular activities after their missions had been completed. He mentioned that luck had been a lady to them more than once, as the secondary targets were often the most dangerous. She was grinding her teeth by now; turning red and feeling an anger that made her tremble. "You okay, Mrs. Thibadeau?"

Aimee shifted gears. "Mr. Lovins, how soon can we bury my husband?" Aimee and her naval officer guests then fell into a routine. She directed Mr. Lovins to the Mr. Coffee maker and the near empty canister of Chase and Sanborn that had been generously laced with Louisiana Chicory, then they drew up their plans for René Thibadeau's remains.

Aimee instructed them to transfer René's body to Arlington for his burial and skip the Travis memorial services. From her chatty next-door neighbor, she was aware that at Travis, his remains would be painstakingly prepared and donned with a new dress uniform complete with two rows of his medals. She would do the notifications for the rest of the family and requested that René's personal effects be sent to his mother who lived in Metairie, Louisiana, near New Orleans. She wanted this to happen as quickly as possible. The small insurance the Navy provided was to be held up until she was settled. The private insurance that René had just bought, and without her knowledge, was a generous $50,000, five times more than if he had not added the extra benefit. The chaplain offered to contact the insurance agency and have the proceeds deposited directly into their savings account.

They also agreed to call their Credit Union, the Social Security office, the Bank of America's new Visa card records department, and the mutual fund company where René had just opened a brokerage account a few months ago. The officers arranged to fly Aimee and her child, when able, to a location of their choosing anywhere in the world. Aimee asked the officers if they would have his decorations held until she was settled, then she would send for them. Aimee was furious that her husband gave his life for six lousy medals; the Purple Heart, Distinguished

Flying Cross, Vietnam Service Medal, National Defense Medal, Air Medal, and the Armed Forces Expedition Medal. A lousy trade no matter how you looked at it. Aimee joined wives, mothers, and loved ones who made that same trade for the 53,000 men and women who would give their lives for a box of lousy medals and a free grave.

When most of the arrangements were completed and after finishing off another pot of coffee, the men rose to leave. Aimee, with typical difficulty of all late-stage pregnant women, scooted and twisted her way out of the couch. Somewhere between gratefulness and loneliness, she hugged both officers long and firm. Now she didn't want them to leave, these reminders of her husband's strong body. After a short sweet prayer, she released her hold and tearfully offered, "Thank you Commander; Mr. Lovins. You have been more than kind."

"You are very welcome and blessings be to you Mrs. Thibadeau. We will be in touch, and please feel free to call either of us anytime, day or night. We'll get through this together." After the men left Aimee with her grief and thoughts, the phone rang. She didn't answer strongly suspecting it would be Kathryn. Ninety percent of her calls were from her anyway and today was not a good day to chat. A big part of her held Eddie responsible for the death of her husband and a conversation with Kathryn would just drag her down more. Aimee instead made an international call to Aubervilliers, a commune in the northeastern suburbs five miles north of Paris, and spoke with an aunt that she had known as a child in St. Dominique.

Aimee and her new child would start a new life, far, far away from the killing fields of Vietnam, compliments the United States Navy. After making a second call, a tearful one to René's mother, she waddled to the cabinet above the stove and retrieved a half bottle of Jack Daniels. She put two cubes of ice in a large glass and poured it a third full of Ginger Ale and the rest with René's favorite Tennessee sour mash whiskey. She patted her belly and looked down with a wistful smile. "It's just you and me now, Junior. You and I are going to have a drink now. One or two won't hurt you, but will make *me* feel a lot better. Bottoms up Sweetheart."   Peter Gosdin and Chester Lovins made the short walk down the cracked and lumpy sidewalk to the black sedan with U.S. Government plates, hopping over the small strip of patchy St. Augustine grass to the curb. They eased into the car, warmed by the afternoon typical of the San Diego November sunshine. "Where to Commander?"

"Chester, take me back to Miramar. I have a load of paperwork that needs my attention, then I have a night hop to Fallon for a lecture at the new Naval Fighter Weapons School. When I'm done, I'll make the hour's ride to Reno and fly home. When I finally do make it back to my rack, I will hug my wife for a long time and say a prayer for Mrs. Thibadeau."

"We'll both say a prayer for her, Commander, and for all the widows that are suffering from this idiotic war." Then the two Angels of Death disappeared into the darkness until their next heartbreaking assignment.

Chapter Eight

*"There is a slowness in affairs
which ripens them, and
a slowness which
rots them."*
~ ~ Joseph Roux

'70s and '80s

As I squirmed around in my personal aluminum privy, the shivering cold challenged me to think harder. My small fuel sump tool that was protruding from its Velcro® pouch near my knee was just long enough to reach my jacket in the back, just behind my shoulder. The three-foot pole with the flanged end might just do the trick. After several attempts, I finally was able to drag it to my lap where I could get some warmth. At least my upper body was feeling better. With a clearer mind, my thoughts returned to turning off the master switch. Too late, I think; the gyro had gotten silent and the radio and GPS equipment remained mute when I tried to turn them on. Crap.

My attention veered to Kathryn, where she was safe, making me feel secure. She was my strength during and after Vietnam. She propped me up me as I journeyed into the business world after leaving the Navy. From flying a sophisticated jet propelled and bomb-laden airplane into harm's way to selling stuff, she was there. When the demons of my dreams were harvesting my soul, she was there to shoo them off and hold me. So what went wrong for her to stray into another relationship so late in our marriage? What did I do wrong? I wasn't the perfect husband or father, but we were happy and deeply in love, at least I was. The questions would not stop.

As I promised Kathryn and myself, after that second and long tour of duty, I saluted the Navy adieu, leaving chards of my DNA sprinkled in airplanes that would become obsolete and gray like me. I had saddled a rhino and realized that I would have to go wherever that naval beast pleased. A career in the Navy would mean moving Kathryn and the kids every three or four years. To move up in rank, it would require a lot of sea duty; plus sleeping alone for too many nights. Owning a home would be unlikely. Building relationships and keeping real friends were also unlikely. My zest for the Navy was only lukewarm on my best days after I lost René, and sooner or later, it would catch up with me. Our family's needs soared so much higher than the altitude of my own yearnings, and that realization made the choice easy.

The privilege of seeking my own path resided on the civilian stage where I traded my khaki and navy blues, for a not too dissimilar uniform, of blue blazer and khaki pants. So, we journeyed to Dallas in 1970 to interview with Ross Perot's Electronic Data Systems, a new computer company driven by the charismatic ex-IBM salesman, the new darling of the fledgling computer world. I was attracted by their motto, *"Eagles never flock, they are found one by one,"* but my only contact with computers was inside a Navy Jet, not marketable knowledge, while my engineering degree didn't knock very loud at the door of this new exploding technology either. We were interviewed (yes, Kathryn, too) at our apartment on Kingswell Drive in Norfolk, our last Navy Duty Station, passing muster all the way to an interview with the prominent Mr. Perot in Dallas. If I chose that line of work, we would be close to Kathryn's hometown of Abilene, and not far from Austin where our folks lived. As a new hire, I would join other neophytes, and for a while, expected to baby-sit computer mainframes in twenty-four hour shifts. The all-nighters of this initiation schedule did not "compute" for me, so I called my dad to see if he might have a contact or two in his industry.

Although we weren't close, I did respect the prosperity he fashioned as a simple furniture manufacturer's rep in South-central Texas. As a kid we had a nice home, two luxury cars, and a little money in the bank. As a teen, I went with him and Mom to a conference in Dallas where he was being inducted into the Roadrunners Hall of Fame, my first introduction into his world. I knew he had risen to the top, or at least a long way from his East Texas farm with only an eighth grade education. The management of prominent national factories like Lazy-boy, Broyhill, and Bassett held him with high respect. His premature gray hair gave him an incongruent cosmopolitan flair and nickname of 'The Silver Fox'.

When I called to see if he knew of any sales opportunities that might fit my folksy personality, he was only eager to reach out and call in a few chips. So, I followed up on his leads to a North Carolina Factory where good money could be had, or so it was presented to me during my interviews. Goodbye Navy Fighters and goodbye Civil Engineering. Hello sales, y'all. I traded my flight gear bag for a briefcase and that was that.

The early '70s Kathryn and I bundled up our wiggly 'Bonnie' and Clyde' and moved to High Point, North Carolina, the international epicenter of American furniture manufacturing. After a half dozen interviews, I finally got an open door, hired as sales representative for an upholstery factory in nearby Thomasville. The training was meager, but the predictably cordial fraternity of old timers took me by the hand and brought me up to speed quickly. They liked my military résumé and sympathized with me for the disrespectful anti-war hippie protesters that greeted a big percentage of veterans when they returned home from Vietnam. I quickly became one of them. All grown up and making a few civilian dollars along the way.

Except for the heavy travel schedule, I enjoyed the challenges and variety of my daily routine. I especially liked being my own boss; a drastic change from military 'spit and shine'. At Kathryn's insistence, I let my hair grow out a bit to accent my fashionable sideburns. I drew the line at the Ambrose Burnside inspired 'mutton chops', but I did keep my black wingtip shoes spit-shined, even in the back. Believe it or not, I was never tempted to get into those hideous yellow plaid bell-bottom pants that a lot of men wore. I just couldn't do it, even on the golf course.

We were very fortunate to locate in the Emerywood part of town near the country club, an older area usually haunted by 'old money' of High Point. My father had a long time associate who owned an old 'fixer upper' on Forest Hill Drive that he used as a rent house, offering it to us for only $22,000, a rare find and price in that part of town.

Scarlett enjoyed the schools there while Kathryn and I both adored the renewed southern hospitality, as we even let the charming southern drawl slip into our verbal vault. It didn't take long for Michael and I to embrace the sport fishing community with the many infinite blue water lakes pregnant with bass, trout, and blue gills. Occasionally, I explored some of the abundant golf courses in and around the legendary Pinehurst area where I honed my skills slashing out of their pine straw roughs. Michael was involved in every sport possible while Scarlett took dancing and piano lessons like most of her girl friends. Kathryn liked the slower pace of High Point, fitting right in with the Community Service League, as well as serving as a major volunteer worker at the High Point Regional Hospital. As the old Elm Street hospital was undergoing a major renovation and had her working so many hours, she thought that if she was going to spend so much of her time out of the house, she should get paid for it. When Scarlett entered the first grade, Kathryn put her education to work and started teaching, first in junior high, then on to high school where she would chair the Science and Math Departments.

More than anything, she and I both especially liked that I was out of harm's way, even though I did travel a little more than either of us cared for. But, that was the way to make the money. Over the next few years, I grew in reputation and skill in the industry. I graduated from Manufacturer's Rep, to Sales Manager, and then leapt to the top of the food chain to the Textiles Industry, where the real money was to be found. I was a fast study, learning to get up earlier, problem solve for the customers, and became skilled at knowing their culture, programs, and their end users. The fit was perfect, as I already knew the retailers, then found ways for them to specify my fabrics from the mill to the factories that I called on. It didn't hurt that I had served in Vietnam with the small lapel pin of my Navy Wings as a great door opener. Another key to my success was getting to know and influence the key managers at the mill, from the Credit Manager, the Quality Control Boss, the Head Designer, to the Shipping Foreman. Knowing the first names of the receptionist and telephone operator paid surprising dividends.

A box of candy, a few flowers and a twelve-pack of discretely placed premium beer paid dividends far greater than the stock market ever could. Most of my customers, who were not heavy in the pocket with extra cash, would do anything for North Carolina University Tar Heel Basketball tickets. North Carolina was just cranking up its perennially successful basketball reputation while hiking up the previously inexpensive ticket prices. I invested in season tickets keeping two in my breast pocket at all times. It always paid dividends; better than liquor or women that my 'good ole boy' competition tried unsuccessfully to oil the buyers with.

In addition to growing my business and

income, I earned the trust and most importantly, the respect of my customers. I was a new player in this a small industry, the payoff being a quickly growing reputation that made me the target for more and more career opportunities. After leading the sales department of my growing textile mill, I earned a chance to interview for a warehouse and sales group manager in the Los Angeles area for a competitor, the biggest in the industry. I jumped on it faster than a largemouth bass on a plastic worm. Kathryn and I had been running back and forth from High Point to Los Angeles anyway, watching Michael grind his way through his first year at UCLA in Brentwood. We were always so proud to see him excel in his blue and gold football and baseball uniforms.

Our familiarity of the San Diego and Los Angeles areas, combined with my previous sales success contributed to getting the offer I am sure. The California move meant managing the west coast sales and distribution office for Fall River Textiles, a Massachusetts mill specializing in nylon woven fabrics that were very popular and in strong demand. Bridging the culture between the New England erudite and laid back casual Californian was quite a chore. Our management came to town in their blue blazers and khaki pants to factory owners in shorts and loud printed shirts that were so popular in the 70's. Our mill created a family of designs reflecting wildly fashionable plush prints, gorging our customers with the popular designs. Due to our bright and talented stylists, I unashamedly made a lot of money for several years and was prudent enough to plow it into five star mutual funds.

After surveying the landscape of affordable housing in Southern California, we planted our family flag in the clay soil of Orange County in the summer of 1984. By then Michael had graduated with honors from UCLA while Scarlett had just completed her sophomore year at High Point Central High. Her pedigree and internal gyro almost demanded that she live in a fast lane like Southern California. She followed to Michael's UCLA two years later, as we all settled into this odd world of Southern California, often described as the land of the fruits and nuts; sometimes an accurate euphemism.

Summer 1989 I still traveled a bit, but mostly ran the business from our west coast office at a sprawling warehouse in the City of Industry near downtown Los Angeles. While living in the small city of Orange, our kids met and married their sweethearts. Michael married his bride Alicia in '85 and promptly had a cute redhead, named after, and a lot like Annie from Little Orphan Annie fame on Broadway. She was likened to the toddler in the Copper Tone billboard ads, but cuter.

They lived only a short distance from us in El Toro, convenient to our customary Sunday afternoon barbeque get-togethers.

In 1989, Scarlett married an archeologist, Aleksander Matthias, a good looking spicy Balkan from Greece whom she met her senior year doing research at Aristotle University of Thessaloniki. Alex adored Scarlett, and she him. They had a gorgeous son, Josh, born with a congenital curse that caused us to make a special trip to Orange County.

At the end of 1989, Kathryn and I moved to Fair Oaks in the Sacramento area, where I was able to run my business from home and travel only every other week. The move to Northern California was to give the kids some space, as we explored the nature driven lifestyle of the northern California foothills. The lack of smog and freeway traffic especially agreed with Kathryn while the endless lakes and trout streams really agreed with my angling tendencies. I rekindled a scaled down interest in flying, buying a small four-place airplane primarily for scooting to Orange County and Monterey to enjoy the charm of Carmel-By-The Sea. It was like a harmless time machine.

When Eddie told me he was calling it quits with Uncle Sam, I was shocked. That terrible tragedy with

René must have really augured deep into his spirit. I was thrilled. I gave him a huge approving hug, well really more than a hug, but I will keep that private. I told my hero that he and I would be good civilians and that I would follow him anywhere he needed to go to find work. My insides were having Mardi Gras, Fourth of July, Rose Parade and New Year's Eve parties all at once. He wouldn't die somewhere in the Pacific Ocean or in a Vietnamese rice paddy after all.

The four of us ended up in a quaint Eastern Carolina town with a traditional small town flavor with good family values. The pace was welcome as we embraced dancing lessons, baseball, and even soccer, a sport that was just catching on. Michael excelled at baseball and football for the High Point Central Bisons. He scored three touchdowns against cross-town rival Thomasville, and was named to the all district team in 1980. He was cheered on by none other than our own energetic Scarlett Parker, the middle school's perkiest Cheerleader.

Eddie even returned to church regularly; 'For the kids,' he said. I knew better as Memorial Day and Veteran's Day rolled around his face would get puffy, revealing his one way conversations with his Maker and his continued search for inner peace. Either his (and my) prayers were working, or time was the real healer. At long last his dreams had become less frequent and violent. After a brief stint volunteering at the local hospital, I put my education to work teaching High School Chemistry and Algebra. I went back to graduate school at UNC in Greensboro for my Master's Degree in Educational Management, all the while loving our two developing youngsters through their sprouting years. Teaching high school became a springboard to school administration, and later, principal of Ferndale Junior High School, only a few blocks from our house.

The best sparkplugs to Eddie's spirit were the kids. Eddie talked endlessly of the fishing trips with Michael, making fun of him shivering in the corner of the boat with only his nose showing. They both chattered like woodpeckers of the 'big one' that got away. Even with his travel schedule, he always made Michael's football games, and most of his baseball games. But fishing was their real passion.

'Really, Mom, you should have seen it. We almost had it in the boat,' on and on and on. The talks energized me too, as the self appointed healer of the World. Eddie and Scarlett had their times, too. Watching those disgusting horror movies, then pigging out on ice cream afterwards. They talked like little old ladies and never revealed to me their secrets.

'Just stuff, Mom, nothing

serious.' (Probably about other girls, puberty, and bra sizes). I just hope that Eddie shared some of the incidents he encountered in the Navy with her. She was such a good listener, glued to his eyes like his used to be glued to mine. The real fun began when Michael and Scarlett grew up and found their perfect spouses. When we moved to Northern California, with Eddie's man-toy the Mooney, we were still only two hours away from the kids. Flying was his yoga; just the extreme opposite for me. Having grandkids was the icing on the cake of our fun forties. Then things began to get complicated.

Chapter Nine

"There comes a time in the affairs of man when he must take the bull by the tail and face the situation.!"
~ ~ 'Pops' Parker

Drifting back

The increasing cold, aided by stronger winds, was an ill-mannered reminder of my worsening situation. It was back to reality, and I was in a mess. It got gradually colder as the night wore on, my legs taking the brunt. There just didn't seem to be a way to get comfortable, as my already small Mooney was made even tighter by the crash. I couldn't get the least bit comfortable and shift any weight off my hip either. No matter how I squirmed, my butt would go to sleep, and if I did shift, that meant I had to stay awake and shiver to death. My butt seemed to sleep more than I did. At least I could dream a bit to ease the torture. Damn it hurt, just like Captain Huddleson predicted. Damn gooks. The only downside of these icy sobrieties was that the travels to the past were getting shorter than usual. Now I can do a dream within a dream?

After my rest and relaxation reprieve in Hawaii, the ghostly visions started in earnest.

I could see blinding lights, lots of screams, and hear René yelling at me on the intercom mike. He was shrieking so loud, it would wake me up screaming with a response muffled in a locked throat. In the F-4, you couldn't just twist around and see your Radar Intercept Officer, but in my dream I could, as if I were in there with him. Thibadeau would be screaming more desperately than any I had ever heard; oversized eyes bulging and spurting bloody tears. There was an object gouged in is head causing rivulets of blood to stream down his contorted face. His expression was of contempt for me. 'It's all your fault,' over and over and over again, with arms waving for emphasis, like a comic book ghoul come to life. He had no hands, just flapping arms and the ends of sleeves where his hands were. Occasionally, the cockpit would be full of water where I could clearly see his oxygen hose, shaped like a seahorse, smacking him just above his wide open bug eyes. There was simply nothing I could do. I was wrapped securely in a tangled shroud of straps preventing my movement. My head was unable to move in any direction. I just straight ahead with eyes better served closed. I often woke drenched with sweat and so tangled in the bedclothes, a sight Kathryn would describe as a murder scene without blood.

Kathryn took the brunt of it for nearly

two years. Little did she know that her vigil was only just beginning. When our ship pulled away from the San Diego pier, I would return with most of the other fliers to be consigned with nightmares darker than any of the night missions we had flown. My team of Navy Flight Surgeons at the naval air station at Miramar said to expect at least six months of the relentless garbage, maybe longer, but that the visions and dreams should ease over time. The doctors were partially right, but my gruesome experience lasted longer than they had predicted.

Finally, they did ease; then they were pretty much gone. With the kids growing up and me busy with work, I guess my psyche reset itself, returning to its usual passageways. My grandmother used to talk of my uncle's nightmares and sweats after his return from the Pacific as a Marine Pilot. Now I was in this unappealing fraternity.

The casualties were not just the pilots, but also the innocents; caring wives like Kathryn and my aunts and uncles, who served in WWII. She felt my pain with each sweaty nightmare when I came home, and endured her own torture worrying about me during the separation. Many war wives, however, weren't as tough as the likes of Kathryn who was blue steel strong. Some women walked away from their damaged husbands or retreated to the whisky bottle, and some even committed suicide. The divorce rate for returning aviators was double the rate of civilians. There were no winners in the war, just the dead and damaged survivors. Curiously, about three years ago, out of nowhere, the dreams inexplicably started again. I went to therapy sessions hoping hypnotism might shed some light on this curse. The therapist was looking for a 'trigger', like hearing from an ex shipmate, a loud noise, or even a TV show with realistic aerial military activity. Nothing. I continue to dream, but I don't wake Kathryn anymore; she sleeps in another room. She seems to accept the arrangement, the price she is paying for my folly as a Navy pilot. We still are intimate, but sleeping alone, by definition, isn't an intimate arrangement.

Much earlier As my cramped up carcass tries to stay awake and keep warm, my thoughts seem to meander back to family where it usually is warm. Kathryn mostly; but Michael and Scarlett more and more. I was lucky to have those two. Good kids, and better parents than I ever thought to be. Thankful that my memory was allowing clearer images, I woke and fell back into the physical discomfort of that cramped little cockpit; shivering and twisting and turning the hours away, except for the brief reprieve of my visions. It was still dark and I was stuck like a rat in a coffee can. At times I wept, thinking that if I were tucked under a lot of brush and camouflage, I would just starve to death and die like a rodent. My legs were not in a lot of pain, but I was tangled up tighter than Bob Marley's hairdo. If I kept still I had less pain, then when I shifted to get more comfortable, the leg would pinch up and hurt like hell. This helplessness is really getting on my nerves. My noggin was still aching and continued to play tricks on my cerebral wiring system. I love my girls. Scarlett, Kathryn, and Alicia. The grandkids. Joshua and Annie. Poor little guy. The visions were getting a bit clearer now, little by little. Seeing better now, but drifting somewhere else.

My mind returned to the blasted letter. It caused my heart to pound so hard it would have fallen into my hands were it not for my chest wall. I needed to deal with this nagging development later, but on this morning, I was driven to get in the air and find my way to Orange County and be there for the marrow transplant for Josh. His situation was far more important than ours, but both weighed heavily. Josh, just a little kid....

1967 until the 1970s "Hey Michael, what's taking so long? At three bucks an hour you're gonna cost me a hundred dollars to get this yard mowed." Now Michael was the smartest, funniest, and coolest kid I knew. As time rambled on, I wished more and more he were mine. He was very little trouble, somewhat reserved, and more inquisitive than a Carolina Coon Cat. Kathryn described him at birth as a perfect little budding rose. Just perfect. The little guy was cute, bright, and always curious. I refused to play chess with him when he was eleven; 'cause I was too busy to practice and he had more time on his hands (I told myself). Kids do stuff like that to mess with your ego. Anyway, he would beat me like a kettledrum, every time. To this day, I will not play him. If he were here now, I *might* make an exception. Things were predictably great with Michael. About the time he was 12 or 13 and the most promising pitcher on the High Point little league Yankees baseball team, he was rolling out honor roll report cards term after term. He was at ease in school, keeping up with his studies while being involved in every student athletic program. All his classmates wanted to be near him and be his friend.

I couldn't have been more proud of him and loved him as much, if not more, as I did Scarlett. He was always a leader, either in Student government, or in athletics. He had the sunniest disposition of any kid I knew, and the only little kid actually happy when he first got up; ready to go anywhere, with anybody, to do anything. He was my perfect cup of coffee on weekend mornings, as it was our special time together.

When he was older we talked about the Friday night high school football games where he normally started as quarterback, who was dating whom, and details of his latest 'honey'. We bought and built the latest model airplane, mostly military styles used in Vietnam or Korea. I never talked with Michael much about my time over there, keeping it general. I occasionally spoke of the skill and determination that it took to fly off carriers and how awful war could be. He seemed to understand and didn't probe. He had several buddies who shared the same understanding with their fathers who served in the same unpopular war and a few buddies whose fathers did not come home. We could always find common ground at a fishing hole.

The most fun we had was when he was around twelve; that in-between age suffered by us all. Our best luck seemed to reside at Lake Norman, near Charlotte. We'd get up extra early and throw together poorly made bologna sandwiches, fruit, stale chips and a six pack of Mr. Pibb. I made a thermos of coffee for both of us, and then was correctly blamed for him taking coffee with him in his lunch pail in the eighth grade. We hit the road and made our way out North Main to Interstate 40, then south to Interstate 77, and finally turn off on highway 50 to the lake, always eager to get our limit of Rainbows and an occasional Channel Cat. When we got home, the family and next-door neighbors always braced for our stories of the 'big one that got away'.

Our usual boat rental was a trusty seven-foot long aluminum hull dinghy, with a seven and a half horse-power, two stroke, Evinrude motor. We had to add motor oil to the gas tank, just like Michael's green Lawn-Boy mower at home, but the smell of that Evinrude exhaust mingling with the marine vegetation and fish odors was just special. A smell that guys never forget. The exhaust that puffed from the little engine mixed with the early morning lake fog created a mystical setting, like being in another world. Then the sounds; the sounds of the 'chug-a-put' motors of ten or twelve others across the lake made a harmony never sang, only stored in the memories of crusty old veterans and new fishermen alike. The fish didn't seem to mind, nor did we.

The boat was so decrepit and cheesy, Bill's Marina folks didn't even ask for an ID or deposit. Maybe we were familiar to them, but any rate, the lightweight craft was barely drainage ditch worthy but suited us just fine. After the fifteen-buck rental fee, we cranked it up just before daylight to nab our favorite spot. We learned where to fish from the old timers who always fished in a contained area below the dam and near the mouth of the Old River Channel. Sometimes, they worked the creek runs of Davidson, Reed and Mountain Creeks, but primarily the Old Channel.

We made our way toward the Buffalo Shoals Bridge as the boat bottom slapped against the calm water where the river and the lake converged. That area almost always attracted the early birds that were up and movin' before sunrise when the fish were having their breakfast. A few hopefuls anchored near the bank where the sandy shoals and rocky banks merged, prime fishing grounds nearly always. Here the fish were larger and easier to catch, especially when the river was fastest just released from the Lookout Shoals dam. The river in that general area ranged from about 30 yards wide, giving us just enough berth so as not to tick 'em off. We positioned ourselves a respectful distance away from the grizzled old codgers, but fished a depth and bottom pretty much the same as them. They knew us, and they respected us as 'the whippersnappers' who were willing to get up really early and stay quiet. We were pretty good pole neighbors. We didn't mess in their sandbox; they didn't mess in ours, and most times we all managed to catch our limit. Sometimes they even nodded or gave us a forefinger salute from their fishhook covered baseball hat rims. Michael always thought that that was 'so awesome'.

With our breath showing a little steam,

just like the old Evinrude in the mist of the cold river, we puttered up to our spot. Little Michael was a perky kid, but still a kid. On the way down the river to get settled in our spot, Michael would be in the far end of the boat with both hands in his fake down-filled coat pockets to avoid his baiting duties. He was so buried in the coat, I could only hope it was Michael and not one of the waifs hanging around the marina for a free boat ride. After a few of Michael's signature farts, I was confident that it was a Parker kid. There was something really, really rotten about that kid's foul spray. Man oh man!

When it was time to swing into action, I wadded two or three sticky yellow fake salmon eggs on a size 12 treble hook, then handed the first pole to Michael. I gave him the honor of being the first to cast his bait into the blue-green Garden of Eden waters for Rainbow Trout. They were stupid fish, planters mostly, but good eatin' trout nonetheless. About this time, the yawning sun would peak through the trees and begin the welcome warming of shivering fishermen all over North Carolina lakes. Michael would begin to get more animated, especially after his personal thaw and expectation of catching the big one; the one I'd been describing to him as a bribe to get him to agree to go fishing with me.

At any rate, we did just okay until that

one time when he did tangle with an unusually nice sized native, but not the really big one of our lore. Damn if he didn't get the surprised Rainbow into the boat, his eyes a big as the fish's. When we got the fish safely on our stringer, Michal's expectations rose so high we started scheming on how big a trailer we were going to need to haul home all the fish we were going to catch.

The trip I will never forget didn't involve 'the big one that got away' or catching our limit of good sized rainbows. We were merely sittin' in the boat just bobbing around in the quiet waters listening to the bottom of the boat slap gently against the surface and feeling the warm sun smiling on our bodies; a state that would put a grown man to sleep. Out of the blue, Michael asks, "Dad, tell me about your flying in Vietnam." I was caught flat-footed, totally unprepared for what to say. We had talked generally before, but he was so young it really didn't register. I didn't have plaques or pictures hanging on the walls or memorabilia anywhere in the house of those years, except for a picture of René and Aimee with Kathryn and me I had taken at Pat Obrien's in New Orleans. No model military airplanes; nothing.

"Tiger, that was a long time ago and a lot of the details have slipped from my memory, but I'll give you my best shot." Michael edged a little closer and made strong eye contact. I wasn't sure I could do this. "The first time I went over there, you had just started school. The cruise was pretty tame that deployment with our air group losing only one airplane, and that was an accident while trying to get aboard the *America*. Our missions consisted of launching from the aircraft carrier and bombing our enemies of the North Vietnamese, mostly their bridges, highways and military gun emplacements."

"Did you ever bomb any kids?" Scarlet, and especially Michael, could come up with the dandiest questions at the most unexpected times and places. This one was the blue ribbon corker. I struggled for a minute, then slowly and carefully did the best with it. "I don't think so Buddy, not on purpose that I know of. The majority of our missions were from a very high altitude and our damage was only determined days later by target assessment teams. I wasn't told of hitting any civilians. Why do you ask?"

"Well, one of the kids in my class, Henry Trung, said one of his cousin's whole family was killed by American Bombs."

"Michael, it was probably an accident from the long-range high altitude B-52s that flew very high, mostly at night. Long before you were born, the United States and England bombed civilians near the end of World War II, a regrettable decision, but understandable because of the terrible things the Japanese and Germans did to our soldiers and especially to the civilians of our allies. Since then, as far as I know, we have not purposefully bombed civilians. That's a fact. My air group even went out of our way not to bomb any target where there might be schools or buildings where there might be civilians."

"Oh. That's good! Can you tell me about that time when your friend Mr. Thibadeau died?" I wasn't ready to answer that question either. My chest began to slowly tighten and I felt light headed. After I took off my baseball cap and wiped the growing beads of perspiration from my forehead with my sleeve, I blinked back at Michael and regrouped for another 'best shot.' As uncomfortable as that was, speaking with my son about those painful events was liberating.

"On my second tour of duty about a year later, René and I were assigned to a low-level night mission. I always hated those."

"Why Dad?" "Well, because at low altitudes you were much more exposed to a lucky shot from smaller caliber guns." "Oh? Is that what happened to you?" "No, Michael, it isn't. We had pretty much dropped all of our bombs, but had just enough left to find what was called a target of opportunity. There was an airfield on the way back to the ship that was responsible for shooting down a friend of ours. We went there, dropped the last of our bombs, and started back to the ship. That's when some lucky anti-aircraft fire or missile hit us. The airplane was damaged and some of the fragments hit Mr. Thibadeau and me. My injuries were not too serious, but a tiny piece of steel about the size of a BB, but very jagged, hit him up under his helmet and caused a small blood vessel in his brain to swell and finally burst. That's what killed him." "Oh. Is that when you got your DFC?" "Who told you about that?" "Mom. She told me not to say anything to you, but I didn't think you would care. Can I see it some day?"

"You're right Michael, it's okay. And yes, that's when they gave me the medal. They gave a lot of those medals out, and I was just lucky; the captain liked me, I think. When we get home, remind me and I'll see if I can find it in my old navy footlocker. How's that?" "Thanks a lot Dad, that's great. And you know what?"

"What?" "I am proud of you and glad you're my dad." I had to turn away and check my fishing pole and line. The little guy really got to me. "Say, I think your cork just bobbed. You better check it out."

When I regained my composure I turned back his way. I looked closely at Michael and saw him differently. He looked older, more sure, and his voice was jumping up and down two octaves in the same sentence. When he fished, he flicked his rod better that the old-timers that we both admired. Maybe the sun was hitting his face just so, but for a fleeting instant I thought I could see myself, like through a distorted carnival mirror. The flash reminded me that when we were shopping for groceries when he was just a tot sittin' in the grocery cart, both legs kicking, when one of the lady shoppers remarked that he was a spitting image of me. Kathryn and I got a big laugh out of that one, especially Kathryn. She never laughed so hard, before or after. The remark provoked my bad self to think, ' Take that Jared, you loser toad. I got your son and now he is mine.' I really did love that kid.

The turning point in Michael's life, and frankly the whole family's life, involved Michael and the law. He was fourteen I think, the summer he was moving from Ferndale Junior High to High Point Central High. We were upstairs fixing each other's tie, or at least he was fixing mine. His teenage neck was growing faster than his shirt would stretch while my oversized fingers just couldn't negotiate the difference properly. "Hang in there Pal, I'm almost done. There, not too bad."

"Okay, I guess, Dad. What do you think the kids at school are going to think of this; of me?" "That's a good question, son. It has been a long time since I was your age, but frankly, kids have short memories and mostly think about what you think about them. Also, a lot of the kids come from other schools and won't even know about all this. If you work hard for your teachers like you have been, they won't care about the past; same with your teammates if you stay with sports."

"I am nervous, Dad, really nervous." From downstairs, Kathryn was reminding us it was time to go. She looked amazing for the occasion that day, hair twisted tight in the back revealing her powerful and beautiful face. The back of her graceful neck was especially appetizing. Eddie took a minute to soak in the unexpected apparition, then continued, as Michael sat patiently on the side of the bed and wondered about what his dad's trance was all about.

"Make it snappy, everybody; we have to scoot and now. You know how the traffic can be on Main and Lexington this time of day. Every tobacco trucker from I-40 and the usual five o'clock traffic will be bumper to bumper. Let's go. Chop Chop."   All four of us were quiet during the 20-minute drive, except for eight-year-old Scarlett who was a nonstop fountain of questions. "Why are we here? Is Michael in trouble? He sure looks like it. Why are we all dressed up?" She went on and on and on. In between all of the interrogations, we reminded Michael to call the judge 'your honor', and to remember his manners.

The old Guilford County Court House

on Main and West Green, was built back in the 1930's, and wasn't all that far from our house in the town of only 60,000 residents. We finally got parked in the small parking lot across the street, and quickly found our way into the massive hall of the Art Deco building. We quickly settled into the wooden slat chairs outside the judges' chambers. The black plastic padded seats weren't all that comfortable, but we didn't plan to be there very long. Scarlett was back on the warpath. "Hush, Honey. You will see what this is all about in just a few minutes. Let's just tone it down, for me. Please?"

"Okay Mom, but I'm bored." It must have been a 100 degrees in the shade that day, and the air conditioning either on the fritz or just incompetent. The courtroom door featured a milky bottle glass window that revealed only shadows of figures on the other side. The neatly stenciled lettering below the glass read: *'Guildford County Superior County, District 18, Judge Brandon James Randles presiding.'*

As Kathryn wrestled Scarlett to sit still, the door that hadn't been oiled in ages squealed open and we all jumped. "The Judge will see you now." We followed an older stooped lady in a long black dress and made it through two sets of doors to an office. She either didn't have an air conditioner in her car, or she forgot to brush the back of her hair that morning, or both. The gust of her Revlon perfume Ciara™ was so strong, Scarlett buried her nose in Kathryn's dress until she passed.

We fully expected to be in a courtroom, with others nervously waiting their turn to stand in front of a tall lectern presided by a distinguished robed judge. Instead, it became clear and blessedly cool, since it was the judge's office. A distinguished looking gentleman, probably mid 40's, dressed in a simple blue blazer, tan pants and white shirt, came through another door across the room with a manila folder in one hand and the other outstretched. "Good, afternoon all. You must be the Parker's? Please, have a seat." As we all found our places, with Scarlett firmly anchored in her mom's lap, he spoke again. "I hope you all aren't disappointed not to be in the big courtroom across the hall, but I think my office is more private and our business shouldn't take too long." He shifted his gaze around the room, half smiling at us all. He stopped at Michael. "You must be Michael."

"Yessir, that's me," still looking at his lap. "Can you look at me, Son?" Michael complied. "Are you okay? You seem nervous." "I am your honor, really nervous."

"Michael I have before me a petition that requires my approval. Are you aware of this petition?" "Yessir." "Are you aware that my decision on this matter could very well influence your life forever?"

"Yessir, I do." His little Adam's apple moved up and down ever so slowly, just getting by the unyielding necktie. I was beginning to squirm now with my own swallowing issues, as Kathryn remained erect with a shrewd knowing expression. "What do you have to say to me about all this Michael."

"Well, your honor, here's my situation. I mean my prob....Ummm. Can I start over, sir?" The judge smiled and nodded. "When I am at school and they have Open House or for any reason that my folks come to school, the teacher or principal always act funny when they refer to my mom or dad as Mr. or Mrs. Parker, then refer to me as Mr. Penrose. I want to be a Parker, your honor. Not just because of the awkward part, but because I want to be like them when I grow up, especially my dad. He is the best man I have ever known." Michael looked left then right to his parents; both of us flush with pride. I had to fight the water works as my chest tightened. The little guy sounded so grown up, pleading his case so eloquently.

"He has always been with me when I play ball and is the best fisherman in Guildford County. When I am sick or get hurt my dad and mom make everything better, especially my mom; she is so special and just has a way, you know... I want to be a Parker, your honor. Don't you see? Please, please, approve our petition, sir. I don't want to be a Penrose any more. I need to be a Parker. I promise that I will make a good Parker. A really good one, I promise."

The judge looked away and took a while to clean his glasses. He didn't linger long, because he sensed the emotional anxiety all of us were feeling. He was a tough judge, had to be. But today the tender spot in his soul had been tapped. He looked squarely at Michael and said, "In reviewing your petition and the court acknowledging that no birth relative or other person or persons has replied to the court's interrogatories as legal protestants, and that no challenge for cause has been entered into the court records, Michael Penrose, from this moment until you die, you are now Michael Edward Parker. Congratulations, young man."

Restless Scarlett, with her eyes on Michael the whole time, was the first. She jumped a foot high and clutched him like the big brother she always loved, pinning his arms as she danced with him like a dervish. When we could break in, all four of us squeezed and cried until we couldn't anymore. Kathryn had such an outburst it took me by surprise. And me, I was a mess, too. The whole scene was just wonderful and amazing. That was such a poignant moment for us all and a time in young Michael's life he too would always look back on with fondness.

During my travel years, he was most helpful with Kathryn holding sway on Scarlett, younger by six years. He was always good company for Kathryn when I was away, eager to do his homework and most of the time didn't mind mowing the yard. He not only had a strong intellect, but good moral judgment in his decision-making. My demanding travel caused me to miss his birthdays due to furniture markets in Dallas, San Francisco, or Atlanta. I've always regretted that, even though Michael always seemed to understand. We were closer during those early years than during the past several. We gradually drifted apart a little, you might say. We are still close, but not like before. Maybe it was just a sign of the times of hustle and bustle of the late 70's and 80's. That's what I told myself, anyhow. I always meant to work on our relationship, but the *Cat's In The Cradle* folk song seemed to have targeted me, and I wasn't sure how to escape the line of fire. Nowadays, he was too busy to make that offshore fishing trip, or even to take in an Angel's or Padres ballgame.

Michael went to UCLA in Brentwood on an athletic scholarship mostly for baseball, but managed to play on the varsity football team as well. He blew out his arm his sophomore year as his football playing finally gave way to academics. This secretly thrilled Kathryn; she, well both of us, always worried about him getting hurt. He graduated with honors, and later married Alicia Farrell, a very bright technician at the nuclear medicine lab where he worked. She was sooo smart, borderline scary smart. Her dad had pioneered the use of radionuclides in the radioactive decay techniques for diagnosis and treatment of diseases. They had the cutest daughter, born with more hair than Harpo Marx ever had. Her name, Annie, suited her personality perfectly; precocious, bright, and like her mom, always affectionate. They were a close family and seemed not to struggle financially in the early years as the two of us did. Still, something just wasn't right between Michael and me, but I just could not put my finger on it. The light of my memory was fading of Michael; back to the cold scruffy assed Mooney.

Early '70s The night wind was picking up for real now, and as I screwed into as tight a ball as I could, I drifted back into the world of kids; this time, Scarlett. Michael was crazy about her and she him. She was always proud of his quarterbacking skill, as she cheered from the stands as one of the play-like cheerleader groupies, as she ultimately became the real deal when she got to high school. Michael's balmy personality was the perfect antidote to her sizzling disposition. She was always noisy. Scarlett's new California manufactured HB snare drums were like a cage full of restless woodpeckers. She always liked the noise of hitting the rim of the darn things, instead of the middle. She was either very clever or just a lousy percussionist, I wasn't sure which. I could see her better now. I know she is mine, because she looks like a cross between Kathryn and my mom. Her orneriness though, most assuredly came from my branch of the family tree. I could see her merge from tot, to teen, then to mom. Each image of Scarlett is more beautiful than before. Her always out of control natural untamed hair framed her soft, innocent features as a seraph of the finest pedigree. Always with a smile, sometimes quizzical, but always a smile like her mother.

As a kid, she loved taking things apart and putting them back together. She was stealthy smart. On the outside a boisterous girl, fully social, but Scarlett was a closet intellectual known only by our family. She skipped the second grade, easily making the transition with the older kids. When Michael was in high school, he would secretly let Scarlett help him with his algebra. She would skim through the chapter relating to the problems, then toss the finished work to him with her fun little wink. Scarlett's future would be assured forever due to her curiosity of life's infinite wonders. She found interest and value in all things and all people. She had a gift, even as a kid, to sense when people were in distress or hurting. Family or friend, she was always there to comfort or aid; got that from Kathryn. At the same time, she was fun loving, even mischievous, always just behind or ahead of trouble; got that from me. She too was athletic and loved rock music, the louder the better. Michael looked after Scarlett, and she him in her own way. While Michael was like his mother in intelligence, Scarlett looked like her mom, thankfully, and enjoyed her mom's good qualities. She was alive, impulsive, overachieving, and lived for the moment. She would often find herself slogging through details, missing the big picture, but never doing so when it mattered.

My favorite time with Scarlett was the movies and ice cream. For her, the scarier and more shocking the better. We watched, *Bay of Blood*, *Alien*, *Amityville*, and *Asylum*, to mention a few. I was willing to watch any chick flick she wanted, but noooo; it was the blood and gore she wanted. My aunt and mom used to do the same, so maybe there's an overall genetic predisposition that fuels the gruesome filmmakers' pocketbooks into family perpetuity. To this day, she doesn't know how terrified I was, sitting there with my eyes closed or excusing myself to take a leak during the scary parts. I didn't always avoid getting scared out of my wits, especially when there was no warning, as was the case most of the time, like in *Carrie*. (It took me forever to watch another Sissy Spacek movie). When I jumped up to leave, I convinced her that my prostate was acting up, a good excuse until she asked what a prostate was. I told her to look it up in the dictionary.

As a young teen, Scarlett would talk to me about stuff she was shy to talk with Kathryn about, or so she says. When our movie was over, we would most always find an ice cream place like the Dairy Queen for a root beer float. In between our slurping, I was asked to share my opinion on a variety of offbeat subjects that I was totally ill equipped to answer. Like the best time to start wearing a bra, whether Tampax ™ or Kotex ™ was the best way to go, and when it was okay to kiss a boy. I was never asked how to throw a curveball or how to hit a golf ball, just girl stuff. Most of the time, I would beg off a week until I could consult with Kathryn during our nightly thirty minutes of bedtime reading. The following week I gave a germane answer to the question, only to be challenged with another, and so it went, mostly about boys. I think she might of had a slight suspicion that I might have been one once.

I am convinced that I was the innocent victim of a mother-daughter conspiracy, but I'll never know. Sometimes that peculiar look from one to the other made me very suspicious. The female species should be considered as the government's weapon for domestic and international negotiations. If they were allowed, the U.S. would enjoy favorable trade balances with the free world, there would no more wars, and the schools would require sensitivity training classes for all boys in the 9th grade. I could never get the best of those girls, back then, or now. I am convinced that God is really a woman.

The personal sacrifice of going to all those scary assed movies, I am convinced, will get me into the pearly gates of heaven. Not fighting for my country, not hitting a home run against an All-American pitcher from Arizona State, or even taking out over twelve tons of trash to the curb over the years. It will be sitting through (most of) the creepy movies that'll do the trick. The only other good reason I could use to beg my way into heaven would be to have used the good judgment to love and protect Kathryn Whitmore Parker.

Kathryn's sweet radiance lit my darkest pathways. Pretty, popular, good sense of humor and most importantly, she was crazy about me. For what reason, to my dying day, I will not know. Given to foster parents when she was three, she grew up full of maturity and style. Valedictorian, Student Council President, and chairman of every group she encountered. I wonder what she saw in me, but hey, who cares? As long as she doesn't figure it out... She could win the Gold Medal of Snuggling and Kissing too, as I could sure use the contest about now. We were married while I was still in the training command in Kingsville, Texas. Got my wings in August and was assigned to..... Ohhhh, Crap. Here we go again.

1:45 A.M. Here it comes, again, the dense pewter fog sneaking in from Newport Harbor; the swooshing sounds, radio static, red lights, red cockpit lights. Am I here or there? Unfortunately here, and I need to turn off the master switch to save the battery. I can't reach the blessed blasted thing, but at least the red glow of the instrument panel might offer some company until the battery gives out. Which damn cockpit? Head swimming again. Jeeeeeez us. The cold oozing marine layer from the Pacific Ocean that rusted outdoor barbeque cookers and had chosen to settle on me was aggravation enough, but the pain from being bunged up didn't help. I couldn't rub an area or shift around to ease an ache and that was just torture. If I had been captured during the war, I would have been a lousy P.O.W.

Was that a woodpecker pecking away in my squashed up Mooney? Nah, probably just the wind tapping the thin aluminum of the broken wing against the side of the airplane. Reality bites. Need to take a whiz again, probably 'cause it's *cold*. Trying to hold the memory of Kathryn but can't; too awake. Wish she were here now. What's this? I can feel the frames of what must have been my eyeglasses. Maybe that would explain why I couldn't see too well; if I could just reach it. Maybe. Ahhh, God is good. They aren't broken. These were last years' prescription, but they would do.

I must have been a cheap bastard, or I would have current eyeglasses for the airplane. I could finally make out my situation better now; still dark, but better. I squinted over my shoulder to the lower part of the passenger door panel, then I saw it. I was as happy as if striking gold by locating the ELT attached to what was left of the right side of the airplane door. I was able to wiggle just enough to reach it, and saw that the small switch was in the off position. We must have bounced twice, since the jolt of a crash is supposed to activate the small transmitter. I can't remember when the battery was changed, probably two years ago when we did the annual inspection.

As soon as I touched the cigar box sized device, I knew something was wrong. Before I could get a good grip on it, I felt it slip through my useless hand and fall into the darkness below. Now was a fine time to learn that my thumb and wrist were badly dislocated and worthless. What really peeved me was having almost bought a Breitling

Chronograph wrist watch that had an emergency distress transmitter built in, sending out a distress signal exactly like the ELT in the Mooney. I could have bought one for $2500, about half the going price. Cutting corners on safety items is biting me in the butt, and I knew better; that's the real pity of it all. I also should have bought that VHF handheld radio, critical for communicating when losing electrical power or radios that go on the fritz. Like *now*. Two backup safety items, that confirms me as a card-carrying dumb ass. Even with all the brush covering the top, front, and side of the Mooney, there was a sudden blinding light. I had to turn away. Then the wind was instantly howling like a small tornado whipping up dust and all forms of debris. It could only be from a spaceship. I hope it's warm and dry up there. Come and get me you cock roaches; at least maybe I will be warm.

Chapter Ten

"Promises and affairs are a lot like impressions. The second one doesn't count for much."
~ ~ *Kristin Hannah*

Sunday Evening

Kathryn crept into her garage after dropping her more and more fussy husband off at the small Cameron Park Airfield, the home of his toy flying machine. She had stopped by Corti Brothers to mostly piddle, picking up their signature Sevile Orange Marmalade, some V-8 juice, and onion bagels to have for a quick breakfast that next morning. On most weekend mornings, Eddie usually made his famous homemade yogurt biscuits, like his mom's, but he was gone and she was in Texas. Kathryn was in familiar territory of being alone, having tolerated the years of Eddie's travel. She convinced herself it was the lamentable price for the creature comforts they enjoyed. Nice house, newer luxury cars, fine colleges, a little money in the bank, and fun getaways to the Caribbean, and lastly, the 'Mooney pit.'

As for the airplane, it was only a couple of hours to Southern California to see the kids, but an eager passenger she was not. She would have preferred to ride the bus instead of crawling into that cramped, noisy airplane. When she did fly, it was either bumpy, hot, or the radio would screech away what little peace she might be having. Eddie wasn't much company in the cockpit as he was poking or twisting the dials, fiddling with something between the seats, or conversing with a controller on his voice activated microphone and headset. He was a very proficient and careful pilot, the best; but that didn't matter. She was scared, and that was that. A lifetime member of the White Knuckle Society, and if it existed, she would be the President.

Kathryn remained baffled with Eddie's most recent behavior. The last few years hadn't been the bliss *Modern Romance* magazine suggests, but after nearly three decades of marriage, things were relatively smooth, even predictable. He was behaving much like he did the first few years after leaving the Navy, but that was a long time ago. Back then he couldn't let go of his memories and guilt. Kathryn and Eddie had both tried unsuccessfully to call Aimee, thinking that the connection might purge the demons still lurking in Eddie's reservoir of dreams. They both concluded that she must have moved back to the West Indies or somewhere far away, probably with family on an island where there was no phone service. Finally, they gave up trying to track her down. She probably, in some fashion, may have blamed Eddie for René's death. Who knows? Aimee was very special, and the best friend that Kathryn sorely missed. Aimee may have assumed that Eddie alone made the decision to make that optional bombing run, the reason they were both hurt. Eddie felt the same guilt even though he and René together discussed and agreed on that decision. Both men routinely found suitable homes for the remaining bombs of their primary mission. Eddie still felt guilty and Aimee was still a Vietnam War widow.

Maybe Vietnam was not it. Maybe he was just going through a middle-aged slump; a condition that all the female activists were convinced was the providence of most married women. Kathryn wasn't a subscriber to that notion and she knew there was too much currency between them for that to be true; at least, in their case. She decided to be patient. Eddie was right there for her when she ignored her heart and married the wrong guy; she needed patience now, more than ever.

They did have their escapes to Martinique or Barbados every year or so, the perfect tonic to make everything better. There was nothing like making love to that special chorale of tree frogs that began exactly at sunset; all in perfect unison. No kids, no trash, no phones, no TV, just the two lovers of old. The cadence of melodious steel drums seemingly from every direction that accompanied the smells of barbequed fish along the beach were like warm oil massaging clarity to their senses. The rhythm was wonderful. The peace was heavenly. The romance only local, perhaps, but romance nonetheless. Kathryn wondered if men went through 'men-o-pause', then chuckled out loud about the notion. Things have to get better.

10 P.M. Kathryn stepped into her oversized closet in the bedroom. She stepped out of her dress, shoes, and underwear; dropping them on the carpet to change into something warm and comfortable. She would pick the clothes up later, maybe. She removed the elastic band from the back of her hair, letting it drop, just covering her shoulders. She wasn't big on jewelry, but never took her diamond wedding band off. Her 18K gold earrings and necklace were unfastened as she let them slide through her fingers quietly into the velvet padded jewelry box. Eddie had picked them up for her in Subic Bay on one of his stops at the Naval Air Station Exchange in Kubi Point, during his first tour of duty in Vietnam. There was the companion heart shaped locket with her photo she had given to him to keep in the side pocket of his flight jacket for good luck. She became emotional as she remembered the circumstances of each piece of jewelry

Eddie had showered her with over the years. The twin ruby ring he bought in Hong Kong and the star sapphire ring surrounded by small diamonds he had made in Burma. She remembered that Eddie took as much or more pleasure watching her opening the gift boxes than she enjoyed receiving the jewelry. He was a good man and she had a determined hope that he would shake his recent malaise and rediscover the Eddie of old. She wore little make-up that Sunday evening, so that came off quickly with just a soft washcloth and touch of Neutrogena Soap. She studied herself in the mirror and thought 'not too bad.'

It had been a long day. She snuggled into her oversized lush terry robe and hood she got from Eddie that Christmas, rubbing the back of her neck and each cheek into its sensuous, generous fibers; almost like Eddie's experienced fingers. As she closed her eyes and drifted a bit, she was startled to feel him. She shuddered as he eased up behind her and rested his head on the side of her neck and buried his face on her shoulder. The adventurous arms slowly encircled her body, his hands sliding into the arms of the robe where Kathryn's hands were folded. He smelled nice, like a freshly showered Eddie always smelled. They began to sway back and forth, to a soft melody known only to them. A lullaby punctuated by steel drums, waves lapping an empty beach, and tree frogs adjusting their serenade in perfect time with their lullaby. Eddie's hands slowly pulled from the robe sleeves, his wedding ring nudging hers ever so slightly. His hands edged slowly upward rounding and nudging her curved breasts; ever so like Eddie. She moaned and tilted her head to the side; his warm breath and familiar stubble finding their niche there. His caress moved back down her side as the expert hands came together toward the gift below. Kathryn began to glisten, as she always did when he was soft like this. Her awakening was so real. She reached back and cupped his buttocks, always firm and easy to grip as the ride intensified. She could feel him nudging against her, so real it took her breath away and aroused her like a desperate woman denied the ecstasy once familiar.

This was the Eddie she craved. Her feelings caused her to recall the black gown he liked best to reach under to feel her completely, then discard over her head almost as quickly as she had let it slide over her head and cover her just barely, her attentive bosoms and yearning fire below. His breath on the back of her neck was just too much. She spun around to demand her desperately needed satisfaction, then *nothing*. As quickly as he had appeared, he abruptly vanished into the mist and lights of the evening fog. He was gone. It was so unfair, this ghost of Eddie. She was soaking in her own moisture, breasts at attention, and her pulse rate at least 100. Her tears of joy for the moment felt, as much for the time imagined, too short. It was a lousy apparition and a hopeless tease, leaving her frustrated and embarrassed.

As for the real Eddie to appear and keep her really warm; she sorely missed that. Missed to the point of an ache that drilled into her spirit. In spite of the recent speed bumps with Eddie, she was still crazy about him. She always felt safe with him and he always treated her special. When she found him in the mood, he was as perfect a lover, as he always was; thoughtful, patient, and always sure that their erogenous engines got to the station at the same time. She had to get through the night without him, dreading waking without him by her side. Kathryn's ache was so raw every breath came with effort. Like breathing backwards; air gushing in, then having to forcibly push it out. At this moment, everything felt backwards to her. Her thoughts just rambled, in no particular direction or purpose.

Eddie always opened the car door for her, waited for her to enter a doorway first, and only missed their anniversary once. What a trip that was. There was never a doubt as to who was the star of the duo was. Pretty, smart and sensitive, Kathryn was the perfect mother and like her daughter Scarlett, everyone wanted to be around her. She grew more beautiful as she drifted through her forties, and undoubtedly would remain so in her fifties and beyond. She knew Eddie was lucky to get her, and she felt the same good fortune. She wondered why he had been so remote lately? She wondered and wondered.... The only time she got grumpy was because of something Eddie did, but always did so in private. She was the sunshine, the rain, and the rainbow of the marriage, giving Eddie the opportunity and environment to find his 'pot o' gold'. She missed him and was curiously fearful about the flight for this evening.

Kathryn was smart, but couldn't put her finger on why their recent relationship had only a whimper of the intimacy and laughter they enjoyed over the years. They were both looking forward to retirement in a few years, and that alone should brighten their outlook of getting older, and freshen the marriage that had grown musty. Should, but it wasn't headed that way. The train was definitely headed down the wrong tracks. Kathryn also noticed a strain in Eddie's attitude with both Scarlett and Michael. Michael had been a dream kid, whom Eddie treated more like a son, than a stepson, and Scarlett, even though sometimes ornery and adventurous, was good at heart and a great mom. She would talk to them both, seriously, after seeing Josh through his procedure. Maybe the three of them could find a solution.

Kathryn's thoughts drifted a bit, from Eddie to Michael and Scarlett. Scarlett, God love 'er. Armed with Alicia's intuitive medical instincts, she was the bulldog that tackled her son Josh's unfair health problems with the required energy and determination that eliminated one dead end after another. It was Scarlett's grit and Alicia's research that led to further testing that corrected the misdiagnosis of chronic anemia to Cooley's Anemia or Sickle Thalassemia. Cleverly disguised as anemia, Josh had abnormal hemoglobin. It was Scarlett's determined decision to proceed with a bone marrow transplant in lieu of more blood transfusions. She wanted a vital and energetic son, not the poor little child who suffered so. In addition to Josh's frequent blood transfusions, he was considered for a splenectomy and removal of the gall bladder, all poor choices for a two and a half year old child, especially Josh.

She wasn't looking forward to the four-week hospital stay where he would be checked four times a day for infection, but didn't complain, even to herself. She was steeled for the daily outpatient visits that would be required to monitor infections and chart the progress of the engrafting progress. For Josh, she knew that even after a successful engrafting, he would be closely monitored for six or seven months, and that it could take up to a few years for the immune system to normalize and get stronger. She was aware of the 25 to 50% chance of long term problems like skin dryness, altered pigmentation, dry mouth and eyes, nausea, and weight loss. The bone marrow transplant would extend Josh's life, and improve his quality of life. Screw the Cooley's anemia. It was messing with the wrong family.

Scarlett finally broke though the mass of medical testing and finally learned that the genes Joshua got from his dad and her; Scarlett's genes from Eddie's family on his father's side and from Alex on both sides. In the part of the Mediterranean where Alex's family all came from, the prevalence of the gene was common. The genes were beta autosoma recessive and affected the production of normal hemoglobin, causing mutations in the beta chain of the hemoglobin molecule. Alex, orphaned as a toddler, was of Greek and Albanian ancestry, and that particular region was the unfortunate source of those genes. Alex was devastated that his ancestry carried this gene, and would have done anything to make Joshua whole. The other part of the puzzle was solved when by definition of the disease; both parents were the requisite carriers. Eddie's grandfather Theodore, it was determined through Scarlett's hours of ancestry research, was the bastard child of a renowned Balkan gypsy and Turkish father who carried the Thalassemia Gene. Both resided along the southern coast of the Antalya region; their ancestors having been there for generations. As carriers only, it was much like them carrying the HIV virus and not having fully developed AIDS. Poor Josh was doomed at the minute of conception and consigned to its miserable consequences.

The most reliable treatment recommended to Scarlett and Alex was successfully tested in the 70's; a bone marrow transplant, and the sooner for Joshua the better. Without it, Josh would continue with his pale, fussy symptoms. His spleen, liver and heart would continue to be enlarged and his bones would become brittle and thin. Besides the years of suffering with fatigue, shortness of breath and jaundice, Josh would not make it past his teens. His heart would just give out, and break the hearts of all who loved him so.

Even though Scarlett or even Kathryn had better odds of being a match for the bone marrow, no one in the family or close friends matched. It was through resourceful Eddie's tireless efforts, that a donor was finally found, a young Navy Pilot that belonged to Eddie's Tail Hook Fraternity. The marrow was extracted from the anonymous saint and made available in Orange County on Monday for the Tuesday procedure. The schedule allowed the whole family to be there for Scarlett and Alex. Joshua needed all the family support he could get.

Josh's plight brought Kathryn back to the present, as she reflected on Eddie back at the hanger in Cameron Park. She could envision him dropping down onto a small little dirt airfield somewhere not too far off, waiting for a 'thing-a-ma-jiggie' part for the Mooney. She could see and hear him sipping 14 hour-old coffee from disgustingly stained coffee mugs with the faded letters of a propeller manufacturer etched on the side. He was laughing and smiling with another airplane old-timer, probably from a vulgar joke. Eddie loved this kind of unplanned buzzing around the San Joaquin Valley in the winter, popping into small airports to enjoy the company of whiskered crop dusters and hounds asleep on a thoroughly dilapidated couch parked near an ancient pot belly stove. This was the real Eddie Parker, salt of the earth who never found a stranger in those little country airports.

Still 10 P.M. Sunday night Eddie was still shivering in his tangled cocoon on the side of a mountain somewhere between hell and heaven, clinging onto every splinter of hope the assuring memories of his family were providing. He was cold, hurt, and holding on to his faith, a skill he learned 20 years earlier in a land many miles away.

As Kathryn contemplated on what was bugging Eddie, her thoughts traveled back to Scarlett again, wondering if she had noticed Eddie's ragged manners lately. Maybe it was all backwards, and Scarlett had said or done something that didn't sit right with Eddie? She needed to call Scarlett, but it was so late, past ten. Maybe she would get to the bottom of the rift first thing in the morning. She knew she could fix her Eddie problem, as she had done their whole marriage.

She knew Eddie could get moody. She knew that when they married and especially after the Navy. There was no question that the Vietnam War had been both physically and mentally expensive for Eddie. She thought of the nightmares and his need of more and more therapy. She hated sleeping alone more than anything.

Put him in an airplane, on a baseball diamond, or in front of a difficult customer, he was as fluid and effective as they come; at home, not so much. There were only brief fits of anger, mostly directed at himself, but more often than not it spilled over to their relationship. It was always something stupid, like a regretful business decision, or a simple mistake like paying a bill late, rare in either case. But between him and the kids, that was different. When any one was out of sorts with him, Kathryn had a way of umpiring things back to normal. Out of nowhere, she thought of René. Dreams again? Maybe? Hmmmm..

With Eddie and Michael, the only reason they might be less than cozy, was that they spent so little time with each other. Whatever it was, it could probably be fixed over a day of fishing off the San Diego coast, or one of those relaxing five day Disney cruises. They had those Lake Norman trips they both enjoyed so much, though not nearly often enough. She mused that was not a bad idea for all six of them to go fishing. Eddie and Alicia got along marvelously, as she brought out Eddie's quirky sense of humor and even drew Michael and Eddie into a battle of endless potty jokes. Annie and Josh would add to the party too; growing into fun kids, and like their parents, had been easy to manage. A cruise and a charter fishing trip, that might just do it. She would check on it as soon as Josh got through the first thirty days of his marrow engrafting tomorrow afternoon. Meanwhile she would talk with her son and Eddie separately. Maybe they were having individual issues that didn't involve the other. She knew that women weren't hard to figure, but men were impossibly different. Women could be seduced with jewelry and a candle light dinner, but men were impossible. It was driving her crazy.

Kathryn was always avoiding her e-mail whenever possible. It was a chore about as appealing as changing a light bulb or taking out the trash. Nonetheless, she shuffled her way into the study to do just that. Maybe it would make her sleepy. The scotch and water was not working; just making her more curious about Eddie. She had an uneasy feeling about him that night; more so than usual as she became anxious each and every time he crawled into that maddening airplane. One would think that doing it for 35 years would be enough. Not for her Eddie though. At least it's only a small airplane and not that hideous Navy Jet that almost cost him his life as it did René's.

About 9:45 P.M. Four hundred miles to the south at the Fullerton Airport, Scarlett was still sitting in her car on the tarmac just outside the Air Combat hangar waiting for Eddie. She called Alex on her cell phone to see if he had heard anything. Eddie had been late before, but not like this. By now she was getting anxious. "Alex, if I don't see him in another thirty minutes, I'll call back and have you call the FAA. I'm not sure who to call, so be looking up the number. In fact, go ahead and call them, and get right back to me as soon as you learn anything." Fifteen minutes later, although expecting that call, Scarlett jumped when her cell phone rang.

"Alex is that you?" "Yes, babe, it's me.

Scarlett, the FAA says your dad left Cameron Park at 6:30PM with an ETA in Fullerton at 9:00PM. They are aware of the slightly overdue time, reporting unusual winds from the southeast that might explain the delay. If they don't hear from him by 10:30, they'll assume communication problems or worse. At that point they will request a search, usually handled by the Sheriff's rescue helicopters. If he does check in with your mom, or us, we are to notify them so they can cancel the search. Give him another thirty minutes and if he doesn't show up by then, come on home. Let's not call Kathryn or Michael just yet and have them terrified over nothing. He's probably just fine. Come on home and I will fix you some of your favorite decaf Oolong. We have a long day tomorrow with Josh. I love you Baby Doll. Try not to worry."

"Okay, Honey, I'll call when he gets in, or if he doesn't show, when I start for home. Either way I'll call. Love you."

11:00 P.M. Kathryn had over 300 emails in her inbox; mostly forwarded jokes and appeals to send post cards to terminally ill children. Forward the message or have bad luck. Ha! 'Maybe that's why I am having such a crappy day', she thought to herself. After grinding through and dumping the unsolicited emails, and an hour later, one that caught her attention was from a friend from the San Diego Unified School District. It wasn't unexpected, but then again it was. She hadn't heard from Chris for a while, so it gave Kathryn an understandably warm feeling as she cupped her chin in her palms and began to read. Her eyes flew over the words half comprehending their meaning. She was very much preoccupied with her AWOL husband; it would probably have served her better to wait until another time.

Dearest Kathryn,

I have missed you terribly, in ways that are indescribable. It has been only three weeks since we were together, but it seems like three years. I miss you so, and need you more than ever. Your companionship and special support has been my oxygen, and I thank God for you every night. I can picture your sweet smile, but I need the real you. You have framed the clarity of our roles in life and it has changed my life.

I wish you and I had met years earlier. My life would have been better, and I trust you feel the same. I know you know that. Let me know when you can get back to Southern California as soon as possible. Twelve months is almost up, and I need your support more than ever. I really need you close by.

In a lifetime, one is lucky to meet that one person you can count on. One special person, selfless to a fault, on call for my every need. You are that person, Kathryn. You have saved my life. Please call as soon as you read this. I know you have been busy lately, but I will wait. You are always worth the wait.

Lovingly to the nth power,

Chris

    Kathryn thought for a minute on how to respond; then abruptly shut the laptop. ' This will just have to wait.'

Chapter Eleven

"Affairs of the heart are the least managed of any other type of affair."
~ ~ *The author*

11:30 P.M. Sunday

Kathryn thought to herself and reconsidered. 'I need to call Chris. It's been a while and I finally have some privacy. I have neglected phoning, but things have been in an awful turmoil lately. Stilll... I should call.' As she reached for the phone, she flinched like it was white hot. The unexpected ring startled her and took her breath away. 'The phone, at this hour?' The caller ID recorded on the handset read 'unlisted', but she took the call anyway. Probably one of the kids, more likely Scarlett's cell phone.

"Kathryn Parker?" "Yes." "This is Bud Bogle, from the FAA in Los Angeles. Are you the Parker's who own a Mooney with the 'N' Number, Two Zero One Tango?" "Why, yes. Yes we are. My husband left Cameron Park sometime around six tonight. He was headed to Fullerton. Why are you calling?" "We have an Edward W. Parker who filed a flight plan from Cameron Park showing him due in Orange County by nine thirty this evening. As you might know, he is long overdue, with his last transmission to the Bakersfield flight controller at 8:45 tonight. Southern California approach control who was the hand off in Los Angeles, never heard from the Mooney." Kathryn simply froze. Couldn't breathe. Her insides felt tied in a granny knot that might last forever. The fears she never allowed herself to feel were real and overpowering. She thought that maybe it was a mistake and Eddie's radio was on the fritz. The airplane was fifteen years old, so maybe that was it. The unimaginable fears were nonetheless flooding her way, and she did not know how to respond, or what to say. She couldn't cry and it took a moment to collect a voice.

"Mrs. Parker, are you there?.....Hello... Mrs. Parker?" "Yes, I am here. What can I do?" "Nothing for now. We can't be sure he didn't have radio failure, but since he hasn't popped up somewhere along the way and called in, we will request a search along his route of flight. We have targeted our search based on his initial transmission when he departed the Cameron Park Airport until the Bakersfield transmission. We are focusing in the Gorman area and near Lake Hughes into the Burbank area. Apparently, he was doing turns for a speed check before he got to the mountains so we are especially concentrating in that area. Anything from there to Orange County would have been reported by now. Mrs. Parker we will depend on you to inform your family members and close friends. I hope that is okay with you. Should we call this number in case we have any news?"

"No. It's better if you try my mobile phone at 916-100-8172 tonight, or later tomorrow morning I can be reached at the Transplant Center at Children's Hospital in Orange. Meanwhile, I will get the family up to date on your search plans."

"Thank you, Mrs. Parker. We will call as soon as we know anything. On your end, if you or your family makes contact with him, give us a call at (310) 725-7560, extension 333, so we can cancel the search. Try not to worry. From what I have heard about your husband, he was a skilled aviator with great survival instincts. Good night Mrs. Parker, and try not to worry."

"Good night Mr. Bogle. Please call as soon as you find out what is happening, even later in the morning, no matter the hour... and thanks." Try not to worry? Not happening. Kathryn immediately reached into the liquor cabinet and shakily poured another stiff Scotch and water. She slumped into the chaise in the bedroom and reached for the phone to call Scarlett. Just as she touched it, it rang again; gnawing unfairly on her already shredded nerves. 'Heavens, I really am going to faint away any time now.' "Hello?"

"Mom, it's Scarlett. Have you heard from Dad?" Without waiting for the answer, she continued. "I waited until 10:30 until I finally went home. Alex called the FAA and they said that he was due at 9:30, but to wait until ten o'clock or so. They said they would request a search by then and call if they had any updates. We're getting awfully worried."

Fighting tears that clouded the view of her floor, Kathryn managed, "Scarlett, oh Baby, the FAA called just a few minutes ago told me they lost radio contact with him south of Bakersfield. They are requesting a search for later on tonight. Maybe his ancient old radio or GPS finally conked out on him and he dropped into El Monte or Riverside. Surely he will turn up soon. You know how he is; always causing worry with his unpredictable changing of plans."

"I hope you're right, Mom. Are you still on that Southwest flight for tomorrow morning?" "I'll be there for sure Honey, and hopefully all this will be sorted out by morning. I don't want anything to interfere with our being there for Josh on Tuesday afternoon." "Okay, Mom, I'll be there to pick you up. If you hear anything tonight, no matter what time, even early in the morning, please call me on my cell if I am on the way to the airport. I love you, and please don't worry. I am sure everything will be alright."

"I love you too and I will see you in the morning. I'll be sure to call if I hear anything. Do me a favor and call Michael for me. I'm not too steady to be doing too much more talking tonight, and especially to be making any sense. Bye, Dear One." Scarlet sobbed, "Bye Mom, I love you."

12:30 A.M. The FAA had two searches going that night, one for a Mooney somewhere between Bakersfield and Orange County, and a low winged Piper Cherokee somewhere in the eastern Santa Monica Mountains in the Malibu Canyon area. The Coast Guard's rescue unit based out of the Los Angeles Airport had just launched its highly regarded HH-65 Dolphin to handle the Santa Monica Piper Cherokee, while the Los Angeles County Sheriff's rescue helicopter, an AS-350 Aerospatiale made Eurocopter, usually called on for mountainous rescue missions, headed toward Gorman and Lake Hughes to look for the Mooney. It was so suited for the mountains the Australian Royal Navy called it ' The Squirrel.' They deployed from the Whiteman Airport in musty Pacoima, near Burbank, in the San Fernando Valley just north of Los Angeles. The sheriff's newer choppers had advanced technology systems that included Forward Looking Infrared (F.L.I.R.), Multi-Band Digital Radio Systems, a Global Positioning Mapping System, and downlink video feed for instant communication to the launching agency.

Sheriff's Deputy and pilot, Captain Dick Duncan, was about Eddie's age, having entered the Sheriff's academy after his

Vietnam tour of duty was up in 1972. He served aboard an ammunition ship, the Haleakala, one of the ammo ships that replenished Parker's *America* years earlier. Dick's Crew Chief, Deputy Sergeant Harry Garcia, handled the harness and litter basket and was a veteran of more than 200 rescues with over 50 during the night. He could see like an eagle, spit like a rattlesnake, and eat like a truck driver. He was the only Rescue Sheriff with the tattoo of a modern helicopter on his left shoulder with the inscription, *We Will Find You!* He was Duncan's favorite crew chief, easily the best in the business.

Harry's handyman and paramedic was Deputy Sergeant Gabriel Hallen. Normally, there were two paramedics, but Harry was shorthanded on this mission, a situation that would not be allowed if this had been a sea rescue. Duncan coaxed the AS-350 northeast toward the narrow pass that connects the Los Angeles area to Northern California called the Grapevine, named after the small truck-stop town at the base of the mountains to the north and five miles south of the I-5 and Highway 99 split.

"Harry, Gabby; you guys keep your eyes peeled to the east as we pass over Gorman. That's the typical route of flight for traffic from Northern California. Our target will likely be between the Gorman and Lake Hughes' navigation transmitter Stations".

Harry and Gabby both replied as they hung out of their doors safely secured by their harnesses; two expectant faces pushing through the cold air to find the missing airplane.

"Wilco, sir. Thankfully, we still have a full moon to work with before it goes down. It'll give us reflections off small bodies of water and other shiny objects in the mountains. Filming this rescue will be tricky though, so be prepared to use those super halogens. Why the department keeps picking on us for human-interest footage is beyond me. The networks have their own choppers but are just too lazy to get out this late."

Garcia was hoping this night would end better than most missing plane rescues, especially in these mountains. The Tehachapi range had lured many pilots and families to their deaths, mostly due to foul weather and fuel exhaustion. Late last summer, Dick, Gabby, and he, scoured the mountainside to find five bodies of a Porterville family from a twin engine Cessna 310 in the very same general area they were now combing. Apparently, the pilot had gotten into the clouds and became disoriented long enough to smash into the side of a grassy knoll just 80 feet below the top of the mountain's peak. Pulling the children out was the worst. It always is.

As the chopper worked its way to the

northeast from Pyramid Lake, the snakelike trail of car headlights illuminated Interstate 5 below, long given way to darkness hours ago. That area of the mountains revealed mostly forestation, with some bald areas from recent fires of the late summer and fall.

Duncan started a north/south search about 10 miles long, working to the east from the Interstate. The chopper had to gradually work higher in altitude to avoid the sheer mountainside. They flew slowly, closer and closer to the top of the peak without any semblance of wreckage.

After nearly an hour of Harry and Gabby's eagle eyes straining for just a glint of the moon's reflection, they were just about to suggest starting over, or concentrating the search further to the south. "Cap'n, I see something shiny at about two o'clock. Come right about 15 degrees and drop about 100. Let's get a closer look." As the chopper neared the object, Harry spotted the shape of tangled aluminum on a small mesa, almost hidden, nestled under thick brush and a few small trees. Behind the wreckage was an out of place, scarred area, about fifty yards long and eight feet wide. As the chopper got closer, it looked liked an airplane had skidded along an old dirt forest ranger road, probably a temporary lane cleared for fighting a forest fire, now almost hidden by mother nature's garden work. The wreckage had burrowed under all the brush at the end of its skid, making it almost invisible to any search efforts, especially at night. Parker was extremely lucky to have Gabriel Hallen and Harry Garcia doing this search; and as they just proved, they were the best.

"Skipper, even with this high beam narrow spot, I can't see well enough from here to see inside the cockpit. It's nearly completely covered with brush and small trees. I'm going to harness Hallen up and lower him down for a 'look see'. From here it looks unlikely that anyone could still be alive.""Standby, Harry. The updrafts and damp air from the marine layer are giving me fits. It's tricky getting near enough to get Gabby in close, because of the shape of the mountain. I have to twist this beast around and come in from another direction."

As the Duncan team neared the airplane again, the downdraft blew debris everywhere, but still did not reveal anymore than Harry had seen before. At least they were close enough to slip Hallen out of the door and start his slow descent to the wreckage below. Being higher than usual and swinging like Tarzan, Hallen couldn't zero in on what was below just yet. He was concentrating on how to stop spinning like a top. Through his helmet intercom he summoned Harry to grab the spinning cable and stop its rotation. He didn't want to have his equipment stressed to the point of failing, as it did in Arizona a few months earlier, killing a popular woman medic. After Harry got Hallen under control with the spinning and swinging, he was lowered down even closer to the wreckage.   "Skipper, I'm going to have to disengage the harness and look on foot. Harry, drop me down just few more feet, but easy this time. You nearly killed me north of Pacoima last summer looking for that 152.... there. I'm unhooked. Take 'er up and have Harry snap on the litter-basket just in case. I'll report back as soon as I can get near the cockpit, but it doesn't look good."

"Roger, Gabby. Be careful down there." Listening to Harry and Gabby exchange ideas, Duncan prepared to update the FAA on what they found. He knew the next few minutes could get tricky, and maybe even messy, depending on what Harry found. Duncan steadied the chopper and pressed the mike button.

"Sheriff Dispatch, Sheriff Rescue Hotel Three, over." "Dispatch, go Hotel Three." "Dispatch, we have a visual on a small plane wreckage near Cherokee Mesa, four miles southeast of the Lake Hughes VOR. We can't tell the aircraft type or see an 'N' number. We have room to hover, and just lowered our paramedic to investigate and rescue or recover. Crew reports unlikely survival based on initial assessment, over."

"Roger, Hotel Three, keep us up to date." The dispatch officer at the Sheriff's Command Center turned to Bennie Merriman. "Bennie, let's get the folks at flight service on the line. It's looks like they found the Mooney with unlikely survivors. This is not a call I like making."

As promised, Bennie Merriman from the Sherriff's dispatch center called the FAA on a secure phone line, as he had many times before. A lady answered the call with a voice unfamiliar to Bennie. "Good evening, this is Bennie Merriman from L.A. Sherriff dispatch for Bud Bogle. Is he available? It's regarding a report on a missing plane."

"Mr. Merriman, Mr. Bogle is away from the phone at the moment and his assistant Beatriz Hernandez is on maternity leave." "When do you expect him?" "To be honest sir, he is in the men's room, and I just can't say how long he will be. This is Leslie Weiner; I work for Documents and Revisions but am subbing while Beatrice is out. Is there something I can help with?" Benny gave her the information, and trusted that she knew the protocol of how to filter the raw information for the family. Weiner knew by reviewing the open search log about both searches and previous contact with families.

1:40 A.M. Kathryn was still trembling from the last call, then jumped a foot when the phone rang again, her runaway heart beating as if to escape her chest. This time it was nearly two o'clock in the morning. Expecting news of Eddie, she sat up on her side of the bed and answered slowly.

"Hello, this is Mrs. Parker." "Mrs. Parker, this is Mrs. Wiener from the FAA; I believe Mr. Bogle called earlier about the search for your husband Edward." "Yes."

"We heard from the Sheriff's Rescue Dispatch Office, as they have located a wreckage that they think might be your husband's airplane. They are not certain it *is* his airplane, because it could be the wreckage of another missing low winged plane similar to the Mooney. The rescue unit is looking for that one further west, so you never know. I am sorry to report that the rescue personnel on the helicopter indicated no visual sign of survivors based on the state of the wreckage."

Mrs. Weiner paused briefly to clear her throat before continuing. She thought she heard a funny mechanical thud, but dismissed it to phone static and finished her conversation. "Mrs. Parker, this is just a preliminary report and they now have personnel on the ground, so there is still a very strong chance that there are survivors. We will call as soon as we have more information. Remember this is very preliminary, Mrs. Parker."

"Mrs. Parker?" There was no response from the other end. "Mrs. Parker, can you hear me? Mrs. Parker?" Kathryn was so shaken; she didn't hear the end of Mr. Weiner's report beyond 'condition of the wreckage.' As soon as she could hold the phone steady and stop sobbing, she hung it up and called her daughter. On the page dated November 23, 1992, the inexperienced Mrs. Weiner entered in her logbook that she notified the next of kin at 1:50 A.M.

A short time earlier, Gabriel Hallen unhooked his harness belt and moved along the mesa toward the wreckage. With his searchlight, he could see a pile of debris and brush almost hiding the Mooney. He thought to himself that if the airplane had landed to the right or left ten more feet, it would have smashed onto the sheer side of a granite wall or dropped hundreds of feet down the continuation of the sheer wall above. It was like the small little shelf had been carved out just for this occasion. Harry had thought right, probably an old forest clearing scraped years ago as a road or firebreak, then overgrown with brush.

As he crept nearer the cockpit and worked the beam of the intense light into the area under the brush where the pilot should have been, he was startled by, "Hey, get that blasted light out of my eyes. You're blinding me!" Hallen's heart was already marching along at a quick pace, but after that voice through the bushes, he could feel his heart really pounding. "You okay in there?"

"I will be if you get that light out of my eyes." Hallen grabbed the smaller usual halogen flashlight, twisted the light to a wider splay and pointed it to the voice. "That's better. Can you get my ass out of here? I am freezing to death and my left leg is stuck under the rudder pedal. I can't move it. My right hand isn't much use. I have a nick on my head and my neck and my back is sore as hell. That's all. Just get me out of here. When you get closer, you'll need to hold your nose; it smells a tad ripe in here." Hallen was now on top of and on the inside edge of the right wing, peeking into Eddie's small aluminum coop.

"Man you were right about the smell. What's all the feathers and goo all about? Must have been an awfully big assed bird? Phew, you have a foul situation here. What a mess." The pun was lost on Eddie, as he was just glad to hear a real human voice, not those imagined that had been his company for hours and hours.

"What's your name partner," followed by, "and if it's possible, we'll get you out of here in no time where it's warm and clean." "Name's Parker, Eddie Parker." "Mine's Gabby Hallen, Mr. Parker. You have tucked yourself into quite a hideout, huh?" Grunting a bit, Eddie manages, "You are a sight for sore eyes, Gabby. Now what can I do to help you get me out of here? I have to get to Children's Hospital in Orange if you can just get me unstuck. My grandson is having a Bone Marrow procedure Tuesday, and I need to be there. Also, can someone call my family? While I am at it, I am as parched as a dried armadillo. I could really use some water."

"Sure thing Mr. Parker." "Call me Eddie." Hallen pushed the button on his walkie-talkie radio and spoke with Dick in the chopper. "Mr. Duncan, we have a male survivor, in our Mooney Two Zero One Tango. Seems like his injuries are not life threatening, but he's banged up pretty bad. I am just getting started down here, but he wants to notify the family. I'll give you vitals as soon as I get closer."

"Good news, Gabby. Get him out of there, and we'll work on the notification. Harry will lower the litter basket as soon you are ready." "Roger. For now send down two large splints to get at least one leg stabilized and a couple of bottles of water. He's shriveled up like a prune.""Wilco." Hallen was fighting the downwash of debris from the large rotor blade of the helicopter. He also had the well intended flood light of the chopper reflecting back into his face from the skin of the airplane as he studied how best to extricate the pilot of the smashed up airplane. Hallen unhooked the splints from their straps that Harry lowered, and then edged closer.

"Mr. Parker, um Eddie, I am going to try and enlarge this opening large enough for me to get in there. When I get finished I am going to lie across your lap and try to get that left leg free. First I need a blood pressure and pulse. Do you have any other injuries you haven't told me about?" "Just what I mentioned before. Nothing serious. I can squirm around a little, so I don't think anything major is broken. Be careful with that leg though, it hurts like hell."

"I have something for that." Gabby wrapped a small cuff to Eddie's wrist. "Try to relax and be still for a minute, Mr. Parker. I need to get your blood pressure and pulse to be sure nothing else is going on." After getting Eddie's vitals, Hallen pulled out a field syringe from his small fanny pack attached to the front of his fatigues, and grunts to Eddie. "This might sting a bit, but you'll feel better in a jiffy. The morphine was jammed into Eddie's thigh and went to work almost immediately.

"Now, I am going to come around to your side and have a looksee, then we'll see how to get you out of here," more talking to himself, as Eddie began to sag. It took longer than he thought but the expert paramedic crawled back to the passenger door and managed to get to the hole in the side of the fuselage where the damaged door had been. He was able to pry the opening a little wider where the aluminum was separated from the steel tubing, just large enough for him to get in. With his warm weather suit and other paraphernalia, he was still as big as a small bear. After nearly an hour, with Eddie's head flopping around like a bobble head doll, Harry had the opening big enough to worm his torso inside.

Scooting his way inside, Gabby stretched out over Eddie's limp torso and lap, managing to work the ankle free of the rudder pedal. If there was any pain, Eddie didn't feel it. The ankle was jammed at an odd angle, and was more like a puzzle than a trap. Pulling and twisting by hand and being able to work the pedal forward slightly, could have only been done by a second person. Gabriel Hallen retreated back through the enlarged window, and gently pulled Eddie to what was remaining of the wing. "Okay, Harry, give me that litter basket now." With one hand on Eddie's collar, he pulled the limp Parker into the stainless steel litter basket. As soon as Eddie was carefully and safely strapped in, he was slowly swinging through the air, rising safely into the helicopter bay door into the safe gloved hands of Harry Garcia. Eddie was leaving his pride and joy down below in shambles for the insurance company to handle. As soon as Hallen was pulled up to the chopper in his harness, the door was closed and the chopper rose above what was left of the mangled Mooney.

Eddie mumbled again that he needed to go to the Children's Hospital, managing to garble a sound resembling Orange County that Hallen recalled when he first talked with Eddie. Something about a grandson and needing to be there. Eddie's words fell thickly, but clearly to Hallen. Duncan called the dispatch officer at the sheriff's office and brought them up to date on Eddie condition, and they in turn would call the FAA through Air Traffic Control. "Dispatch, Sheriff Rescue Hotel Three, over." "Go ahead Hotel Three."

"Hotel Three has a middle aged male survivor, Eddie Parker, from the Two Zero One Tango Mooney reported missing. Victim has minor facial contusions with small lacerations on left forehead and left heel is sprained with possible fracture. Victim complains of neck and lower left hip pain. Right wrist and thumb stabilized with flexible splint with possible fracture or dislocation. Survivor has moderate hypothermia with body temp of eight niner degrees, BP one zero eight over six five and heart steady at six seven. Patient was given one zero milligrams of morphine subcutaneously at the extraction and four more in present saline drip for hydration. Although he is pretty sedated, he still mentions he is expected at Children's Hospital in Orange County; request permission to skip UCLA Medical for CHOC.

We have used CHOC before and heliport can be ready within ten minutes notice. Over."

"Standby, Hotel Three." After several minutes Captain Duncan, Harry, and Gabriel got their answer. "Hotel three, Dispatch, proceed direct to Children's Hospital in Orange. They have been notified, and will expect you within two five minutes. They are advised of passenger's injuries and vitals. They will transfer patient to St. Joseph's Trauma Center next door. Contact South Coast Approach Control, on one two six point two zero. CHOC Unicom frequency one two three point zero seven five and continue to guard Dispatch this frequency. Over."

"Roger. Leaving you for South Coast on one two six point two zero, CHOC heliport Unicom one two three point zero seven five. Thanks for the service tonight. It's been a tough one. Out."

After getting the update from Duncan in the chopper, the dispatch officer turned to Bennie again. "Bennie, call the FAA again and be sure they update the family." With several rings and no answer, Bennie surmised that they were either shorthanded and the hour was in the vacuum period of the night; they would have to depend on the hospital to contact the FAA. They radioed Duncan back and instructed him to be sure the hospital personnel notified the FAA of Eddie's arrival and condition.

Eddie finally managed a weak smile, then fell into a deep sleep. The crew gently washed his face and immobilized his neck, leg and wrist. They had him smothered with a thermal blanket to get his body temperature back to normal. He was sedated, and even with the blanket his body was still shivering. To further minimize the effects and damage of hypothermia, they massaged his arms and good right leg vigorously.

"Captain, did you ever hear the story of this guy in Nam?" "Yep. Anyone remotely interested in the Naval Aviation part of the war over there knows of Lt. Commander Parker. He and his RO pounded an anti-aircraft emplacement that had been giving the B-52's hell during their nightly bombing raids in the North. During the mission his Phantom had been so badly shot up that no one aboard the carrier expected him to land safely. He managed it, but lost his back seat man and best friend with shrapnel wounds. Before he rotated out, he had one confirmed MiG kill and another probable. Both guys got the Distinguished Flying Cross. Quite a guy this Parker. All that combat and to be smacked down by a dumb bird 20 years later.

I'm not sure about this last part, but rumor has it that Parker was recommended for the Navy Cross for the MiG, but he had the recommendation squashed. Said the enemy jet just popped in front of him from nowhere, and it was a lucky kill; that he didn't deserve the medal. Old timers say there is way more to the story and he should have gotten the medal." The story of Eddie's reputation and heroism affected the crew as they treated him like a reverent champion of an ancient war for the last few minutes of the flight, fussing over him like a boy hovering over a baby bird fallen from its nest.

As they swooped up and to the south into the darkness, they were all amazed that he survived the rubbish they left behind. The moon, having done its job, quietly dipped below the horizon as the chopper made its way south to Children's Hospital in Orange. Eddie's struggles were finally over, as Eddie's parade of family memories embraced him and kept him whole throughout his 'fowl' ordeal.

When the sweet nectar of the morphine seduced the neurons of Eddie's nervous system, he drifted back to the family again. They were always there, all of them, especially when the chips were down. There was Alex, the special Greek who felt guilty about Josh's exotic blood disorder, trying in vain to find out more of his ancestry. The orphanages in Macedonia had few records about birth parents, feeling that the kids were lucky to have food and a place to sleep as sufficient reward for their circumstances. When Scarlett met Alex, she knew he was a winner. He was kind, honest, and loving. Through the historical turmoil of Yugoslavia's political climate, Alex studied hard, learning Albanian, Turk, Bulgarian, and neighboring languages that proved helpful at the University of Thessaloniki in Macedonia. It was an exchange program in their physics department that brought him and Scarlett together, a merger that increased the family's worth significantly.

Michael's catch with Alicia was another perfect fit for the Parkers family. Her exceptional pedigree was veiled beneath the red wavy curls and clever sense of humor. She was short in height and petite in dimension, but had a heart bigger than the Rose Bowl. She and Michael were a perfect match. They rode motorcycles, took frequent trips to rally's in Las Vegas, and fished harder than the Dutch Harbor crab boats in the Bering Sea. When baby Annie appeared, they simply got a sidecar and continued the fresh air adventures that only they could understand. They camped, fished, biked, and had it all.

2:45 A.M. Monday Everyone in the family tossed and turned in their beds with worry except for Eddie, Annie and Joshua. Annie was securely plopped between Michael and Alicia as her parents imagined what the morning would bring of Eddie's fate. Josh was anchored between his mom's breast and knees while Alex covered them both with his large caring arms. Alex whispered, "I Love you," into Scarlett's available ear that was surrounded by her strategically draped thick curly hair. All she could say without betraying her anxious soul, was a whimpered, "me too."

In Northern California, Kathryn tossed and turned, twisting the bed sheets into a wad like an overloaded washing machine after the rinse cycle. She imagined Eddie's body smashed into a half conscience state, trapped as the Mooney's engine began to smoke and finally the airplane bursting into a flaming tomb. She could hear his muffled shriek as her own scream stuck in her throat, causing her to sit straight up in her oversized king bed. The leftover scotch didn't help that much, so she watched re-runs of The Johnny Carson show that went off the air earlier that May until she drifted back into a restless slumber. Her alarm went off at exactly 4:30 A.M.

The Sheriff's Rescue Helicopter touched down safely at the hospital's heliport in Orange without incident. Eddie was gently lifted out of the helicopter as the rotor blade wash pounded the crew and the medical team on the pad. Hallen jumped out of the chopper to be sure the attending doctor had Eddie's vitals and was emphatic for them to contact the FAA so the family, in turn, could be notified. The woozy aviator was immediately ushered through the tunnel from CHOC into the emergency room at St. Joseph's. Satisfied that the medical team had everything they needed, Hallen climbed back through the doors of the AS-350 and buckled his harness. As they lifted off, Duncan spoke to both Deputies. "Great job men. No one else on earth could have spotted the Mooney except you folks and thank God for the moonlight. We had some Divine help along the way tonight, I am sure of it. The world is a better place with men like Parker and I can't help but think that God must have a purpose for this guy down the road. I hope he has a great recovery. Let's go home and have a cup of that nasty law enforcement coffee."

Eddie's wounds were examined as carefully as befitting his war hero status. His X-rays revealed no fracture of the ankle, but a small hairline fracture of the calcaneus, or heel, with swelling just in front of the heel near the cuboid bone. The MRI of the head revealed no skull fractures with "non-appreciated" injury to the brain, meaning no problems with the noggin. His thumb and wrist received minor fractures as the lacerations were sewn and then set in a semi-flexible band with the wrist. The C. T. scan also revealed that Eddie suffered severe neck trauma, damaging his cervical spine, threatening the nerves. If that wasn't enough, his lower back had also taken a pounding. He would need corrective surgery in both areas as soon as they could get the on call neurosurgeon located. The attending physicians were puzzled about his hip complaints. When they found that Eddie's medical records were in their system, and that the pain he was complaining about was in the area of scars on the lower left buttock, they realized it was from shrapnel wounds suffered in Vietnam.

After hours of probing, testing and more exploratory examinations, the doctors and nurses finished working on him, two hours before the sun was to make its grand appearance over the lush Santa Ana Mountains into Orange County. The charge nurse made her call to the FAA offices. She reported specifics of the injuries and hoped the FAA could reach someone, even at this early morning hour.

Bud Bogle was back at his post and thanked the nurse profusely for the good report, as the news was contrary to his expectations, and unlike most of the outcomes he has to report. Right away he called the cell phone Mrs. Parker had given him, but was immediately directed into her voice mail. At 4:45 A.M, she was probably sound asleep, he thought. He left a detailed message he knew would be met with tears of joy when she checked her voice mail. He felt good about these kinds of reports. Real good.

Made the stale coffee almost taste good.

Dawn The FA-18 Hornet pushed by the sun from the east, descended into the landing pattern of the El Toro Marine Airfield. The experienced pilot gently touched down near the threshold of runway 25L, a near two-mile stretch of asphalt assigned for southwesterly winds. As the pilot taxied where he was directed, the name LT. Cdr. R. Lefevre could be seen stenciled just below the canopy. Just under the name, were two small flags the chief did not recognize, one with red, white and black stripes, with green foreign symbols written in the middle white stripe. The pilot stepped on the brakes as the jet stopped and his engine slowing from a whine to a purr and become quiet. The expectant crew chief spoke to the tall thick haired officer with the angular jaw, as he climbed down from the cockpit that had been his cradle for the past five hours. "Been a long night, sir?" Stretching as after a nap, "Not so bad Chief, long but not bad. Is my ride ready?" "It is for a fact, sir. As soon as we get you changed into civvies and check in with the Commanding Officer of the 3rd Air Wing, Colonel Seymour Bowes, you will be on your way back to Pensacola." The chief pulled a small overnight duffle bag from the jet's small fuselage compartment, then the two men walked to and through the doors of Hangar

244 to a locker room where Lefevre changed into a turtle neck sweater, levis, New Balance™ running shoes, baseball cap, and a Members Only™ jacket. He and the chief then made it to an upstairs office overlooking some of the vintage warplanes showcased below. The doors were prominently marked with:

DO NOT ENTER. OFFICIAL BUSINESS ONLY.

"I'll bid you 'good day' Commander, and will see you again tomorrow. I'll have your bird refueled and ready to go by 1600 today." They exchanged salutes as the chief unceremoniously spun around for his return to the flight line to handle the myriad of military jets scheduled for arrival and departure that day.

The Lieutenant Commander knocked on the fittingly marked door, immediately hearing, "enter."

Commanding Officer
Colonel Seymour J. Bowes, USMC

"You are right on time, Commander, as the Colonel rose and energetically shook the navy flier's hand. Have a seat and let me get you a cup of coffee. Feel free to use my bathroom through that door if you need to," nodding to a discrete door in the corner.

"That would be great Colonel, it's been

a long flight." After a few quiet moments and the pilot refreshed, the Colonel spoke. "Mr. Lefevre, I heard about what you are doing, and have to offer a hand in admiration. In my opinion, what you are doing requires more courage than most combat firefights. I've learned over the years in my job that we all have a little hero in us, but we seldom have the opportunity to let it out. You are letting yours out big time, Sailor."

The dark haired Lefevre blushed and before he could reply that several had volunteered for the mission, the Colonel quickly changed the subject. "I trust your journey and assignment to the facilitating authority will be uneventful and the team will let you leave the clinic tonight instead of tomorrow; the usual length of stay after an undertaking like this. I talked with the Chief of Staff last night and she thinks they will get you out the door late in the afternoon as long as I assure them that we would keep an eye on you for at least 24 hours, especially before letting you back in that Hornet. I assured her that we have an excellent group of specialists here that would take good care of you. This is such an unexpected operation for you, and for the U.S. Navy, as a matter of fact, as it deeply affects one of our own.

The element of today's secrecy is very important, we know. However, as well briefed as all of us here have been, I don't have authority over the people where you are going, so a careless citizen could blow this whole operation. Your identity revealed could have unintended consequences. Failure is not an choice for you today, Commander." "I hear that, sir. I really would like to stay longer Colonel, since I flew with several of your men from Fighter Squadron-314 in Iraq during Desert Storm and have stories of their tireless bravery to share. I know I'll likely be back here in a few weeks, so we can catch up later."

The Colonel picked up his telephone and spoke only, "We are ready." Looking at Lefevre, the colonel was short and to the point. "Lieutenant Commander Lefevre, if you need anything, and I mean anything, do *not* hesitate to call. There are people in the pentagon watching this very closely who have a lot more juice than I, willing to step in if necessary. I wish I could go with you, but two's a crowd where you are going, so God's speed and get back to us tonight safe and sound." The visitor stood, put his Anaheim Angels baseball hat on, saluted, then spun around and exited the Colonel's office. The Colonel fell back into his tall backed chair and thought back to his brief stint on an aircraft carrier over twenty years ago; he swelled with sadness and pride over an event one night that he could never forget.

The drive north into central Orange

County and to a dull pinkish three-story building was a short one. He was escorted through an unmarked door and taken to a sterile room where a grim faced white clad staff was waiting. Lefevre changed into a gown of sorts, and promptly laid on his stomach for his procedure. An hour later, he was wheeled to a recovery room where he was aroused 45 minutes later. The male nurse was at the foot of the bed when he woke. "How goes it, sir?" Groggy, the aviator answered, "Okay, except I feel like someone kicked me in the back with an iron boot and my hip feels like it has a cigarette lighter screwed into it; other than that, no complaints. I hope all this fuss is not all for naught, especially after all the effort and sacrifice put forth from folks like you and the volunteer teams of the Navy and Marine Corps. Are we still on schedule for me to get out of here and back to El Toro tonight?"

The nurse nodded affirmatively. "As long as there are no signs of bleeding or other complications, you should be out of here by six or seven. We will load you up with gamma globulin and antibiotics for insurance. You'll be sore for a couple of days, but it shouldn't interfere with any of your flying or 'husband duties'." Lefevre just shook his head. 'Bedroom humor at a time like this,' he thought. As good looking as the aviator was, he was used to it and laughed it off.

'California, just being California.'

Just as the aide had predicted, that evening just after dark, Lefevre was unhooked from his IV and heart monitor wiring, got dressed, and exited two sets of double doors restricted to incoming police, ambulances, and other first responders. The same military car and driver that delivered him to the hospital picked him up. In less than an hour he was back at the marine airbase in El Toro where he spent the night under the close supervision of the on-duty flight surgeon. Well rested the next morning, Lefevre was refreshed sufficiently to undergo an extensive debriefing. After a brief nap, he was back in the air by dusk with the lowering sun at his back. He felt ten feet tall and more exhilarated than if he had ended the Iraq war. It was a good day for the Lieutenant, a good day, indeed. In two days, the nation would know of his unusual mission that could impact the lives of several very special individuals.

Chapter Twelve

*In the office of affairs,
the heart has a
wee different
tongue."*
~ ~ *The author*

About 2 A.M. Monday

After the brief one-sided conversation from Mrs. Weiner from the FAA, Kathryn awoke flat on her back, gazing at her ceiling slowly spinning to a stop. As Kathryn became clear headed, she began to be anxious about the message of the phone call. She heard mostly the words, 'Wreckage located, but no apparent sign of survivors,' then Kathryn dissolved into the carpet, a puddle of humanity and nightgown. As soon as she pulled herself onto the bedroom's loveseat, able to hold the phone steady and get control of her sobbing, she called her daughter.

Scarlett Matthias was still awake, curled up on the family room chaise in their quaint Tustin mission-style home. Mostly, Scarlett was just restless. After all the months of misdiagnoses and the anxious search for a bone marrow donor, Joshua was finally going to have his day; a day that would change his life from sickly to healthy. The firm date and time of his procedure were set. It was such a relief. A letdown almost. She just couldn't fall asleep on this eve of Josh's trip to the hospital.Her sweet and adored husband Alex, was tossing and turning in their nearby bed with his head under his pillow; likely anxious about Josh and the days ahead. When the phone rang, Scarlett intuitively felt it was her mom's call. They often talked late into the night like high school chums. 'Mom is probably restless too, or wants to be sure I'm on time to pick her up at the airport later this morning.' She turned on her side, pulled her hair from her face to the back, and picked up the phone.

"Scarlett Baby, they found your dad's airplane. The FAA just called. They found the wreckage and said they didn't expect to find any survivors." Now Scarlett was really awake, not expecting to hear those words.

"Oh God, no, no no.. It can't be true. It just *can't* be. Why Dad, why us, why now? Oh dear, I just can't believe this. Alex, wake up, they found my dad!" He immediately was, sitting erect, feet on the floor, with wide eyes on Scarlett in disbelief. "Mom, I am so sorry! He was always so careful. I gotta sit back down; I'm not sure what to do or how I can help."

"There is not much you can do for now, Dear One, unless you can bring your dad back to life; back to me. I am lost without him." "I will be lost without him too, Mom." The usual steady Scarlett trembled and fought back tears as the image of her father's possible death overpowered her. "None of us will be the same. He was so strong." Kathryn and Scarlett talked for another 20 minutes, talking in a wide circle of the same whys and hows, sprinkled with fresh hope and frightful musings. With Kathryn's early morning flight just a few hours away, they finally agreed to wait until later in the morning to tell Michael.

"Mom, as much as I wish you were here to hold on to, for now though, let's both try and get some rest. I have a feeling tomorrow is going to be a long day. I can't wait to see you. And you know what? Dad always said that nothing good really dies. He was a good man and just the best father in the world; I will not give up hope, no matter what."

"You're right Honey, he was, I mean he really *is* a good, good man. We both have to be optimistic and wait to hear back from the FAA. The report of 'likely' doesn't mean dead. Get some sleep, if that's possible, and I'll call you in the morning when I get settled at the airport boarding gate. I love you, Scarlett, and can't wait to see you either. I'm looking forward to a much-needed hug. Bye for now, Honey."

"I love you, too, Mom, and thanks for calling. I'm glad you called, even if the news wasn't the best. Bye for now." Through her weary pink eyes, Kathryn looked at her Lady Movado™. It was 2:30, dark, and a very dark *time* for her; the darkest since just before Hawaii in the 60's. 'Okay', she thought. 'Maybe I can still get some quick sleep, shower, finish packing, and get to the airport in plenty of time to catch my six o'clock flight to Orange County.' She had pretty much packed, but added an all black wardrobe of that below-the-knee length sheath Eddie liked, black slip, black camisole, black bra, black knee highs, and black suede sling back heels. Instinctively, she pulled out her black and gray pearl necklace that Eddie had bought for her when they were in Tahiti two summers ago.

It was the last evidence of the serious romance they had enjoyed in a long time. She quietly wept as she tugged and coaxed the suitcase to close. 'Son-of-a bitchin' damned old Mooney.' It was one of the few times Kathryn ever cursed, but when she did, it always seemed to involve her husband. Kathryn slipped under the covers of her oversized bed and closed her eyes in hopes of even a little sleep. Feeling more alone than ever in her whole life, she was immediately greeted by quivering sobs. She had been alone before, but this was marital isolation of an ill sort. She finally dozed off with her cheek matted to the pillow with her half dried sticky tears.

A.M. Monday Kathryn showered and dressed, wondering why the FAA people never called again. They promised to get back to her. Probably have to get the body and do whatever they do to make a positive identification. If the plane burned, that would take longer. The one sided conversation continued. She sobbed as she rambled, feeling less alone, recalling that loneliness had not been her friend when Eddie traveled a lot, but *really* was not a friend for sure just now.

'God, I just can't stand it anymore. First Josh, and now Eddie. Thank God there was real optimism for Josh's recovery and genuine healing.' She should try and focus on something positive. She couldn't wait to see Scarlett and Michael. She needed them more than ever now, and them her as well.

'Here we go again; my cell phone is dead. Drat!' Eddie had always nagged her about not keeping the phone charged or even turned on. He said the cell phone should be treated like an emergency device.

'Well phooey on him. He's not here to nag about that or anything else any more.' Then she sobbed to herself that if he were still alive; somehow, she would never let the phone die again. She vowed to recharge it as soon as she found the chance. The fearful part of her wasn't in a big hurry to hear the news that might be on her voice mail. For now though, she parked the cell phone, as well as the charger, deep in her bottomless oversized Louis Vuitton handbag. The purse was so cavernous that Eddie had given her a penlight for Christmas one year to put in it so she could find things quicker. She couldn't even find the penlight now, and for sure the batteries in it were probably dead anyway. 'Damn purse, damn light, damn phone, damn battery, damn it all!'

Early A.M. There wasn't much traffic on Highway 50 or I-5 on the way to the airport just north of Sacramento, especially that early on a Monday morning. As soon as Kathryn got checked in and near her gate, she plugged in her cell phone charger and called Scarlett again. She figured correctly that Scarlett would probably be awake. Her phone was still muted from Church on Sunday, so she didn't hear the tone alert for her new voice mail. Created mostly for business use, voice mail was a fairly new feature for cell phones, so Kathryn gave herself a pass on not checking it as she should.

"Mom?" "Yeah, Baby, it's me. How are you holding up?" "I'm going crazy here. Have you heard anything more about Dad? Have they found him yet?" "Nothing yet, Honey. It's only been a few hours since they first called. I'm hopeful, but not very optimistic. Did you call Michael?" "Yeah, I did. I actually drove over there to do it. He and Alicia are really, *really* depressed. They hope and pray there has been a mistake. You know how really close Dad and Michael used to be... He reminded me that we were all meeting Alex at the hospital as soon as you and I get in. Josh is checking in for last minute tests, and that's the best pla...."

"Oops; Honey, they are calling my flight, gotta run; I'll see you in a jiffy." "Okay Mom, I should be on time; Southwest flight 2359, 7:15. I'll drop Alex and Josh at the hospital and will meet you at the gate to conserve time. Bye, love you."

Kathryn yanked the cell phone cord from the wall and stuffed it and the phone back into its hiding place and tripped down the boarding tunnel to her seat in the nearly empty airplane. As she noticed all the vacant seats, she guessed correctly that Southwest was positioning the airplane into the newly modernized Orange County's John Wayne Airport for Monday morning's schedules. Since the new modern airport had opened barely two years ago, it was still a secret for Los Angeles business travelers as most flights were mostly empty, especially from Sacramento. True to her word, Scarlett was at the gate an hour and fifteen minutes later as Kathryn walked off the airplane.

7:30 A.M. "Oh, Mom, am I glad to see you. This is just *terrible*." They hugged twice, rocking side to side to comfort each other. They felt safe now, clutched in the powerful mother-daughter bond. Passengers deplaning veered to both sides of the crying women, unaware and uncaring of their plight. After they wiped most of their runny mascara with the heel of their hands and cleared their watery eyes so they could see, they trundled to the baggage claim carousel, snagged Kathryn's bag, then made their way hand in hand to the car. Along the way, they nervously giggled at each other's puffy face from all the crying. Then they fell back into reality as Kathryn made a comment that her tears tasted bitter, like death.

As they left the airport and headed north on the Costa Mesa freeway, Scarlett asked Kathryn if she was hungry. Only until asked the question, had she thought about her appetite. "I'm not very hungry now, but I'll get a bite at the hospital later. I'll be famished by then for sure."

"Mom, have you heard from the authorities on the search for Dad? A news report on the radio this morning has reported the recovery of a body found last night from airplane wreckage in the Santa Monica Mountains. I'm hopeful there's been a mistake, but deep down, my heart fears the obvious."

"Mine too, Honey. Mine too," as her voice tailed off. "Oh darn, I've got to get to an outlet and charge my cell phone so I can touch base with the FAA or whoever.... When they called last night, that's the only number I gave them. I wasn't thinking very clearly." Kathryn was furious with herself, and not typical of her critical thinking ability that she usually demonstrated.

"You know what, Mom? I am such a knot-head. I have a car charger that fits your phone, the same as mine." As soon as Scarlett turned the radio down with Garth Brooks banging out *That Summer*, Kathryn's hand squirmed down in the abyss of her purse and finally found the phone. She plugged in Scarlett's charger and fired up the phone. She listened for a minute then it was Christmas come early. The blinking light of her voice mail caught her eye. It was the voice mail from Mr. Bogle with the FAA assuring her that Eddie was not dead, but was bunged up a bit and close by. Kathryn covered her mouth and started a guttural sob from way down deep; she brushed the hair off her face and covered her eyes as she shook. Then, Kathryn's piercing screech startled the be-Jesus out of Scarlett, causing her to bounce over the curb exiting the airport.

"No way? Oh my God. Thank you God! You've got to be kidding? Oh Sweet Jesus. Thank you God." Catching her breath, Kathryn huffed and puffed that Eddie had been rescued and that the news report was of another plane that had been missing. Eddie had been transported by helicopter to the trauma center at CHOC earlier this morning, and moved next door to St. Joseph's Hospital. He wasn't in grave condition, but still banged up. The caller did not elaborate. He did though, but Kathryn in her excitement of hearing that Eddie was alive, snapped the phone shut. She was infused with joy and thrilled to know her gritty old lover was okay. She was so thrilled to know he was alive and was filled with amazing relief. She couldn't wait to see him.

"Scarlett, your dad is alive, and can you believe it? St. Joe's is right next door to CHOC. Oh, let's hurry. Maybe they'll let us see him as soon as we get there. And God, I am sorry about all the cursing. I promise.... Well, I'll *try* not to ever do it again. Go with me Scarlett. I'm terrified of what I might see."

Sobbing almost as much as her mom, she managed, "Of course Mom. Of course! This is such *fabulous news*. I can't wait to call Alex. I'll give him a jingle so he won't worry any longer. I'll have him call Alicia and Michael so they won't worry any longer either. They're probably already at the hospital with Josh. His prep is scheduled to start at nine and they always want to be a little early."

The morning traffic couldn't have been any more uncooperative as they crawled along the 405 freeway averaging only about

20 miles an hour. They jumped from the San Diego Freeway to the Costa Mesa Freeway, to surface streets, but it was all the same. The ten-mile ride took 40 minutes, but it seemed like hours. Scarlett and Kathryn were so excited, they shrieked all the way to the hospital, either joy from the good news or of anger at all the other drivers they regarded as slow pokes or other bleeped names. As soon as they screeched into St. Joseph's emergency room parking lot, they ran to the emergency room.

At the same time in Lake Forest at Michael and Alicia's, Michael is being urged to get ready so they can get on to the hospital. "Com'on, Michael, we are going to be late getting to the hospital. You know how traffic is at this time of the morning."

"Lis. Come look at this, *hurry.*" "What is it Babe?" "It's about Dad's rescue. Look at the ticker at the bottom the screen."

At approximately 2 AM this morning, the Los Angeles Sheriff Department's rescue helicopter located the wreckage of a single engine private airplane in the Tehachapi Mountains. The name and condition of the middle-aged victim is being withheld pending notification of next of kin. The pilot was a Vietnam aviator with over 200 combat missions. More details at KBCS News at Ten.

"This is *not* good news, Alicia, not good

at all. We have to call Mom before she hears this." After two tries and going straight to voicemail, they gave up. "Let's get on the road and help Scarlett and Alex get Josh settled. Maybe we can beat Mom and her before they hear the news. You take the Beemer and I'll follow on the Harley. I have to get some work done on it today, so it'll be a perfect chance to have you follow me to Huntington Beach later in the day." Fighting her own tears, she sobbed, "No problem, Honey. You go on ahead while I straighten up our bed and get Annie a bite to eat." After Alicia finished her handful of chores and situated Annie into her child restraint seat, she had just pulled out of the driveway only to be jolted by her cell phone.

"Hello, Alex?" "Hey, Alicia. Sorry to bother you on the road. You're probably on the way to the hospital. I tried to call the house and Michael's cell, but no luck. Can you pull over? I have some news about Eddie."

7:45 A.M. With both hands trembling and a barely audible, 'oh dear,' Alicia eased to the side of the street. When Alex gave her the good news, she became so ecstatic, she startled little Annie strapped into her infant seat in the back seat of the car. It was 'YIPPPEEEEE', all the way to the hospital, with Annie's 'YAAAAAAAAY' from the amen corner in the back pews. She sped like a woman possessed to the parking lot at Children's Hospital to check in with Alex and drop off Annie. She parked under the hospital entrance and jumped out to be greeted by a reliably expectant Alex, with his signature bear hug and his Hollywood smile. Alicia squeezed Alex back with a smile that signaled restored hope.

"Oh, Alex, isn't this fabulous? Eddie is alive and right here. I am sooo happy." Alex smiled more, then stooped over and directed his attention to the little passenger.

"Hi, Cupcake, how you doin' this beautiful morning?" Annie lit up like a lantern on Chinese New Year. "Ain't it great news about Pops? What a tough old boot. Now, we can focus on getting your cousin healthy." Alex always knew just the right words at difficult times.

"Annie, it looks like you and I are going to hang out together some this morning." Annie smiled even wider, as she was crazy about her Uncle Alex.

"Boy, this is such fabulous news for sure, Alex. I can't wait to see him. How are you doing with Josh? How was his evening?" "Josh made it through the night just fine, Alicia. He has just had a mild sedative that is causing him to mostly sleep. The conditioning regimen this past two days has involved so many drug concoctions, mostly immuno-suppressors that sometimes make him a little woozy. He's part Parker, and we both know how gnarly they are. Josh is a tough little kid and is probably the least worried of us all. Truly though, Scarlett and I are still a little nervous about the little guy's procedure, as is everyone. It won't be easy on him for a while, but long term, I know it's best. By the way, while I'm thinking about it, you and Michael are dears to come this morning. Just being here means a lot to us. Why don't you run on over to St. Joe's and check on Eddie and I'll bring Michael up to speed when he gets here. Annie will be fine with me. By the way, where is Michael?"

"The guy should be here by now; he's so A.R. about being late, you know. He left ten minutes before I did, probably stopped to pick up some donuts for everyone. He just *had* to ride that new Harley™, his early Christmas gift. I found the candy apple red he was dying for, but I had to have it trucked in from Chico sight unseen. He already has some warranty issues and wanted me to follow him to the shop in Huntington Beach when things settle down later today. He should be here any minute. Anyway, I'll run on over to the other hospital and find Eddie if you'll give my hubbie directions on how to find me when he gets here." She waved 'bye' with, "It's going to be a fabulous day." Little did she know....

Michael was more than thrilled to know his dad was safe. ' The tough old bird was okay.' Michael promised himself that as soon as Eddie was able, they would renew that special time together. He had agonized that his father was probably dead, and never got the chance to reclaim that closeness he once enjoyed. For now though, Michael was anxious to get to the hospital and see him. He sped west along surface streets to avoid the early morning freeway commuter traffic. The 18-mile journey would be safer and probably quicker that way. He jumped on Irvine Boulevard then north to Tustin Avenue and then west on Chapman taking him into Old Town Orange.

He dreaded that ancient roundabout in Plaza Park of Old Town. He had to watch three intersections at once wile working his way first to the inside lane then back to the outside to exit south on Glassell Street. This morning all was fine, except that his front wheel twisted sideways from a small branch not cleared from the night Caltrans trimming of the many trees in the circle. His view changed from the pavement to the sky, to spinning trees and back to the pavement. Then nothing. His new Harley Davidson was twisted with the front wheel spinning next to his ear, motor coughing to idle.

His first awareness was being strapped on a large board and being lifted onto an emergency vehicle. "Stop! Where's my bike? Where are you taking me?"

"Easy sir, try to lie back and relax. Your bike will be fine. We'll notify your family and they can claim it for you. For now though, you need to be still. According to witnesses, you really smacked your back hard against the curb. We are just a few blocks from the hospital where they can take care of you." As the pain began to set in, Michael didn't protest. He was only thinking of how Alicia was going to kill him.

With her skirt creating its own wind and arms crossed like a farmer's wife on the way to the outdoor privy early in the morning, she and her low heels clicked down the sidewalk and across Pepper Street, to St. Joe's. Her ringing cell phone tucked in the handy side pocket of her purse slowed her to a near halt. "Mrs. Parker?" Out of breath as she entered the hospital through the automatic swinging doors, "Yes, this is she. Who is this?" "This is Sergeant Chavarri from the Highway Patrol." "If this is regarding Eddie Parker, you may have the wrong Mrs. Parker. I am his daughter-in-law, and you probably need his wife. Can I give you her cell phone number?" "Mrs. Parker, we are calling about your husband, Michael." Her eyes immediately grew wider than a teacup saucer and she stopped as if she hit an invisible glass wall. "What? Oh, dear God. You have *got* to be kidding! How bad? Where are they taking him?" She snapped her phone shut and muttered under her breath, 'What the hell else could go wrong? *Enough* already.'

8:30 A.M. Alicia found the emergency room waiting area and still out of breath, arrived just as the ambulance was pulling the gurney into the foyer. Michael seemed dazed, his Levis torn and black with grease, was strapped to a board of sorts with an IV needle tucked into the back of his hand and a large brace bound tightly around his neck. As Alicia edged closer, Michael became aware of her presence and tried in vain to raise his arms but found them tied down like the rest of his body. Alicia was gently nudged back, and urged by the ER nurse to go to the waiting room a few doors down the hall.

"We'll be a while, ma'am, and we we'll take good care of him; don't worry. He injured his back, but everything else seems fine." Alicia held firm. "Ma'am, I will talk to my husband. I know he is in no grave danger and I will not be long. He needs to know about his father who was fished off a mountainside this morning." They pushed the gurney next to the wall and asked Alicia to try and be brief. They watched intently as she tenderly drew near to him and spoke softly into his ear for about two minutes. His eyes seemed to relax. She kissed him on the cheek and while wiping her nose on her sleeve, walked back to the nurse. "Thanks for the privacy. I want to see the doctor as soon as possible. Please." Not content with just sitting, she asked one of the ER nurses where she could find another ER patient, Edward Parker, admitted in the early morning. "He is my father-in-law," as emphatic as if he were the President. The twenty percent boot camp sergeant from Alicia's mom was kicking in.

"Please page or send word for me, as soon as they are finished with my husband. I will be with the other Mr. Parker in ER recovery." Down the corridor she chased, past the bank of vending machines and the elevators to the second floor ER recovery room, and ultimately to the ER recovery waiting room. There she found Kathryn and Scarlett huddled into the middle of the oversized waiting room. Both staring through the windows glued on the room across the hall, eyes on the team of doctors crowded around a bandaged and wired image of her father-in-law. The three Parker women could not take their eyes off the large glass windows, revealing the ritual of the doctors and nurses, as they studied radiology reports, probed, tested, retested, and braced Eddie's limbs and torso. Eddie looked sedated and very still. "Mom is he going to be?" "Oh, Alicia, Honey, we don't know too many details yet, but we were told he doesn't seem to have any life threatening problems. They said they were about ready to take him to his room and the doctor would meet with us in a minute.

Alicia, don't cry so. He will be okay. Wow, you are really taking this harder that any of us."

"Oh Kathryn, it's Michael. He's here too, in the emergency room. I just saw him. He wrecked his bike." Scarlett dropped her paper cup of vending machine coffee and scarcely noticed that it splashed all over her mother's ankles. Both Kathryn and Scarlett shouted almost simultaneously, "No! Please. Dear God, no more." Kathryn drew a big breath and asked as she exhaled, "Is he hurt bad, Honey? Is he going to be okay? Can I see him now?""Not right now. They're cleaning him up to see how extensive his injuries really are. The E.R. Nurse told me that as soon as he gets settled, she would call the Charge Nurse here so we can see him.

The officer I spoke with said that Michael must have hit a slick spot in the road going around that dreadful circle in Old Orange and flipped into the curb. He hit his back pretty badly, and maybe his arm or wrist, I'm not sure. When I saw him as they wheeled him in, his nose was all skinned up, but that's about all I could see. He was strapped to a board and had on a neck brace and at least tried to nod my way. When they get through with him, I imagine he will be somewhere in this wing; then we'll know more. I am worried about Dad Parker. When do you think we might know something? Isn't this just insane, and not knowing..?"

Full of grit now, Kathryn said, "You are right about the not knowing, so let's see what we can do about that." She pulled Alicia closer and spoke to her sweet, sensitive, daughter-in-law and said, "Don't you worry either, Sweetie; everything is going to be all right. Scarlett, why don't you go back to Children's Hospital and sit with Alex and Annie. You can bring him up to date on Michael. It'll be a while before we will know much about him or your dad. In fact, why don't the three of you grab a bite to eat; Alicia and I will come over when we find out what's happening with the guys."

"Okay Mom, but let me know as soon as you know anything. This is just terrible, just terrible." With that, Scarlett marched down the hall towards the elevator, burdened with the worry of her son, stepbrother, and father, balanced on her freckled shoulders.

Kathryn turned her attention to Alicia. "Alicia, I know this seems like such an impossible mess." She sat with her distraught daughter in law, scooting her chair up close to hers, then wrapped both her calming hands around Alicia's small shivering hands. "No matter what, Sugar, we are all going to be okay. Don't worry yourself so. Your Michael Parker and my Eddie Parker are tough as nails. They likely came out of the same heavenly machine shop, and they'll get through this in great shape. I'm sure of it. So far, so good. Everything points to full recoveries so we can get to Fashion Island and do some serious Christmas shopping. You sit tight while I find a charge nurse that can pull all this together so we're not chasing all over the hospital." When she stood, she reached down and gave a hug only a loving mother-in-law could impart. She squeezed Alicia so completely; the tension seemed to drain from the junior to the senior. Then Kathryn marched down the corridor to find that charge nurse.

Kathryn's expression did most of the talking, as the floor nurse understood immediately and promised that the specialists repairing Michael and Eddie would make their visits to the family in a single waiting area, each doctor as soon as they had information to share. Then Kathryn marched swiftly to find her Michael, the son that kept her in one piece only a few years ago. 'He just has to be all right. Why me God, why *me*? Quit picking on me. Just quit it!'

There were none who could question that the six and a half hours from the time Kathryn received her call from Mrs. Weiner at the FAA, until Michael's admittance into the emergency room at The Sisters of St. Joseph Hospital, were most unkind to the Parkers.

Chapter Thirteen

"People are hurt in love affairs
and never recover; more
than in boxing
~ ~ George Foreman

Same Day 10 A.M.

As Kathryn and Alicia huddled in the waiting room, Doctor Dunlap finally greeted them. At first glance, he looked like a black custodian with his white coat and dreadlock hairdo. Then when he turned to them with his lanky outstretched hand, they immediately liked him. He was dressed to the nines, Johnson Murphy's shined like an ebony porcelain bowling ball, and a mile wide smile with teeth as white as fresh snow. When he spoke, his deep brown eyes lit up, complimenting his clear and proud resonant voice.

"Hi, I am Doctor Clifford Dunlap." Looking at Kathryn, "You must be Mrs. Parker number one," and to Alicia, "You must be Mrs. Parker number two." As they both nodded, he said that he just guessed, and that they could have passed for sisters. Kathryn fluttered while Alicia delighted in her mother-in-law's girlish reaction. It didn't happen often, but Kathryn was caught off guard. He shook hands with both and patted the seats of nearby chairs. "Let's take a seat so we can all be comfortable. Man, your guys have kept me really, really, busy for most of the last several hours." With widened eyes for emphasis, he offered, "Interesting guys, your Parker men. First, let me properly introduce myself. I am a board certified neurological orthopedic surgeon. I graduated from Loma Linda twelve years ago and I specialize in neck and back injuries. I also work with pediatrics for orthopedic abnormalities when surgery is needed such as kyphosis and scoliosis. I grew up in Louisiana with Creole parents and love my heritage as the king of the crawdad lovers. I am on loan from the Stanford Neurological Surgery group, and was on call when your husband came in early this morning."

He turned to Kathryn. "Most of your husband's injuries were not serious, but when the x-rays came back, they revealed some cervical, or upper neck problems. Also, the lumbar or lower region of the back was bruised, but nothing serious. Boy, the images of his lower region revealed some nasty wounds from his service in Vietnam. At any rate, for the neck, the discs between C-3 and C-4 regions of the vertebrae were crushed, either from the accident last night or from an earlier incident years ago. When the admitting doctors learned who he was, we were faxed his navy medical records. They verified the damage and deterioration of his discs from trauma way back in late 1969.

As for his cervical issues, we had to surgically remove the damaged tissue of the herniated discs and replace them with porcelain spacer prosthetics. This will give him full movement and relief, an improved outcome from the old way of fusing the spine. The old fusing technique required the patient to turn the whole body to get the head from one side to the other. I developed this procedure two years ago, and I'm confident of his full recovery. Because there is a risk of damaging the spinal cord cutting directly into the back of the neck, we went through the front, a much safer approach. He will be a little hoarse for a few days and need to wear a flexible neck brace, which he won't like. We had to move the larynx to one side for the duration of the procedure, so he'll sound like a cross between Gabby Hayes and Chill Wills for a few days. He will have to wear the neck collar for two weeks, maybe less. Any questions? If not, follow me and I will take you to his room."

As they moved towards the door and down the hall, Dr. Dunlap fell in stride with Kathryn and Alicia. Turning to Alicia he continued, "Mrs. Parker, we are still in the process of evaluating Michael's condition. We are running more tests, and just need a few more hours. He has several issues with a team of very experienced doctors looking sorting them one by one. As they know more, I will be their spokesman, at least for a while. I can tell you with certainty, he has no life threatening injuries, or paralysis, but his lower back took quite a licking. He is comfortable and immobilized to ensure the spinal cord is not threatened. Give us another hour or two, and we will be back to you. We have to get and review the radiologist's report of the MRI and X-rays, study the images, then if surgery is needed, and I think it might be, we will know exactly what needs to be repaired." That report and his genuine smile lifted a very heavy burden off Michael's mother and wife.

"Alicia, please give Scarlett a call and bring her up to date on her dad and our Michael. Tell her we will be in Eddie's room." The Parker women then followed Dr. Dugan to Eddie's room to have a look-see at the very lucky Mr. Parker. They were greeted with a menagerie of hardware and miniature trapeze paraphernalia. His left ankle was in a cast up to his knee, and elevated with a device of rope and a high bar attached to the foot of the bed.

His right wrist was in a cast halfway to his elbow, and his head wrapped in a bandage like a shoot 'em up victim from a John Wayne western. He had a neck collar and a small plastic oxygen mask strapped to his mouth and nose. He was still a little dopey, but managed a weak smile and wiggled his left hand fingers when his wife and daughter-in-law smothered him. Relieved by Scarlett, now watching over Josh at CHOC, Alex had just entered Eddie's room with that predictably bigger than life Greek grin.

Kathryn moved closer to the bed, as she inched down toward her husband. As tenderly as a human could ever be, she wormed around the hoses, wires, and cable to get her cheek where he liked it most, just under his chin, by now scratchy and smelling of ether. It didn't matter to Kathryn. He was safe and no one could harm him now. She managed a teary "I love you", gave him a peck on his forehead, then blew her nose and moved back. Her tears tasted much better than before, when just hearing of his feared fate only hours ago. In a rising crescendo and altered expression, she changed the cadence, volume, and choice of words.

"You scared the life out of us, you knucklehead. *That's the end of your flying days,* Mister. We were worried sick. We thought you were dead!" Eddie rolled his eyes in his twilight haze and comprehended none of what his wife was saying. Kathryn babbled on how her mobile phone was dead, and she didn't know, it was her fault, and on and on. Suddenly she pulled the back of her hand to her mouth and remembered. "Oh, Honey, Michael has already turned that new red

Harley over, and hurt his back. They are running more tests and stuff now, to see just how serious the damage really is. It's just awful, but thank God he's alive and they think he probably won't be paralyzed. You both should be shot. Between the two of you, I am getting ulcers, wrinkles and gray hair. Dang! What else could go wrong?" Then she moved the oxygen mask aside, kissed him, this time on his crusty lips, taking the breath out of them both. He knew exactly what had just happened! Then she let the mask snap back, but ever so gently. She blew her nose and let the burdens of the world drain down her torso to the bottom of her feet. "Thank you Lord. You always come through for us."

Monday morning 11 A.M. With both men and Joshua in good hands, the three women hiked down Stewart Street to Main, invading the nearby Happy Doughnut, for coffee and a pastry. Knowing that both of the men were alive and should heal, they realized just how famished they were. That late in the morning it wasn't very crowded, so they were able to easily fit into a private corner booth. Having not eaten since yesterday afternoon, Kathryn blurted, "I am starving people. How about you?" Alicia and Scarlett both nodded. They agreed on orange juice, black coffee and a dozen bear claws. Alex and Annie would be super hungry and could devour any number of sweets the Parker women would have left over.

Kathryn's cell phone barked out a muffled song, just as she was in the middle of their sugar fix. Her *Water Fall Atlantic* ring tone sounded better buried in her handbag than on high volume. She mostly listened and nodded her head while choking down her bear claw. After hanging up and through the half chewed pastry, she managed to report to Scarlett and Alicia.

"Doctor Dunlap is about through with Michael and wants to see us." The phone was snapped shut and returned to its dungeon home at the bottom of Kathryn's hopelessly stuffed purse. Almost forgetting to pay the check, it was three hyper-propelled women with their pastry sacks tucked into their purses, flying down Main, back to Stewart Street, on to the hospital for hopes of a good report.

After what seemed like an eternity, the ER physician Dr. Richard Finley and Dr. Dunlap entered. As Finley was removing his rubber gloves, he asked for Michael's wife. "I am his wife." The doctor sat down in a chair facing Alicia, Scarlett, and Kathryn, all frantic to hear the verdict. "Michael is in X-ray again, at this very moment, so it will be a while before you can see him. We checked him over pretty good and thankfully he suffered no serious head or limb injury. There are absolutely no signs of paralysis." While the girls exhaled slowly and furtively, the doctor looked at them both, and in a measured and gentle tone continued.

"Our biggest concerns right now are his kidneys. According to the CHP, he somehow flipped over his handlebars and landed squarely on his lower back when he hit that curb. While there is good news of no spinal cord damage, we think there is possible damage to his kidneys. The contusions were severe, so we will just have to wait. The renal flow is spotty and weak, so we have to give it a while.

As for his back injuries, we are lucky to have one of the best orthopedic surgeons in the country, Dr. Dunlap, looking after him. He will go over his surgical needs in just a minute. This guy can do miracles and we are lucky to have him. Do you have any questions?" Alicia wanted to know how long would it take to know more, and was Michael aware of his condition. "He is heavily sedated to relieve his pain, keep him stable, and as immobile as possible. We have not talked with him just yet." Doctor Dunlap moved in closer and weighed in, knowing of their complete fears. "While you are waiting to know of Michael's kidney situation, let me be quick so you can rest easy about his back injury. Michael has an injury to his lumbar region and in one area there is a need to do a minor decompression repair, maybe two. This involves removing a small portion of the bone over the nerve root and disc material from under the nerve root to relieve pinching of the nerve and provide more room for the nerve to heal. We call it a micro-discectomy and it's quite routine. Your major concerns are the kidneys, but I did want you to know the details of his back surgery so you wouldn't worry about those issues. They are still testing and evaluating. Then the big smile. Don't worry, he will be fine."

There was nothing they could do, but sit in the shadow of despair. Kathryn, Scarlett, and Alicia were frustrated, not knowing the fate or future of their men and little man. Was it a cruel prank or just a terrible dream? The Parkers were all such good people. Decent, smart, generous, faithful, successful, and nurturing parents, grandparents and spouses. Not fair, not fair at all.

Scarlett excused herself to rejoin Alex, Annie, and her son, at Children's Hospital. As she worked her way down the hall to the exit of the hospital, Kathryn turned to Alicia and put her hand into hers. "Let's stop by the chapel, Honey. Maybe we can find some answers there." They checked in with the charge nurse and told her they would be in the chapel, and asked that the doctors or nurses call for them there. After two lefts and a right, they found the small chapel door and went inside as the only two occupants. They knelt and held hands as Kathryn whispered to the higher power she knew and trusted. "Please, please, Lord, make them okay, especially Michael. Make our guys good as new and keep Joshua in your arms as he is transfused with wholesome bone marrow cells. Please, oh dear me, please.....oh, and thanks again for bringing back my husband, safely, again. Amen." Alicia nodded.

Monday Noon The hospital's Chaplain, Sister Ann Elizabeth, quietly moved into the dimly lit Chapel and down the small aisle towards the kneeling ladies. She was adorned simply by her holy habit, the black serge tunic wrapped only by a black woolen belt where her wooden rosary beads dangled. Her silver cross, supported only by a black cord, was cradled on her chest as a black veil swept on each side of her head and her face. Her cotton cap was secured by the bandeau and wimple that framed her small little face, revealing this peaceful servant of her personal Higher Power. As she neared the kneeling girls with their gift-shop scarves neatly placed over their heads, she placed her small hands on each of Alicia and Kathryn's shoulders. They were both trembling and half asleep as they were leaning forward on the back of the bench in front of them. Half in prayer and half in an ethereal state of hope, they felt ever so helpless. Both women were in unfamiliar waters of not being in control. When the Sister cleared her throat, they winced a bit and leaned back into the pew. The girls blinked to clear their eyes and turned, looking up with expectant eyes. The gentle Sister felt their pain, but was powerless to ease them just now. She said a silent prayer, gave the girls a reassuring smile, and whispered.

"Sorry if I startled you Mrs. Parker", nodding to Kathryn, and again to Alicia, "Mrs. Parker. The doctor is ready for you. Before you go, may I say a quiet petition for your men?" Almost in perfect unison, causing them to look at each other and smile, "Of course, please." The sister took each of their hands and soft as a dove, but sure as an eagle, whispered, "Oh Lord, You are good to those who seek You, and those who are faithful. This family who is truly faithful, has full trust of the evidence of Christ's assurances he gave to His disciples after his resurrection. You, who are the only source of health and healing, the spirit of calm and the central peace of this universe, grant to this believing family such a consciousness of Your indwelling and surrounding presence. We pray for Your blessing and healing power for Joshua, Edward, and Michael, and grant them health, strength and peace, through Jesus we beseech Thee. Amen."

She rose and gave each of them a card, with a Bible verse on the back and smiled. "God be with you and give you peace." She kissed her cross and smiled to the heavens as if to speed her prayer while the two wives, girded with renewed faith, left the chapel as quietly as they had entered.

When they got back to the waiting room, Dr. Finley was waiting and sat them down. He scooted his chair close to them and smiled. "Here is the situation. As you know, Dr. Dunlap found that Michael has two crushed discs in his lower back, one between L-4 and L-5 and the other between L-5 and S-1 near the base of the spine, which he will take care of that in surgery later today. The spinal cord injury is unremarkable, while the nerves are just very angry, but that's all. He won't do any fancy dancing for a while, but he will heal as his lower back is blessed with a good protective muscular shield. There is some disturbing news, however; not life threatening, but serious." Kathryn and Alicia frowned and grabbed each other's hands. "While I am thinking about it, when we get through here, you need to catch up with Michael's nurse and sign the consent forms for Dr. Dunlap's surgery.

When Michael landed on those handlebars he also hit the curb right on the same area of the back. In the process, he traumatized both kidneys severely. He has internal bleeding from both, so we have inserted a catheter to drain the blood. Our surgery did confirm the trauma, but it will take a while to see if one or both are going to function properly. The trauma was deep; all the way to the Renal Medula. They took quite a jolt, but we just have to see how badly. Usually kidneys are pretty resilient, but if the damage to both is too severe, he will have to undergo dialysis three times a week until we can find a replacement donor kidney. Hopefully, at least one of the kidneys will be okay. Right now, they are only filtering at a rate of 50 to 75 Milliliters per day, way short of the 400 plus that is a normal urine output. Until we get some more information from new renal scans, and his output increases, he will be undergoing dialysis on a regular basis. Hopefully the nephrons that produce the urine will kick in and Michael will get back to normal. We just need to see an upward trend, but so far it has just been flat." It took a while to sink in. They only thing they could say was to repeat their earlier plea.

"How long till we will know something?" "We should know something by first thing in the morning. If they don't kick in soon, they will just shrivel and become non-functioning. You might consider getting a bite to eat. I know how to find you if there are any surprises. In the meantime, you might get in touch with Dr. Hindman in the kidney transplant department on the third floor. The donor applications are extensive, and require some medical history. The process takes time, and you might want a head start if the news is not what we all hope."

"Thanks Dr. Finley. You have been very kind." That's all Kathryn could think to say. Alicia was in a composed daze. "Alicia Honey, could you call Scarlett and see if she wants to get out and get a bite to eat and bring her up to date on Michael? As for me, I can hardly swallow and for sure can't eat. I'm just going back to Eddie's room and stay as long as I can. If I'm not there I will be in the waiting room. He is still a wee bit dopey and won't be much of a conversationalist, so I'll probably just watch *Disney Afternoon* or some God-awful soap opera.

Chapter Fourteen

*"Stupid is a great force
in the human affair."*
~ ~ P. J. O'Rourkethirteen

November 23rd, Monday 1 P.M.

As arriving passengers from New York
on Delta's flight 2663 were staring at the TV
monitors in the gate area of the Los Angeles
International Airport, one lady in her mid
forties pushed forward; intensely glued to the
news. She was tall, olive skinned, and sported
a pulled back half up, half down hairdo. Her
hair combed back on the crown of her head
pulled everyone's eyes from her striking
features to her forehead then to her brilliant
raven jet-black hair. With her rich mahogany
wide set eyes, she could have easily been
confused with any number of Hollywood
luminaries, especially in this airport.

Stan Chambers from the local KCBS
news channel was featuring footage of the
miraculous recovery of a pilot that had been
missing. The surviving pilot was found in a
small airplane in the mountainous region of
the Los Padres National Forest and Tehachapi
Pass areas north of Los Angeles. He had been
reported missing late Sunday night when the
pilot failed to report to the Los Angeles Flight
Center radar controllers. The story had
gained momentum when it was learned that

the pilot was Edward Parker, a Northern California businessman and Vietnam decorated fighter pilot. He was pulled from the wreckage of the Mooney aircraft by a rescue helicopter from the Los Angeles Sheriff Department's Rescue Team, then flown to the Children's Hospital of Orange and moved next door to the Sister's of St. Joseph's Hospital in Orange. A reporter correctly questioned the reasoning as to why that particular hospital was chosen, since there were several trauma hospitals with Helicopter Pads much closer to the crash site and the usual sites designated by the Sheriff's Department. Apparently, his grandson was in that particular hospital, awaiting surgery for a blood disorder on Tuesday. Parker's request had been approved due to the circumstances and his non-life threatening injuries.

She took in a deep breath and slowly exhaled. The stunningly beautiful woman knew this Eddie Parker and knew about the grandson's need for a bone marrow transplant. Months earlier her son, a Navy pilot, had heard of the situation through a Navy magazine article. Then and now, Aimee's mind raced back twenty-five years, opening wounds of regret. After her husband had been killed, she never returned the Parker's letters or phone messages. It was partly because she felt Eddie had some responsibility for her husband's death, and partly because Eddie and Kathryn, as great a couple as anyone could meet or know, would remind her of her loss. She had a new life now, happily married, with four handsome boys, whom she missed already. She was trembling somewhat, but told herself that she had to see him. The trip to Maui would have to wait. Luggage or not, she went to the front of the terminal and queued into the taxi line.

"St. Joseph's Hospital in Orange, please", she shouted. Loud was the culture at the noisy airport as she pondered what would she say, especially to Kathryn. Before René died, Aimee cut ties with the Parker's. Kathryn had been her best and dearest friend for many special months, and now, regret begin to really set in. A bit of anxiety teased her conscience as she pulled into the hospital's unloading foyer. At the admitting desk in the hospital, she learned that Eddie Parker was in surgical recovery as Eddie and Kathryn's prodigal friend was directed to the waiting room.

She didn't hurry, but found the room soon enough. As she scanned the room, she spotted Kathryn talking quietly to a twenty or thirty something woman she thought to be her daughter, Scarlett maybe? She was amazed at how little Kathryn had changed. Still beautiful, poised and slim as ever. She walked quietly and as she got closer, Kathryn glanced her way, and the puzzled expression turned into a growing smile a mile wide. At the same time, Kathryn jumped a foot off the ground, did a tiny fist pumping Jennifer Beal's styled flash-dance, and let out a reflexive squeal of happiness.

"Aimee Thibadeau, is that you? Oh my gosh! It really is. It's really you." After they hugged and hugged more, Aimee kindly corrected Kathryn, "it's Aimee Lefevre now, Kathryn, Aimee Lefevre." "Its so wonderful to see you. God, you look great. Really, *really* great. What are you doing in here, in Orange County?"

"Actually my husband and our boys are in Hawaii, partly business and partly vacation. The flight from Paris required a plane change in L.A. where I saw the news report on Eddie. I just had to see you. It was long past the time to do so."

"Oh, wow," she oozed. "I am so glad you did. Where do you..... Oh, silly me. My manners. Aimee, this is my daughter-in-law, Alicia. Honey this is Aimee Thib... I mean Aimee *Lefevre*. She and her husband René, Eddie, and I, were best friends when he and Eddie were in the Navy in the 60's. You remember? We talked about both of them forever, after you and Michael were married."

Alicia held out her hand, "It's really great to finally meet you. Mom and Dad have told all of us of your fun times in the Navy. I am really sorry about your husband, Mrs.

Lefevre." She stopped there when Aimee's expression began to sag. Not now she thought.

To the rescue, Kathryn gave Aimee another hug and exclaimed, "Aimee, Aimee, Aimee, wow. Let's sit a while and get caught up. First, I need to bring you up to date on the crazy goings on here at the hospital. In addition to Eddie's accident, we are here for Alicia's husband, our Michael. You remember little Michael? Well, he was injured on his motorcycle on the way to the hospital early this morning. Our daughter Scarlett, who you will meet in a few minutes, has her son next door at Children's Hospital getting ready for a bone marrow transplant tomorrow to alleviate a rare blood disorder. We now have three of our boys in here." "Dear, Kathryn, you obviously have your hands full here. Let me meet Scarlett and visit a bit with Eddie, then I will be on my way."

"Nonsense, Aimee, you are staying put, and will at least spend the night. You are like family, and I want you to get to know my kids and grandkids as best you can, even if it's here in the hospital. I want to know all about you and your family and life in France. In a little while, we'll check in on Eddie and if Michael is awake, at least say 'hi' to him. Scarlett and her husband Alex are next door with their Joshua. They will love you, having heard all the Navy stories through the years."

"Okay, if you insist. Kathryn, you always did get your way." "Alicia, dear, would you get us cup of coffee please?" "Gladly. How do you like yours, Lefevre?" "Aimee, please, Alicia. You know me, Kathryn, extra strong if there is any close by. My Creole blood still demands that jolt of thick chicory flavored java! And thank you, Alicia."

Alicia discretely bowed away and was off to find a local Starbucks coffee shop, the popular gourmet coffee company brand new to the Orange County and Los Angeles markets. "Kathryn, dear Kathryn, it's been such a long time and truthfully, I think about you and Eddie more than you know. We had such good times, until... "

"Hurry back, Honey." Aimee started over. "Kathryn, I hardly know where to start. After I learned that René had been killed, I went into a two-year funk. I was pregnant with René Jr. as you well know, and after he was old enough to travel, we went to France and moved in with an old aunt who had emigrated from Dominica. She was widowed and perfect company and even better, a great nanny. We didn't talk much, which suited me just fine, just enough for me to learn French. You know me, a slow student if it requires memorization. We watched TV and crocheted during the evening, and by day I worked for an investment bank.

After a few boring months, I went back

to school then sat for my CPA at NYU, then in Paris for my D.E.C. or what they call *Diplôme d'Expertise Comptable* exams in '72 and '73; of the exact years, I'm not for sure, but about then. As I interacted with smart outgoing people, especially men, I finally turned into a human being; a French human being. I met and married my boss, who had lost his wife to leukemia a year earlier. We had a son together and with his own two boys, I have enjoyed life as I never thought possible. My husband adopted René Junior, and to honor his father's memory and legacy, retained Thibadeau for his middle name. Several years later, Junior was able to go the Naval Academy in Annapolis, the wonderful legacy from his father, and guess what? He is a stupid Naval Aviator. Go figure.

Many times I wanted to contact you guys, but we were so far away, it didn't make sense, especially during those first years. That's a poor excuse, I know. The past was the past, and a part of me blamed Eddie for René's death. I had to blame someone. Not René for picking a dangerous occupation, and not me for marrying a Navy Jet jockey. Over time I grew out of the silly blame game, especially when I came to the realization that you could have been the widow and René was able to come home to me."

"Oooo, thanks for the coffee, Alicia. Smells heavenly. Not hospital coffee, I think?"

"No ma'am. I found a Starbucks just two blocks down, and knew they would have the strong kind you would like. It's a double espresso, or at least it is supposed to be. They didn't have any chicory stuff to put in it."

Alicia managed to get the door open with her foot and fanny, as both hands cradled the three cups of coffee in their paper mâché holder. "It smells divine, Alicia. You are too kind. Where was I? Oh, yeah. Honey, when I saw the TV monitor at LAX, I was spellbound. It most especially reminded me of my foolishness. You and Eddie were so special to me; I hoped I could come here and reconnect. Maybe restore old times."

"God, I am so glad you did, Aimee. You are such a sight for sore eyes, as today our circle of friends has narrowed to family and only a few others. I know Eddie will love to see you, and like me, hope you will stay much closer to us in the future. It is so good to see you. Eddie is still banged up, and probably under the residual effects of sedation for a while longer. By staying the night, you can catch him tomorrow morning when he is more aware. He would kill me if you got away before you two could chat, and I need more time with you as well." When Alicia excused herself to trash the empty Starbucks cups, Aimee whispered, "There is something you need to know, Kathryn." Her expression told Kathryn that it was must be serious.

"Kathryn, dear Kathryn. Before you and Eddie were married, we were a couple. We slept together as convenient lovers, and then became best friends; that is, until he met René. We just thought we were lovers, if you catch my meaning. After Eddie met René, at that instant, he knew he was not in love with me like René and I could be. So, he introduced us. The rest you know."

It got quiet, and then with eyebrows slightly raised, Kathryn's expression merged into a curious grin. "You still want to be friends now, Kathryn?" Kathryn thought for a long time, and replied with her trademark warm Kathryn smile.

"Aimee, Eddie told me all about you and him, a long long time ago just before we married. He said you dated for a while; then he introduced you to René. He just knew you guys should be together, and I agreed. You two seemed perfect for each other. And he was spot on right. I'm cool about it, Kiddo. Seems like we all have our little secrets, huh?" Then Kathryn made a curious laugh, tilted her head back a bit, and smiled even bigger. Aimee's smile was wider. "I know you, Aimee Thib.., uh, Aimee Lefevre, and doubt there is little you could do to hurt our friendship. I am so glad you came." They hugged big; rocking back and forth with each having smeary mascara issues. Kathryn smiled and thought to herself. 'I was the first with Eddie, and I will be the last. Ha.'

"As to being friends again, Aimee, nothing would make me happier! You are special and we need to reconnect as soon as we get our guys back on their feet. I can't wait to meet your family. We will have so much fun." They enthusiastically agreed.

5 P.M. Same day During the afternoon, Aimee met the rest of the family, and even slipped into Eddie's room to give him a slight hug. He was still drifting through his sedation, but alert enough to smile and wink. He knew exactly who the beautiful visitor was. She patted his good hand, pushed a shock of his hair away from eyes and whispered, "I will see you tomorrow, handsome, and we will talk." Another smile from Eddie's still cracked lips and a weak squeeze from the hands she had known all too well.

When Alex found everyone all together, he offered to spend the night at the hospital and keep and eye on his son, Michael, and Eddie. The Parker guys all. When Alicia and Scarlett balked, he insisted, reminding them that tomorrow night might be another long one, and he would gladly step aside for someone to take his place. There would be plenty of time in the days ahead for each to take the duty at the hospital. Sensing that Aimee had just a short time left to visit, he knew that an evening with Kathryn and the girls would be appreciated.

It was decided. The girls and Annie would grab a bite to eat and spend the night at Michael and Alicia's home in Lake Forest. There was plenty of room and everyone would fit into the car. Kathryn, Aimee, Scarlett, Annie, and host Alicia, left the hospital into the chill of the late afternoon to the hospital's parking garage. Alicia opened the car doors with a chirp from her remote and slid behind the wheel of their BMW 750. She pointed the car south to Lake Forest and turned on the radio to the classical FM station from USC and a little Vivaldi to relax by on the way to her sprawling casual house, homey and just right for this occasion. Kathryn popped into the front passenger seat while Scarlett, Annie, and Aimee eased into the roomy back seats. Kathryn let her head bob against the headrest as it seemed to be just enough of a massage for her to slip into a drowsy never-land. Alicia was still thinking of Scarlett's unselfish Alex; tending her husband, nephew, and her father-in-law. There would be plenty of nights when she and Scarlett could exchange the hospital vigils. Tonight though, she could enjoy a much-needed rest. It had been a long day for everyone.

From the back seat of the car, Aimee was pressing Scarlett to learn more of her life as a Parker and a Matthias. From her mom and dad, Scarlett had heard so much about

Aimee and René during the Navy years that she felt comfortable enough to share a little history. She directed her family background to Aimee, starting with the drowsy years in North Carolina, sharing the fun she had with her dad, especially their weekly nights at the movies. Aimee was pleased to hear of her penchant for scary movies, as she thoroughly delighted in the European horror movies such as the European version of *The Shining* and *Mr. Vampire*. Scarlett browsed through her library of memories of her school and college days, then slowed to talk about Alex. "You know, Aimee; may I call you Aimee?" "Of course, Dear. The Mrs. thing makes me feel ancient."

"Well, Aimee, the biggest chapter in my little diary was when I traveled to Greece to wrap up my UCLA degree at the Aristotle University of Thessaloniki in Macedonia. My first few weeks were awkward to say the least. Most of the others spoke perfect English, but when it was Greek on Greek, it was all Greek to me. Ha!" "I know the feeling, Scarlett. It was the same for me when I first snuck off to Paris. Exact same thing. Go to the country or the grocery store, it was all French."

"That is so cool. Anyway, thankfully, the university had a program in English for my physics studies and a small section of their library that had great resources for archaeology, one of my main interests that drew me to Macedonia. During my first semester I was at the library browsing the Archeology section, a subject that I had planned to study as my last elective, but even more so, as I felt a connection right there, in the cradle of civilization. I was struggling to find English reference materials and getting very discouraged and frustrated. I muttered to myself, a little louder than I had realized, when this black haired Greek idol introduced himself. When he started talking, I heard nothing. I was fixated on his cologne, his dimples, and the biggest set of perfect teeth on earth. And that *hair*, oh dear. When he finished talking, I went dumb. I gave him my name, and then like a ninny, had to ask for his name, again. 'Aleksander Matthias, Alex will do,' he told me.

"When he learned of my frustration, we moved to a small study table where he was able to direct me to English volumes that would be helpful. I asked how he could be so familiar with this particular field of study; he casually mentioned that it was his passion and also his major. He and I were both seniors, both liked archaeology and didn't have a dating steady. He helped me learn Greek and I helped him brush up on his English.

"At first, we were just very good friends. As I learned of his orphanage childhood and later the teen years with a loving foster family, it became clear that somewhere in his ancestry, he had to come from royalty. His impeccable manners and sharp mind did not come from humble beginnings. He stood out of the crowd of any male student, as well as any of the Greek men around town. As worshiped as the school soccer players were by the girls, they were no match for Alex. The dark eyed and narrow boned Greek co-eds, most of them Greek goddesses in their own right, were insanely jealous of this red headed American who had hi-jacked one of their men. I loved it. Alex had only meager sketchy details of his birth parents that the orphanage provided to his foster parents. Apparently, his father had been mostly Albanian with some Italian heritage, while his mother was Greek. Being from Albania, they joined other Albanian blue-collar refugees fleeing from the 1967 campaign of dictator Hoxha's banning of religion. They settled in Strumica, the largest city in eastern Macedonia, near the Novo Selo-Petrich border crossing with Bulgaria. The town of 100,000 had a fairly large community and church of Methodists founded by 19th and 20th century missionaries working out of Salonika.

"His parents, the Matthiases, joined others who were hungry to obtain and determined to enjoy the freedom of religion. The move ruined any chances of prosperity, an expected consequence, but they did not expect abject poverty. Soon after the birth of Alex, and with an older son, they felt that they had a better chance of raising just one of the boys. They turned to the orphanage in Macedonia, a place considered safe for Alex. According to what Alex learned as he grew curious about his parents, they had promised to return some day and reclaim him. He was told that they put him there with love and that his name was to be held precious, as his family was 'special', whatever that meant. They never returned. Alex confessed that the searching of his family name's heritage stirred his interest to dig deeper into the world of archaeology, principally history of Alexander the Great. Just a few weeks ago, we made an agreement that as soon as Joshua is on the mend, we would go back and unravel the mystery of his parent's family.

"Alex and I became almost inseparable from that first moment of meeting in the school library as we enjoyed exploring together the treasures of the area. We loved to investigate the mysterious hidden Markets of Thessaloniki and sometimes went to the nearby Archaeological Sites of Aigai in nearby Vergina, only sixty miles east on E90, an easy trek in Alex's little Peugeot 505. Aigai became famous when a Greek archaeologist discovered the burial site of the Kings of Macedon, including what he claimed to be the tomb of Philip II, the father of Alexander the Great."

As Scarlett took a breath to continue, she noticed Aimee's eyelids struggling to stay open, and her mom's head beginning to bob, then jerk up. She turned to Aimee; "I had better quit. I am sure this must be getting boring." Aimee argued, "Quite the contrary, Scarlett, tell me more. Your charming Alex sounds like a one man international mystery!" Alicia echoed the same sentiment, "don't stop now Scarlett, I hadn't heard about a lot of this stuff. Keep going."

"Well, okay, just a little more. Like Mom, I'm pooped. We are both running on fumes and my memory is getting a little sketchy right now, but I'll try. Aimee, we traveled all around the area on long weekends. We went north into Serbia, east to Bulgaria, southeast to Turkey, and south to Athens and the area around Corinth and the Corinthian Gulf areas where Paul fought valiantly to spread the Gospel."

"Wow, you guys really got around, and I thought I traveled." "Thanks, Aimee. I think our favorite getaway was the little island of Thassos, just a ferry ride from Keramoti. You could float on your back in crystal clear turquoise water and see snow covered mountains in the distance. It was simply fabulous. Anyway, we rented a pan car, a sort of beach buggy, to explore all over the island.

We enjoyed the fabulous beaches, as well as me getting to witness first hand Greek culture and tradition. We poked around the goldmines, marble quarries, and always loaded up on olive oil and honey that's made there. By January of 1988 we were deeply in love, but it was Alex who insisted that we marry before we made, uhhh, before we were real intimate. Now that was driving me crazy. I was so attracted to him I just couldn't stand it. Those hairy arms and chest; Wow! The little two-day shadow of a beard didn't hurt either. Then the smile; was like a panty vaporizer. Still is." Now Kathryn and Alicia were wide awake after that last remark. Alex's unshaven beard would never be the same to them.

"We didn't quite make it to the wedding in the intimate department. It seemed so natural and Alex was so right for me, it didn't matter. We moved in together and married in July just after we graduated in '89; Alex with a degree in Archaeology and me wrapping up my degree in Physics with a minor in Greek Culture."

Scarlett was turning red now, thankfully disguised by the shadows of the late afternoon. "Scarlett, you sound like a floosy up there. Shame, *shame*." "Oh, *Mom*. I thought you were asleep, and *you* should talk. Give me a break." They all laughed as Alicia pulled onto El Toro Parkway, the way to

Lucille's Smokehouse Barbeque in Lake Forest. After dining on two baskets of slow smoked baby back ribs generously slathered with Lucille's Carolina style barbeque sauce, they demonstrated their approval by the splotches of sauce scattered on their clothing.

The girls slipped back into the BMW and made their way, by now, only a short drive to Alicia's house. Kathryn and Scarlett knew the drill and found their rooms, leaving the spacious guest bedroom for Aimee. When they got settled and put on their robes, they adjourned to the 'great room' and tried to find a suitable nightcap from Michael's generous bar. Alicia was the last to join, but still she still had her clothes on.

"Ladies, I just can't do this. I have to go back and be with my husband. I worry about him being alone, and even if he doesn't know I'm there, I still want to be with him. He would be there for me, and I want to be there for him. I just can't help it. When I see Alex, I will send him back in the morning to pick up everyone. I hope that's okay?"

Scarlett nodded, "It's okay, Honey; I know how you feel. I would do the exact some thing. We'll all have our turn to be up there for all-nighters, that's for sure, but you go ahead. We can visit a while here, then turn in so one of us will be fresh to take the helm tomorrow. While you are there, keep an eye on your father and give me a call if there are any changes."

"Will do for sure. I am positive that Annie will be okay with you Kathryn. You are almost like a second mom to her. You okay with that?" "Of course. Shoo. Scat." After another merry- go-round of hugs, she was gone. Aimee couldn't help noticing Alicia's sweet spirit, and dabbed her eyes when Kathryn and Scarlett weren't looking.

"Kathryn, you have a special girl there." "Don't we know it, huh Scarlett?" "Yesiree; without a doubt." Kathryn continued. "All parents hope their kids find just the right partner, and with the divorce rates as they are, and with all the shacking up and stuff these days, Eddie and I were delighted with both Alex and Alicia. Scarlett filled you in on Alex; so let me give you a short history of Alicia.

"She grew up with her parents in the Pacific Northwest near Everett, Washington, 25 miles north of Seattle. Her father was a professor at the University of Washington's Medical School, specializing in Biophysics as well as spearheading the growing WWAMI program, a multi-state educational outreach initiative that included Alaska, Idaho and Montana. His passion though, was fishing, an enthusiasm eagerly shared by Alicia. From the time she could walk, she joined her dad every available weekend to the waters of Puget Sound. When she got a stick of deodorant one Christmas, she thought it was some new kind of stink bait.

"They bottom fished for Lingcod, worked their down riggers for Coho Salmon, and lured Spotted Halibut out of the water into the small 17-foot Bayliner Capri™ they owned. If they weren't fishing, they watched seals, sea lions, and if they were lucky, Orca whales. They prayed for lots of birds, flat water, and sunny skies, which made for the perfect father/daughter experience. If their fishing luck was not so good, they could always get their limit around the south end of the outer bar of the Sound. On the rare chance they were skunked, they still came home with new appreciation of the amazing views of Mount Rainer, Mount Baker, the Cascade Range and the Olympic Mountains. We never tire of Alicia's stories of being with her father. Although her mom only fished when the weather was just right, she was the moral backbone of the family.

"She was characterized as eighty percent nun and twenty percent boot camp sergeant when the situation demanded, describing Alicia's personality to a tee. I am not for sure, but at least one of her parents had a great down to earth sense of humor. A surprising feature of Alicia was her keen interest in her dad's work in medicine. She had good grades, earned a scholarship to and enrolled in UCLA, where Michael was enrolled. Believe it or not, they met on one of those commercial sports fishing day trips at *Davy's Locker* out of Newport Beach, just down the highway from here. After they motored to their usual fishing waters, he noticed this small girl in her foul weather gear, looking more like a thirteen-year-old orphan who misplaced her *will work for food* sign. His impression changed when she began to catch more fish and get them cleaned better and faster than the crew.

"The closer he got to her, he became more and more drawn to her quirky smile and strong confidence that she radiated. When they were down below getting coffee they shared a booth where he got to know his future wife. When she threw back her foul weather hood, she revealed a shock of hair like Scarlett's and a natural facial beauty like the Eurasians, described by many as the most beautiful of all women. She was smart, enrolled as a pre-med student, and had learned about Michael through the school newspaper.

"Like Eddie, he was the promising baseball star from high school, but was injured and had to hang up his Bruins Baseball uniform. Oddly enough, when Michael first talked about her, he was attracted to her laugh and sense of humor more than her intellect. Add beauty and you have great ingredients for a strong friendship and now marriage.

"They had a few dates off and on for the first two years, but then in their junior years started going steady. We all fell in love with her, and her folks felt the same for Michael. Like Alex and Scarlett, they married just after graduation, and promptly had Annie. When Annie starts Elementary School, Alicia wants to do further study in nuclear medicine like her father, and maybe teach at U.C. Irvine. For the time being, she is content as a mother and wife, and a loving daughter-in law. We are crazy about her and lucky to have her in the family. Her real metal shined when she reinforced Scarlett's determination to find out what was really killing Joshua."

Scarlett inserted a big amen. "I would have been lost without her. We were one hell of a team." A few yawns signaled that they were all feeling the toll of the day's events and turned in, totally exhausted and anxious about what the next day would bring.

7:30 A.M. Early Tuesday morning True to Alicia's promise, Alex picked up Scarlett, Aimee, Kathryn and Annie at 7:30 on the dot. When Alex kissed Scarlett good morning, Aimee saw firsthand the effect of that two-day-old stubble. She wiped her forehead, pretending to be messing with her hair, thinking, 'aye yai yai!' On the way to the hospital, Alex elaborated about all three guys resting without incident. Alicia crept back and forth between Eddie, Josh and Michael, then slept in the lounge chair next to her husband, holding his hand much of the night. The few times that Michael or Eddie stirred, Alex had a short assuring visit with them as they crept out of their fog of sedatives and began to slowly regain their strength. Alex caught catnaps in each room, but was vigilant most of the night, shushing the cleaning crews and nurses as they chatted and laughed a little too loud to suit him, especially as they were clocking in and out of their shifts. With the family in place at the hospital, the hours ticked slowly towards Josh's infusion of healthy new blood cells. The afternoon was closing in as little Josh had completed his pre-op regimens of blood workups and was pronounced fit for the procedure. He was resting quietly in Scarlett's lap with the juvenile intravenous line already poked into the crook of his small arm.

1 P.M. The Pediatric Hematologist came into the room with his surgical mask tied around his neck, resting loosely on the front of his scrubs. "It's time." He patiently went over the process again. He described the specific procedure as a Hematopoietic Stem Cell Transplantation. The donor's cells, or progenitor cells, would be expected to reconstitute normal bone marrow function and fix Joshua's congenital immunodeficiency disorder. Because Josh did not have the complication of toxicity from the usual chemotherapy to deal with, it was expected that he would have fewer side effects and a speedier and heavily prayed for recovery.

Joshua was gently laid on the gurney, and with Scarlett by his side, rolled into the transfusion center down the hall. Scarlett was prepped, then allowed to remain in the OR with her blue hairnet, mask, and blue scrubs, holding his little hand the whole way. Her chest swelled and her tears began to trickle down her freckled cheeks, as the bone marrow from the mysterious anonymous donor was primed with a granulocytecolony stimulant, designed to increase the stem cell count and speed the transfusion process. The precious filtered gooey marrow slowly dripped into Josh's chest vein for about thirty minutes. By then the stem cells would be completely transfused into his blood stream.

The total process took only about ninety minutes with little discomfort to Joshua. Hopefully, the donor's marrow would migrate into the cavities of Josh's bones and produce normal numbers of healthy blood cells. The energetic leucocytes were off to the races; now the waiting. The stem cells were determined to push up Josh's blood count, enabling his immune system to strengthen. It would take Josh weeks and maybe a few months to regain his full strength, but he would have a highly trained staff of hematology specialists monitoring his progress and cheering him on.

Scarlett and Alex knew that the seventy percent success rate of a healthy recovery were far better odds than more tedious blood transfusions, as well as possible spleen and gall bladder removal. For now, the constant doses of folic acid, and other medicines to decrease Josh's iron output had been necessary. His little body could tolerate only a few more years of this harsh treatment, then the doctors would throw in the towel and Joshua Parker would die. The outlook now was so much more optimistic.

The first three months would be critical, requiring trips to the hospital every other day for outpatient care. With Alicia and Michael's love and support, it would be a shared burden less heavy, and Joshua was a Parker equal to the challenge. As soon as Josh was returned to his room, Alicia and Kathryn adjourned to St. Joes to focus on his uncle Michael. Aimee agreed to stay with Scarlett's family for a little while, as Alex and Scarlett were consigned to the waiting game, again. But this time, finally and thankfully, a game with many more winners than losers. The fortunes of the Parkers seemed to be shifting.

3 P.M. The news for Michael was not the answer to prayer the family had hoped for. His wife, sister, and mother, were all devastated. Both of his kidneys suffered end-stage renal failure, too damaged to do their jobs. He was put on the kidney databank waiting list and scheduled for dialysis three times a week. His wait would be three to five years, maybe sooner with his health and youth. Kathryn, Scarlett, Alex and Alicia were crushed at the thought. The idea of this virile active man having to be chained to a dialysis machine was unthinkable.

When they regained their composure, the Parkers gathered to compare blood types, to see if any might be at least a blood match and be able to submit samples for further testing as matches. Unfortunately, Michaels' blood type was A negative, narrowing possible matches to those with A negative or O negative. As a sibling, Scarlett was the best hope, with a twenty five percent chance of being a full match, but she had AB negative. No help. Kathryn remembered that Michael's birth father Jared's blood type was not a match, leaving the only candidates to be Eddie, and Alicia, both with compatible O negative blood types. Since Eddie and Alicia weren't blood relatives, Michael would for now, be dependent on friends and members outside the family for help. Even though a remote possibility, outside donors who matched and specified the recipient would be Michael's best hope. Kathryn asked Alicia to leave Michael just briefly; to follow her to Eddie's room for an important discussion with the three of them. That morning the nurse noted that Eddie had not used his morphine, so she disconnected the medicine bag from the I.V., leaving only a saline drip for hydration and antibiotics. He was fairly lucid and curious to hear what Kathryn had up her ever so long sleeve.

Kathryn went straight to Eddie's bed. "Scoot over a bit Honey, and let me sit here." Kathryn proceeded to ooch her husband over as if a sack of pillows. He looked at her as if she had lost her marbles. "So, here's the deal", slinging her words left and right so both could hear. "Michael needs a kidney. It may sound far-fetched, but you are the only two who have compatible blood types for Michael, the first step in determining full compatibility for a kidney transplant. I know the lineage is not the same, but better someone close, even a friend. If one of you, by some miracle, is a match, we can do what we call a 'directed donation' and avoid the huge 4,000 long waiting list with the National Organ Procurement and Transplantation Network that could be a three to seven year wait. Giving up a kidney is no small thing. It's a really big deal. Alicia, I would understand if you might want to pass, but..." Before Kathryn could say more, Alicia blurted, "What do you mean might want to pass. If I only had one kidney, I would donate in a heartbeat. He is the love of my life. Case closed."

"Okay Honey, okay. That doesn't surprise me. You are such a treasure. Edward William Parker, here's your situation. For you to match would also be long a very, very long shot, but nevertheless a chance. The doctors explained to me, that in addition to the blood match, there is tissue matching which requires a six-antigen match, as well as cross matching that define how Michael might respond to your particular cells or proteins. It's a crapshoot all the way around with such overwhelming odds, but it's up to you. What about it, Love?"

Eddie maneuvered his cast and managed a thumbs up. In a husky voice, he muttered "okay", and with a strong smile, his eyes shouted, "Absolutely." He loved Michael as his own, and would do anything for him. He would give his life for him, as well as any of his kids or grandchildren. Kathryn knew this, but it felt good to see it in his face. "I'll get with his doctor and set up the tests."

Chapter Fifteen

*"In romance, the 'secret affair', sooner
or later, becomes an oxymoron."*
~ ~ *The author*

4 P.M.

Aimee slipped in to peek in on and chat with Michael, a man now. Nonetheless, she could still see that adorable little round face she knew so well years ago in San Diego. The longer they talked, the more clearly a vision of the little boy emerged. Even with such a short visit, it was clear through that Parker smile, his smooth manner and politeness demonstrated that Eddie's influence on him was deep. She could have talked with him all day, but knowing his condition and convinced she would be back, she excused herself, wished him good luck and every happiness, then tiptoed out of the room. After a while, she walked down and around to Eddie's room where she could be with him alone. True to Kathryn's prediction, Eddie began to show some color and animation.

After scooting in as close as the hardware would permit, she gave him a kiss on the forehead. He woke from a light nap and smiled. She whispered, "Eddie, I love you and owe you an apology. After René died and as soon as he was buried in Arlington, I ran away, all the way to France. I worked in an office during the day, and took French lessons from my aunt by night. I was bitter that our country took the love of my life away. I even wondered if it was you who took the unnecessary risk, and that was why he died. I had to blame someone. I thought of awful things, day and night. I was selfish. To be honest, I was really surprised to hear that he was dead. I didn't think that death would have the patience to take him. At that moment, it all turned to 'all about me'. I was so very foolish for a very long time, until now." Sounding like he had just swallowed a six-pack of small gravel, Eddie twisted more to her and managed a reply.

"Aimee, I love you too, and we both have missed you terribly." Eddie had to wet his lips with his tongue and clear his dry throat. "When we got that telegram that René didn't make it, we cried for days. We didn't eat for three days. When I left the squadron to meet Kathryn in Hawaii, I was assured that he was going to be all right; at least that's what I told myself or wanted to hear. Kathryn and I were both crushed, but it was harder on me than I ever could have imagined. I lost several good friends in Vietnam, but René was different, like a twin brother. Both of you were my family. I imploded. I couldn't think and didn't want to fly anymore. Thankfully, the captain was kind and sent me on mostly benign missions, probably saving my life. I ran into a MiG one day from a routine recon mission, and almost peed myself before getting a lucky shot off. I just wasn't the cavalier Parker as before. When my tour was finally over, I punched out of the Navy, and slipped into the furniture business, the quietest of industries. I could have flown for any airline and made 200 grand a year working three days a week, but I just couldn't bring myself to get back into that cockpit or any cockpit for that matter, at least for a while. I just lost my soul, my Mojo, and wasn't the same husband Kathryn signed on for. I, we ...."

Aimee gently interrupted. "Darling Eddie, just listen to me and give me a chance to finish. By the way, your voice sounds like sandpaper, so you need to rest it anyway." She leaned closer with one hand on his arm, and the other over his chest. Her French 'do' had come loose a bit, with a thin clump hanging just across her left brow. Eddie scrunched up a little, as best as he could, wired, roped, collared, and with casts and braces everywhere, to hear better. Aimee, with an expression that would tame the devil, leaned in closer still to her former lover to be sure he heard and understood every word. His eyes grew larger waiting to hear what she was about to say.

The colorful Haitian exchange nurse puttering around the end of Eddie's bed noticed Eddie's monitoring equipment showing a blip in his heart rate and blood pressure. Looking at the cozy couple, she smiled and muttered aloud to herself, "Hmmm, a little sumpum, sumpum going onnn?" The mahn's new friend be really bootiful and he a war hero. Hmmm? What about de Parker woman? Whoooppeee. Ha."

Aimee was tuned in to this 'sistah'. Quicker than a cat, she spun around to face her with a glare more powerful than if she had poked a Voodoo doll in her face. She cracked a short sentence in Pidgin French that caused the nurse to spin and trip her way out of the room, bumping on the edge of a chair on the way out, still looking at Aimee with a terrified expression, eyes wide, the size of fried eggs."Now where was I? Oh, yeah. Eddie, as time wore on and I began to see life for what it really was. I realized several things. For a while you and I were a couple, and I loved you, or thought I did until you introduced me to René. That was a wonderfully unselfish thing for you to do. You and I could have been just sex buddies, mutually convenient, but especially so for you. You gave that away. Wellllll, and me, too, I suppose. I really, *really* liked you and especially the *'it'* we had. I told you that then, and I am telling you that again. No doubt we could have made a great couple.

Sacrebleu, I am embarrassing myself

now. Here's the thing, Eddie, you taught me the difference between love and lust, although the latter wasn't so bad. You gave me René for twenty-four karat years of indescribable happiness. You were solid gold." She fanned her face to cool a slight blush and to hide a big smile. "I thank you for that and much more for the months I was married to René. As for losing him while in that airplane, I see it this way. His injuries were the luck of the draw. It could have been you that took that shrapnel. You could have been killed. Maybe René could have been the one nursing that airplane back to the carrier and you were the one to bleed to death. He could have done it, too, you know. I knew you let him land a couple of times, number three wire each time, and he never told a soul, except me. Maybe he would have ejected safely. There were a ton of maybes. Fate just bent the twig, Eddie; it just frigging twisted both of our twigs.

What happened just happened. Eddie, you could have punched out and ejected René with you for the two of you to be rescued. You knew he was hurt, and despite your own injuries, you got that damn plane on the ship. I have no regrets, Eddie. And as for regret I learned a valuable lesson from an old proverb that said, 'regret never mends a broken urn.' Then from the writer, Barbara Bloom, I was reminded that the Japanese believe that 'when something's suffered damage and has a history; it becomes more beautiful over the years as if the cracks are filled with gold.' I have restored that vase, Eddie, filling the cracks with gold, building a life clear of guilt and grief.

All that aside, I still have to ask your and Kathryn's forgiveness for not making contact with you after a decent amount of time. I am ashamed of that. What treasures we have missed not talking with and seeing you, Kathryn, and your family. What *good times* we could have had.

Anyway, René died, and I got to say good-by to him. My memory of him was a sweet face at peace, a vision not possible if he were at the bottom of the South China Sea as fish food. I still visit his grave at Arlington every time I am in Washington. I had girl friends whose husbands smashed into Vietnamese hillsides and others whose husbands drowned, still in the cockpit of their airplanes at the bottom of the muddy seawater. I have to thank you, Eddie, for letting me say good-by to him that was critical in my healing. In my journey of life after René, I now have a husband who I love dearly, my precious son René Jr., a son with Jean Baptiste Lefevre, Gilles, and my two stepsons who I am crazy about. I have the privilege of having loved deeply *twice*, and that would not have been possible without you, Eddie Parker." As her eyes drove deeply into his, she brushed the top of his lip, moving down to the lower one with her finger, then leaned in just a bit closer. She was reflecting back to that Tiki Bar years ago and without thinking, whispered in perfect French the words she knew to be regrettable, but nonetheless, they trickled out as, "Maybe three times, no" Then she checked herself. 'Oh dear, I *need* to get back to my *husband* before I do something stupid..again.'

She shifted back a bit and put her restless hands in her lap. "Eddie, the friendship between the four of us was the definition of a perfect friendship. Not many people ever have that, my good man. After René and I were married and when you tied the knot with Kathryn, we had such good times. Healthy times. We played cards, slipped off to Vegas, and prowled René's and my hometown like four juvenile runaways. As an old haunt of yours, you even showed us a few places we didn't even know about. I'll never forget the fun times running up and down Bourbon Street drinking from our Pat O'Brian Hurricane Glasses full of that awful rum drink, peeking into Preservation Hall, then watching the sun come up while eating Beignets and drinking Chicory coffee at Café du Monde on Jackson Square. You and René taught me how to have fun, real fun. I loved you for that.

One more little matter, Eddie, and you

will have to cross your heart to keep what I tell you just between the two of us, at least until I leave the hospital. Can you promise?" Eddie nodded, mostly with his eyes, now watery and more widely open from his curiosity.

"My son, René Jr., is a very private and humble person. He heard about your grandson's bone marrow transplant through the Tail Hook Association's gossip line, and is the very proud donor of the bone marrow for Joshua." Eddie's jaw dropped about a foot as Aimee smiled big and continued. "The 'why's' and 'how comes' will have to wait until my son is ready. Ultimately, you will have the opportunity to thank him, but I wanted to tell you first. God has a plan for all of us, and He knew we would all be here at this time in His master schedule. If you had not introduced us, there would be no René Jr., and maybe no Joshua. So *there*." Then she gently kissed his furrowed fifty-year-old forehead and then onto his dried lips, slightly moistened with a single teardrop that rolled from her cheek.

It got quiet. Eddie was blurred by Aimee's tears, Aimee with Eddie's. The fist that first grabbed his heart when Kathryn left him to marry Jared and grabbed it again when he read that telegram from Captain Huddleson years ago in Hawaii, finally eased its grip. His universe felt restored, whole, and finally began to make sense. Aimee had sculpted their history most wonderfully.

Huskily and slowly but very clearly, Eddie managed, "Aimee, what you said, ummmm, well, you just restored my sanity. I haven't been worth a nickel as a father or a husband since I learned that René died. I have had a few good moments, but I have had nightmares and cold sweats on and off ever since. I have had visions seeing René's bloody disfigured laughing face as he disappeared into the sea. There are dozens of images that I won't frighten you with. I wake up with a pain in my butt where the shrapnel hit, as if it just happened. I felt like a killer; the murderer of my best friend and the husband of you, my special friend. You have rendered the torturing devices inside of me harmless with your words. Only you alone could have done this. And your son's unselfishness; it all fits. You are an angel, Aimee. Hold my hand. Hold it tight. I suddenly feel sleepy."

She stroked her other hand over his unshaven face and rubbed her thumb under his swollen eye, as they both felt more serenity than they had ever known. The cerebral and emotional afterglow bathed their senses with the sweetness of understanding. He would now finally make peace with the forces that had haunted him for so long. Aimee felt the same release with the gift she had just conferred on Eddie. Aimee also knew that someday, the Parker family would come to the realization that René's DNA would reside in their family for generations. His presence would be remembered on more and more branches of the Parker family tree. At that, she smiled, coming to that conclusion only that moment.

It had been a long day, but a good day. Aimee smiled, kissed Eddie on the forehead, got up, retrieved her purse, and walked out of the room knowing what she had to do next. After a good sneeze and having cleared the happy salt water from her eyes, Aimee walked down the corridor feeling ever so majestic. She looked in on Michael, who was sleeping again, or at least letting the sedatives do their thing. Then she stepped outside for a walk. The brisk cool air felt good as she began to look forward to meeting her Jean Baptiste Lefevre and sons in Hawaii.

She called to speak with Kathryn, but only got her voice mail. "My dear Kathryn, I am sorry I missed you, but I'm going to head on out early tomorrow morning. I found a seven o'clock flight to Maui, so I can catch up with my fabulous family and you can concentrate on getting yours back to good health. I will stay the night at the Airport Doubletree and not impose on anyone here for transportation. I wanted to tell you what a miracle it was for me to see the TV images of Eddie on the morning news. It drove me to see you both, something I should have done years earlier. I will always apologize for not getting in touch much, much sooner. Anyway, I hope that we can stay close, and visit at least once or twice a year. You will love Jean Baptiste and the boys, and they will love you and your family as much as I love you and your wonderful family.

And *most of all*, thank you from the bottom of my capricious little heart for being so gracious. You are a special friend, one that I love more than ever. I am so impressed with your family; I know I will love them more and more. You have my phone number, so catch me up when Josh, Michael, and Eddie are on the mend. When we come back through LA in a few weeks, and I am so very hopeful that we can spend at least one day together. I would dearly love to relive those special times. Oh, and for Eddie, tell him, 'Laissez Le Bon Temp Rouler.' If he's talked about his and René's times, you will know the meaning. If not, he will still get a kick out of it. Bye for now, my *special* Kathryn. I can't wait to see you soon. Good luck my friend and God bless you. Amie"

Chapter Sixteen

"When the urge to cheat is
so strong, there are no
promises, no shame
and no fear.
~ From "Follow
Me" by
Uncle
Kracker

Friday November 27th 9 A.M.

Tuesday surrendered to Wednesday and Thursday melted into Friday. It was only six days until Thanksgiving, and no one in the Parker family expected their prayers to be answered by the holidays. Scarlett and Alex were with Joshua at Children's Hospital watching the boy get stronger and stronger, while Kathryn was catching up on her casual magazine reading in Eddie's room next door at St Joe's. Alicia was parked down the hall, tending her man Michael mending from his successful lumbar surgery; waiting to hear from the Kidney Bank for an estimate of how long they would have to wait. Eddie's phone chimed on his nightstand. "Hello, this is Mr. Parker's room, may I help you?"

"Mrs. Parker, this is the Kidney Transplant Coordinator. Will you hold for Dr. Hindman?" "Why yes, of course." "Good morning, Mrs. Parker, this is Doctor Hindman. Could you come to my office on the fourth floor to discuss Michael's apparent donor match for a new kidney?" She didn't drop the phone as before. She had an anxious but good feeling about the meeting and crossed her fingers when she hung up.

Kathryn walked briskly up the three flights of stairs to the Nephrologist's office. She needed the time to settle her nerves a bit to hear what he had to say. This was all so ethereal and dreamlike, even for this tough old broad. 'But a match so fast? Can't be. Something isn't right. Did someone pull strings to get Michael a kidney so fast?'

"Mrs. Parker, what I have in front of me is a highly unusual and unexpected test result." He was squinting over his 'granny glasses' that were perched on the tip of his nose. With his knuckles tucked under his chin, he dropped his right hand and ever so slowly to open the thin leather folder on his desktop. "Your husband, Edward, matched perfectly with his stepson." He continued slowly and deliberately. "The blood group, the antigens of the tissue, and the cross match was as close to perfect as any match."

Kathryn tried to swallow, but there was no moisture, only the beads forming on her upper lip and the tears stampeding to the doorway of their ducts. Sweat began to gather then roll down the small of her back and disappear into the waistband of her cotton underwear. She sat expressionless. She couldn't make her eyes blink for fear she would wake up from this amazing dream. She bit her lip just to be sure. It was not a dream. The realization allowed her to exhale an eternity of tired breath.

"If Mr. Parker's final lab reports come through as expected, and his and Michael's condition improve for a couple more weeks, then we can do the transplant. This will also allow us time to do the necessary screening of your husband's medial history. It will also provide the time to complete a thorough psychiatric review. Are you okay? You don't seem very excited, Mrs. Parker?"

Startled out of her fog and trying to put some expression into her words, she exclaimed, "Oh, I am Dr. Hindman, I am. I am thrilled beyond words. It's just that I have a lot on my mind about my grandson, son, and husband. I am a little wrung out right now. Forgive me, but you have made me the happiest woman on the planet. This is truly an answer to our prayers and is a miracle of miracles. I can't believe it's really *true.*"

"Good. I am sure you want to be with your family and share the good news. I will have the Transplant Coordinator call you in a day or so to go over some paperwork and schedule the surgery. Ideally, we should plan this while both men are still here in the hospital. They both will have recovered sufficiently from their injuries and any subsequent infections to be healthy enough for surgery at about the same time. All in all, I think these guys, beat up as they are, to me, are very lucky. Your husband by all that is holy should not have survived an airplane crash into a mountainside, and your son could have just as easily been killed on that bike. The biggest stroke of luck was the fact that a stepfather could be such a good match for a kidney transplant. That is a mystery to me, but in medicine, all shapes and sizes of miracles, never fail to amaze me. Last year a wife of 46 years matched and gave a kidney to her husband, so I try not to be too amazed when something like this happens."

He tried to peer into Kathryn's eyes, but she had retreated from his gaze, protecting the secrets her eyes might reveal, which they usually did. She continued looking into her lap, fiddling with a half crushed tissue pack. Not having much luck engaging Kathryn any further, Dr. Hindman asked, "Unless you have any questions, Mrs. Parker, I'll let you run along and share this good news with your friends and family. I am sure they are on pins and needles, as I would be in your situation."

"Thanks Dr. Hindman, thanks a million. I'm on my way." She breathed a huge sigh of relief and reached for her purse. As she rose to leave, exactly like Peter Faulk's *Columbo*, he continued. "Oh, just one more thing, Mrs. Parker. I have a question for you."

Dr. Hindman was leaning back in his black leather swivel chair, rocking slightly and moving from side to side; hands clasped across his belly. He bent forward, now, leaning across his desk, ever closer to Kathryn.

"Oh?" "I mean no disrespect, Mrs. Parker, so for forgive me if I seem off base." Over his granny glasses again, he glanced down at his folder and took a deep breath and slowly exhaled. He puckered his lips in a funny way and scratched the right side of his neck with his left hand. "Is there any chance that Michael could be your husband's son?"

Kathryn just stared, her lungs barely moving. For a second her heart quit beating and her inhaling and exhaling were no longer a reflex activity of the autonomic nervous system. She had to push air out to make herself breathe. She slumped a bit, drooped into her chair, and hid her eyes again. 'Dear Lord.' After what seemed like forever, she swallowed to clear her throat and whispered, "Yes. Yes, he could. I actually hope that he is."

The quiet was punctuated only by the faint dings of patient call buttons, custodian's cleaning buckets, far away phone rings, and nurses' pages for doctors. Dr. Hindman gave it some time. He was wiser than most. "Mrs. Parker?" "Yes sir?" She was really watering up by now. She felt like a prostitute that had been busted for years of sinful behavior and hidden secrets. He wisely gave her some time as she attacked her tissue pack. "Would you be offended if I suggested a paternity test?"

"No, sir. That actually would be great. Let's do it as soon as it can be arranged. How long will it take?" "Two days if I put a rush on it." "Great! Dr. Hindman, and if it's possible, I would like to keep the test and our conversation just between you and me until we get the results. I might have a lot of explaining ahead of me in case it is positive. It would mean a lot if you could do this one thing for me, Doctor."

"You have my word, I totally understand. Mrs. Parker, try to relax bit. Take a deep breath. You have a lot to be thankful for and a mature family that will support you and your husband, no matter what."

Kathryn, rose, then nodded a grateful smile and turned to leave. Then she turned and inexplicably ran to the doctor and gave him a great big hug, almost knocking him over and nearly ruining his granny glasses. "Thank you Doctor Hindman, you are a saint." Then she left his office and began slowly down the same route that took her to Dr. Hindman's office. There was never a time in her life when she had faced so many tempests all at once. She was on a simultaneous high and low that was ripping her apart. She just needed to get through these next few days; even the next few minutes would be exceptionally nice.

She worked her way into Eddie's room and found him asleep. She pulled the hospital's flimsy plastic chair up close, eased her purse to the floor, and dropped carefully into the seat. The bed had been lowered and the side rail was down. She edged her way closer so she could lay her head on the pillow next to him. Most of the tubes and trapeze paraphernalia had been removed, and except for the pillow supporting his ankle, he looked almost normal. His voice had mostly returned and the neck brace had been changed to a smaller soft collar. Eddie stretched and almost knocked Kathryn's glasses off with his elbow. "Oops. I'm sorry Babe, I didn't know you were here." With his signature smile, he whispered, "what's up?"

"I love you so much, you will never know. So much it hurts." She rested there for a long time until Eddie fell back into a pleasant sleep, without nightmares this time. Kathryn pulled the family together and casually lied that the doctors had conflicting results on the first run of the Kidney Match Tests and had to do a second run, a routine procedure in a lot of cases. It would be Sunday night or Monday before those results would be known. Everyone was already reconciled to having to depend on the waiting list for Michael to get the new kidney, so they weren't too concerned one way or another. Their expectations were light-years away from Kathryn's.

8 A.M. The Following Monday From the adjacent waiting room, Alicia watched through the glass window into the office of Dr. Hindman. Kathryn had asked her for a few private moments with the doctor, which seemed a little odd, but Kathryn had promised to explain her reasoning later. Alicia could see the doctor showing her a paper as his mouth moved to explain. Kathryn had her back turned to her and only saw her head nod up and down and then sideways. The Doctor had a faint smile, then gestured toward Alicia to come in. Dr. Hindman gave Kathryn a long, big bear hug, again. This time it was he who felt warm and fuzzy. Kathryn was wiping her eyes as she turned back towards Alicia, also waving her to hurry in. As she took her seat next to Kathryn, the doctor spoke to Alicia.

"Mrs. Parker, by a miracle of The Almighty and Lady Luck beyond this old doctor's imagination, your father-in-law matched perfectly with all aspects of your husband's blood type. We want to schedule the transplant for a week from Friday, on December 4th. There are still a few tests your father-in-law has to undergo, however, we expect no problems. He is a healthy man and will be thrilled to be donating his kidney to his.....uh, to be giving his kidney to Michael." Then Alicia got in on the three-way hug carousel. They were bouncing, almost dancing. "Honey, you run tell Michael, while I tell Eddie. Meet me in Eddie's room when you get through, then we can call Scarlett and Alex to come over from Children's Hospital."

"Thank you, Doctor Hindman. You have been a godsend," Alicia managed, wiping away more fresh tears. He just smiled, like Sherlock Holmes after solving a big mystery. "You are more than welcome, Mrs. Parker. Your husband and father-in-law are deserving of this miraculous news."

"Let's go Alicia", as they both gave Dr. Hindman one more squeeze. As soon as they were off the elevator, Kathryn scurried down the hall a little faster than Alicia. She swept into Eddie's room as he was twisting his good hand around a piece of slightly burned toast, trying to get a smear of packaged strawberry jelly on it. "Here, let me help, Hon." "Oh, hi Babe. Thanks." The husky whisper had given way to a near normal voice, as he had talked the nurses into letting him take off the neck brace if he promised to put it on when getting out of bed. Making sure she had full eye contact, "You matched, love; you matched Michael's tissue, the cross match, everything. Unless you flunk a routine psych evaluation, you will be giving Michael one of your kidneys." Eddie sat up a little more in his bed, blinked several times; then looked quizzically at Kathryn while the uneaten piece of toast dropped from his gaping mouth. "Say something Ed. What are you thinking?"

"You're kidding, right. That was a million to one shot." Kathryn began to tremble. Finally, she drew up close, put her hands on both of his cheeks, pushed his hair up and out of his eyes, and gave him a kiss. She stayed close eyeing every pore and every wrinkle of his battle worn face. A face that had seen fun, pain, joy, success, death, all of it; and he was her soul match since before they were born.

"I need to tell you something; something I should have done a long time ago. About six or seven months after Michael was born, Jared began to act strange. First of all, our relationship cooled not too long after we got married. As you are aware, it just wasn't a good fit. All of his family and friends were fanatics, almost militant churchgoers. If you didn't believe just like them, you were going to hell. No if, ands, or buts. Jared was just like his overbearing father and began to try to rule every step of my life. As you know, I was not only doing most of the A-hole's schoolwork, I was raising Michael, taking 18 hours at Stephen F. Austin, and working part time. Stubborn me, I was determined to make it work. Most of the time I turned over my paycheck to Jared." Eddie, with a puzzled expression, started to say something. Kathryn shut him off.

"Let me finish, Sugar. As I said, when Michael was about six or seven months old, Jared started getting paranoid. He already knew how I had felt about you and imagined that I might still be seeing you. He was always jealous, even though you were some 500 miles away and flying seven days a week in Florida or Alabama. He was such an idiot. There was just no way I could have gotten away long enough to go anywhere, much less out of his sight long enough to see you. Not even if you had been in Nacogdoches. Most of the time, I didn't even have access to a car or a telephone. His paranoia escalated almost by the day. At any rate, he was so sure I had been seeing you; he accused you of being Michael's father and ultimately slapped me so hard it left that scar on my left cheek you have always been curious about.

The rest you know about. I immediately left Nacogdoches and returned to Austin with Michael, then filed for the divorce giving me a huge feeling of relief. Thankfully, Jared's paranoia made him eager to get the divorce, too, which explains why he showed little interest in seeing little Michael since.

That's how it ended. When you and I made love that last night before I left you, I secretly hoped and prayed that I would get pregnant with your baby, especially having sex only a few days after my period. I wasn't optimistic about the wish coming true, but at least if it did, I would have part of you always. I wished it, but doubted it for all these years. It was the most selfish act that I have ever been proud about, if that makes sense.

Eddie, we just did a paternity test here at the hospital. Michael is your son, Eddie darling. He is your son and Annie is your granddaughter for real. Somehow, I think Jared knew. I don't know how, but I think he knew. To me, when we became one spirit that night in Austin, we were married. Jared was just a lousy affair."

Eddie felt numb but smiled broadly; he was speechless. Kathryn watched a tear roll down the side of his face while he squeezed her hand, holding it tight as if he was about to fall off a cliff. "Kathy, Honey, this is such good news." His voice trailed off and he had to clear his throat to continue. "No, it's *great* news. We should have done a paternity test a long time ago, but I guess we both would have been reluctant to do it, fearful that Jared was really the father. Who knows? Who cares? He is mine and Annie is mine too. How great is that?" Eddie then let some of what Kathryn said soak in. "Does Michael or Alicia know?" "I haven't told him yet, about the match or the paternity results. Alicia only knows you matched for the transplant. I will talk with them both as soon as I leave here." Eddie moved back into his pillow a little and looked at Kathryn. There was still some scar tissue clinging around inside of him, and he might as well talk about it.

"Kath, speaking about affairs, there is something that has been eating at me for some time. Do me a favor and look for my pocketbook and calendar inside my leather coat pocket hanging in the closet. There is an envelope in it that I wish you would get for me. Be careful of the dirt and grease, among other disgusting dirty debris." As she moved away from the small built-in closet, Kathryn was holding her nose and with one hand the other hand holding the mangled envelope by the very corner.

"Pew! You really need to burn that jacket." Eddie adjusted himself a bit to take the envelope. "I told you so. Thanks. I'm sorry to have to ask you this, but would you go back to the closet and see if my locket is in the zipper sleeve pocket." Kathryn shook her head from side to side, not relishing the second round of disgusting smells she would have to endure. She was in a bit longer than the errand demanded, and when she emerged she was wiping the tears from her cheeks with the back of her hand.

She had forgotten about the locket that Eddie always carried when he flew, even in the Mooney, and having it in her hand was like touching a miracle. She was unprepared for its powerful effect when she clutched it. Eddie took it and carefully opened it to see the picture of her, thinking that it might somehow have escaped. He closed it and smiled as Kathryn returned the smile. "Hon, if you would, open the envelope and read its contents, please. It is a copy of an email I found a few weeks ago. Would you read what it says?" Still puzzled, Kathryn carefully opened the envelope and unfolded the single paged note.

Dearest Kathryn,

I have missed you terribly, in ways that are indescribable. It has been only three weeks since we were together, but it seems like three years. I miss you so, and need you more than ever. Your companionship and special support has been my oxygen, and I thank God for you every night. I can picture your sweet smile, but I need the real you. You have framed the clarity of our roles in life and it has changed my life.

I wish you and I had met years earlier. My life would have been better, and I trust you feel the same. I know you know that. Let me know when you can get back to Southern California as soon as possible. Twelve months is almost up, and I need your support more than ever. I really need you close to me.

In a lifetime, one is lucky to meet that one person you can count on. One special person, selfless to a fault, on call for my every need. You are that person, Kathryn. You have saved my life. Please call as soon as you read this. I know you have been busy lately, but I will wait. You are always worth the wait.

Lovingly to the nth power,

Chris R.

"So you were prying in my email folder? I didn't think of you as a snoop.""No, I wasn't prying and I'm not a snoop. I opened your folder by mistake. I thought I was in the Keynotes folder, and clicked the Kathryn folder next to it by mistake." With very little expression, Kathryn furrowed her brow and just looked at Eddie. She calmly said, "What about it? What's all the drama?" Eddie scooted up a little further and drew back a bit. "Is that all you can say. What about it?"

"Yeah, what about it? It's a note from Christine Russell, the school administrator who has just retired from San Diego Unified and is fighting her way through the addiction of alcoholism and other junk you don't even want to know about. She is a sweet lady; even though she gets a little emotive more than most, she is a good person. You would like her, and I do need to call her."

"Huh? I thought it was that Christopher Riley guy with the State Accreditation Board from San Diego who you used to spend nearly every month with in meetings." "You gotta be kidding? I haven't heard from him in months and months. Anyway, he divorced and remarried a year ago. As to Christine, she has been going to Alcoholic's Anonymous, but is struggling with the twelve-step program that's a critical part of the recovery process. As a struggling Christian, she is hung up on steps three, five, six and eleven where God is involved. I'm trying to reach her by reminding her that all higher powers work through people, and that she could give credit however she wants. Stuff like that.

She is really stumbling over the steps that require making a list of people she has wronged and the making of amends to them all. Get this; her ex-husband killed himself from all of her drinking and carousing, and his family will not even speak to her. She can't even ask forgiveness from them. My being there for her when the urge to drink is stronger than her own willpower, has been my part time job, since her real sponsor relapsed and was killed while driving drunk on interstate eight on the way home from a Chargers' tailgate party. That's a huge burden for anybody, don't you think? As soon as she finds another sponsor, she will depend on me less and less, and then just be a good friend. You remember me telling you about that?" Sheepishly, "Oh yeah, I do."

"Eddie, her guilt is so deep, you of all people should understand all this from your own dad's problems. Her whole emotional system has been eviscerated for crying out loud." Then Kathryn locked in even more so, waiting for Eddie's eyes to settle on hers.

"Honey, she has been leaning heavily on me for the past few months since all of these recent disastrous problems. That grief of her ex jumping off the Coronado Bridge, her sponsor's death, and the yearlong recovery process has been stressful for Chris. It's been really hard. You do remember that recovering alcoholics claim a very high percentage of suicides, especially when urged by circumstances like divorce, loss of a business and the like. All of this has been a real mess and more than really sad. Edward William Parker, I have been trying to be as good a friend and temporary sponsor to her as you would in the same situation. Both of us are qualified, you know, Eddie. Remember when your dad went through this just before he died? Anything else on your mind?"

Eddie Parker knew he was in trouble. Feeling about three feet tall, Eddie sighed. He thought back, as his dad the salesman of salesmen, and his inability to overcome the scotch and water sugar teat that nourished his confidence all those years. He tried to quit. He pooh poohed the Alcohol Anonymous program as he and Kathryn studied its design and tried to customize its principles of co-founder Bill Wilson, for Mr. Parker. Still no luck, and finally, the booze had its final hurrah, as he died in late 1988, a shriveled reminder of alcohol's hideous power.

"Can you forgive an old fart, and give him another chance? Sitting on that cold mountainside in the Mooney flushed out a lot of memories, Honey, with you and the kids always at the head of the class of the good ones. What do you say? Throw that silly note in the trash and let's start over. I have a real son now, and I'll do whatever it takes to be a real husband; be the man you married."

"Okay, Cowboy, but you are going to have to pay a lot more attention to this old girl. What do you think?" "Ha, just watch me. Cross my heart and hope to die. By the way, call Christine as soon as you can." The 'makeup' kiss was one for the ages; another promise, that one. Aye yai yai.

"Okay, then," rearranging her hair. Kathryn caught Alicia as she was turning the corner to come into the room. "Give Eddie a quick hug, and let's go back to Michael's room. I have something to tell you both, then I have to go across the street to Children's Hospital."

Chapter Seventeen

*"The best love affair is one which
is conducted entirely
by post."*
*~ ~ George Bernard
Shaw*

Friday, December 4th

Twelve long days later, at six in the morning, Eddie and Michael lay side by side at St. Joseph's hospital for the always-tricky transplant. Both were shivering, earning them both heated blankets. The nurses were fussing over the men, treating them like celebrities. There are no secrets in hospitals, so the entire staff of doctors, nurses, and even those noisy custodians, were emotionally immersed in the Parker love saga. The snickering smiles, giggles, and thumbs ups flooded throughout the transplant ward. Their story was better than *As the World Turns, All My Children, Days of our Lives* and *General Hospital* all rolled into one.

"This won't take long Michael. We will be back in a jiffy with a slightly used but long lasting kidney," assured the nephrologist Dr. Sigala, who was handling both operations. Eddie was wheeled into the OR and soon began drifting off to sleep with his last sounds being the periodic beeping of monitors and hissing of oxygen equipment.

Surrounded by his team, Dr. Sigala made two tiny incisions in the left side of Eddie's abdomen. The doctor carefully grasped, cut, cauterized, and guided by a tiny endoscopic camera in a third incision, snipped the ureter tube, clamping it and the artery that feeds blood to the kidney in Eddie's abdomen. In less than an hour, the left kidney was removed and lowered into the endocatch bag by the procurement specialist. Michael's new kidney was flushed with an icy preservative solution, and taken to the Operating Room next door where Michael had been prepped for his surgery. More clamping and cauterizing would follow for Eddie, but the major work had been accomplished without a hitch. Eddie was parked in the surgical recovery room set up for the two patients.

7:07 A.M. The prep team began its surgical preparation for Michael. The anesthesia team was ready to ease him into a Propofol universe of a no pain or memory. When instructed, Michael was told to count to ten, but did no better than four. Dr. Sigala, after dictating the details of Eddie's surgery, and swallowing a quick cup of coffee, emerged with fresh sterile hands, new rubber gloves, and began his magic show once again. After opening Michael's abdomen, Dr. Sigala quickly removed Michael's useless right kidney, tying off veins, the main artery, and his ureter tube. After cleansing and prepping the area, Eddie's warmed left kidney was lowered into Michael's right side. The right side was preferred because the blood vessels in the right side were more horizontal and easier to connect The renal artery of Eddie's kidney, branching from the abdominal aorta, was connected to the external iliac artery in Michael. The renal vein of Eddie's kidney, previously draining to his inferior vena cava, was connected to Michael's external iliac vein. Dr. Sigala stepped back and watched. In mere seconds, the kidney pinked up, gaining verbal approval and applause from the whole surgical team, including Dr. Sigala. "I never get tired of watching this miracle, I just love it." With smiles hidden behind their masks, the whole team nodded in agreement. The surgical procedure took less than two hours. Another half hour or so was spent stitching and closing the tiny incisions. Michael and Eddie were both wheeled into the same recovery room, side by side.

In the recovery room, Eddie woke first, then an hour later, Michael roused. They both murmured and groaned for a while, napped, and woke once more about an hour later. Michael turned his head slowly to his father and just looked at him. When Eddie turned his way, with a smile as big as a recovering surgical patient could muster, Michael whispered, "Hey Dad. Ready for a little fishing?"

"I'll consider it if you will trade that silly looking blue hair net you are wearing for an Angels cap." They both laughed as best they could, considering the surgery.

"By the way, thanks. As much as your kidney means, it's your heart that that means the most to me. I love you more than I can say and always have. You know that, but I just wanted you to hear it. Also, just knowing you are my real dad, and have been forever, that's just the best."

"Me too," Eddie blubbered. He managed an emotional commitment that he would let Michael never doubt it, no matter what. Kathryn from her listening post in her little plastic chair was weeping like a newly elected high school Homecoming Queen. Her men were going to be okay, and they would reconnect like they did at Lake Norman. Even better. Alicia bent over and gave dopey Eddie a kiss on the cheek and asserted firmly that he was the best darn father-in-law in the whole wide world. For real.

News cameras were filming through the glass in the hall so that the viewing audience could cry as well. The local TV news stations as well as the Orange County Register, Los Angeles Times, and Riverside Press Enterprise were all over the place. CNN, the national networks and even BBC had reporters and cameramen all over the hospital, as much as the staff would permit. The Parker's were famous now. The feel good story of Eddie's rescue and donation of his kidney to his stepson was a relatable story felt by every family with a special needs' child, a marriage that needed mending, or knowing someone on the waiting list with the National Kidney Foundation. The Kidney Banks around the country became swamped by calls from citizens wanting to test as potential kidney donors. The good news story was needed after the day-to-day blow of the Gulf War the year before.

At an opportune time only a few hours later, Kathryn and Alicia went back to the chapel to thank Sister Ann Elizabeth for her prayer and support. They found her just wrapping up her afternoon devotional. Knowing of the good recoveries, the three hurried to each other's outstretched arms. "Sister, Alicia and I just had to see you before we get out of here, and thank you again for your strength and prayers."

Alicia weighed in, "And we especially appreciated your Bible verses. The messages of Exodus 15:26 and Deuteronomy 7:15 were just what we needed. They were perfect reminders of who the Real Healer is. And guess what? Dad, I mean Mr. Parker, wants to go back to church again. Isn't that great? Perfect proof that God does answer prayers." The sister was humbled and reaffirmed of her often-unappreciated mission at the hospital.

"You are thoughtful to come, and I have thanked the Generous Father for all your good fortune, especially with the kidney transplant. Most people who pray for a kidney have to learn patience and understanding. God is mysterious, so we don't question what we don't understand or how He does answer our prayers. He always does and we are always thankful that He is present all day, every day. If you ever get discouraged again read Second Peter Chapter Two, verses 1:4 of God's promise."

After another round of hugs, Kathryn concluded the warm meeting. "Sister, for just the very short time we have known you, we both agree that you have had more impact on our lives than anyone we know. We will never forget you. We need to run now, Sister. We have to scoot up to Doctor Hindman's office right quick, for he is nearly as wise and special as you. He deserves a very special hug." They hurried around the doorway, and adjusted their mascara before scampering up the ever-familiar stairs. The elevators were just too sluggish for these two energetic and bone-happy women.

10 A.M. December 17th The search and rescue helicopter's landing skid bobbed around lightly, then settled on the heliport deck at Children's Hospital in Orange. The pilot told his crew, "Okay men, this will be one trip to this hospital that we will all remember. Let's go." As the main rotor blade slowly decelerated, the pilot and two crewmembers exited the aircraft. They had changed from their flight suits into more formal attire.

After a few steps, Commander Shadrach 'Shade' Pearson, the Commanding Officer of Miramar Naval Station in San Diego, fondly nicknamed Fighter Town USA, greeted them. He was the nephew of Admiral Elmo Pearson who served as Commander of the Pacific Fleet during the Vietnam War. Another figure exited from the back of the helicopter, a white haired civilian unknown to Kathryn, his eyes hidden by the popular military pilot's sunglasses. They all held their hats down to keep them from being blown away by the slowing rotor blades.

Kathryn met the contingent, along with the Navy photographers and two reporters from the Orange County Register. "Thank you all for coming. You guys are so wonderful. Eddie will be so surprised, and thank you Commander Pearson for putting this together. Let's go on in, shall we?" The helicopter crew fell in step with the Commander as they headed for the room of her husband and son. Kathryn moved to the white haired gentleman, and held out her hand. "I didn't catch your name, Sir?" "Just call me Dick. Dick will be fine." He gave a grin that was warm and disarming. She nodded, recalling a faint familiarity in the voice. Yet... for now she needed to catch up with the others. She had them ushered into his room.

As soon as they all entered the room, Eddie scooted up in his bed to see who these men might be. "Excuse me fellas, I think you have the wrong room." Then Gabriel Hallen spoke. "Remember us?" In the other bed, Michael concealed a knowing smile and sat up a little higher.

"Can't recall guys....Wait... The Voice. Gabby? That you Gabby? Gabby from the helicopter?" "The same, Mr. Parker."

"Sweet Jesus. Come closer. Now I can see what you look like." After a mutual energetic handshake, Gabby then introduced Captain Richard Duncan and Harry Garcia and their important roles from that highly publicized night only a few weeks ago. Eddie just remembered getting that morphine shot and that was it for any memory of the rescue. He wanted to hear every detail. Duncan promised to send a copy of the detailed report he filed after they debriefed early that morning before his shift ended at sunrise. Then there was that video from Harry. The one he shot that night and one that Mrs. Parker received to surprise Eddie and the family with later.

When Kathryn introduced Commander Pearson, Eddie didn't know if he was to salute or kneel, neither of which he was in shape to do. "Wow, Commander. It's a privilege to meet you. Are you related to Admiral 'Shade' Pearson? I met him at a summary briefing in Da Nang during the war." "Guilty, as charged Mr. Parker, he is my father. When we were arranging this little surprise I spoke to him about it. He told me of stories from our ground forces, especially the forward air-strike controllers that filtered to the fleet, as some of your bombs saved a significant number of our ground pounders." Then the Commander stepped aside to let the Sheriff deputies tell of the details of that night as he quietly slipped over to Michael's bed and shook his hand, noting a subtle similarity of his smile with Eddie's, then moved aside for a while. Everyone in the room was anxious to get a minute with Eddie, and he knew they would have time together again in San Diego, as soldiers have a tendency to do.

The crew each went over details of finding him, Gabby's descent to the mountainside, getting his leg untangled, and their decision to honor his wishes to be flown to CHOC, even after being woozy with the morphine shot. After a careful embrace, Eddie got a little emotional.

"You guys are so darn nice to come by. I really appreciate it." His voice weakened a bit. "I was in quite a mess that night, so I probably didn't even say thanks. Now I can, but it's still not enough."

The pilot, Dick Duncan finally spoke. "If all goes well Mr. Parker, and if Mrs. Parker approves, we plan to write a book, a first person account about the rescue. We can speak to so many fronts and with our ghostwriter's help; it should be a best seller. He turned to Kathryn. It'll give the department a chance to toot its horn and remind the public of the sacrifice your husband and many like him gave in Vietnam. Most of the sales will benefit a new trust fund we are building that will support widows of fallen Sheriff Deputies, and California widows of fallen soldiers from the Iraqi War. If you like the book, you would honor us by signing our copies. It will be a treasure for all our families and our kids' families." Duncan pushed Harry a little forward, so he could speak.

"Mrs. Parker, we were just doing our job. After we learned who your husband was, we took special pride in that night. Any small gesture on our part, like this book, would just boost our pride and hopefully spotlight your husband's and his aviator comrades' military legacy." Kathryn just smiled. "I don't quite know what to say, but we will do whatever it takes to advance those causes." Eddie blurted, "Harry, what was the shape of the Mooney?"

"You don't want to know, Mr. Parker. I

think Gabby might have salvaged a condor feather if you are interested." Eddie's 'yuk' got a huge laugh from everyone in the room. Then Harry turned down a trade of the feather for Eddie's nasty leather jacket. Another round of laughs from the family who threatened to have the jacket burned.

Just as they had all had made their personal talk with Eddie, the white haired man emerged from the shadows in the back of the room. He looked to be in his late seventies, but still erect and fit with a waist decidedly smaller than his chest. He moved slowly to Eddie's bed as the others slowly gave way. "Hello old timer. What's all the fuss about, Pops?" Eddie scooted up in his bed and squinted as if he were seeing a ghost.

"Skipper? Captain Huddleston?" In an instant the men embraced and both shook a bit, sniffling, then at arms length. "Man you look great. Really great. How,..where..I mean..oh darn, I can't think right now. It is so great, so very great to see you. There is so much to talk about." And they did, at least they began.

"I know Eddie, I know. I'll hang around a while and we can get caught up." The two warriors with smiles as wide as a piano, talked in muffled tones, interrupted by either bowed silence or gentle laughter. The others in the room treated the two in total reverence as whispers roamed the room between those who knew the connection and the few who did not. They embraced again and agreed to keep in touch, as souls of war often like to do; need to do. Only those who suffered the daily fear of death and the struggle to keep each other alive could understand their bond.

After a little more small talk, they all left, with Dick Huddleson trailing behind. Kathryn escorted them into the hospital corridor as they vowed to keep in touch while she thanked them again for the meeting. She told Captain Duncan that the family would discuss the book proposal, and assured them it probably would be approved. She even knew of two renowned ghostwriters that might have an interest. She also volunteered to Admiral Pearson that when Eddie was truly mended, and after a little R&R somewhere private, he would be honored to speak to the new Top Gun class at Miramar. She mentioned that the past few weeks after his rescue had been such a catharsis; that a month ago, he didn't have any interest in anything that reminded him of Vietnam. He appeared now, to be the whole man she married.

As the chopper began to board its passengers, Kathryn hugged Dick Huddleson, and cried. She didn't intend to, it just happened. She was back in Hawaii with her shot up husband, learning of René's death, and the beginning of those awful nightmares.

She knew it was all in the past, but the memory was refreshed by his presence.

"Thank you for coming, Admiral." "Just Dick or Richard, Mrs. Parker." "Okay, well, your coming meant a lot to Eddie, ...and to me. I am not sure how you heard about this little get-together, but Eddie was as touched as I was. We never really met, although, I remember as if it were yesterday, your kind voice from the *America* telling me about Eddie's wounds, and your reassurance not to worry was extra kind. I will never forget it, and never forget your coming today. Thanks ever so much. I wish you didn't have to rush off."

"Naval aviation is a small community, so as soon as I heard, I had to get here. After your men are healed, we can get together in Santa Cruz, maybe this next summer. I have a small fishing guide service that your men will enjoy and a quaint but warm house on the beach for the gals to relax in and remember the good times. Bye for now." He gave her a soft squeeze on the elbow and slipped into the chopper as it lifted, slipped on its side, and whomped into the sky with Kathryn's hair and tears mingled on her cheek. She waved and turned back to the others. At the end of the day, it was a good day. Eddie was restored and he would not be going anywhere but home. Not to war, not to a sales meeting, but home with her. Just home. Just with her.

During Eddie's medical evaluation for the kidney donation, his medical records were reviewed thoroughly. The attending psychiatrist group interviewed all of the family, Eddie's nurses, friends, as well as Eddie. After a thorough evaluation, the shrinks concluded that Eddie had a not too rare onset of Delayed Post Trauma Syndrome Disorder from his Vietnam experience that caused his recent grumpiness and remoteness. They also concluded that the events of the crash and kidney donation had such a profound positive effect on Eddie, that it would preclude any of the usual therapy or counseling. The Mooney incident purged Eddie of more demons than a year's therapy sessions could. They went over this in detail with Kathryn and Eddie. They were both relieved that Eddie wasn't losing his mind, and as Alicia suggested, was not having mid life crisis problems. A few days later, Eddie shared with Kathryn how Aimee's visit had affected him.

Just before Michael and Eddie were discharged from the hospital, Kathryn was in a chair nearby reading Eddie's discharge papers and doctor's orders regarding his follow up appointment and the do's and don'ts of post op behavior. The phone rang, and although Kathryn had hoped to intercept the call, Eddie beat her to the phone.

"Hello? Yes, this is he. Yes she is. Just a moment." "Hello, Mrs. Parker." "Yes, who is calling?" She listened for a minute and asked if she could call back a bit later. "Who was that, Babe?" "Just the insurance adjuster about the Mooney. I told him I would call him back." "Oh well, all the better. You talk to them. The plane is gone and that's that." Done talking, Eddie turned towards the wall and feigned falling asleep. Kathryn was the wiser, marching out of the room to make that call. She knew how to fix her man.

After being discharged from St. Josephs and convalescing at Scarlet's and Alex's, Eddie returned to Sacramento to begin the regimen of permanent healing. Only a few months later the following spring, Aimee Lefevre and her bunch piled into Orange County for a couple of days to catch up. Kathryn and Eddie flew commercial the prior day to meet up with them all. The Lefevre boys teamed up with Scarlett and Michael for a day at the beach. Eddie learned that Aimee's oldest, René Thibadeau Lefevre Jr., graduated from the Naval Academy in Annapolis. He was extremely bright and the youngest to graduate in thirty years. He had returned from duty in Iraq only a year ago, having served aboard the USS *Saratoga*, a ship only too familiar to Eddie. There, attached to the Sundowners, Squadron VFA-81, René in his F/A-18 Hornet Strike Fighter, shot down two Iraqi MiG-21s with a sidewinder missile, two of three enemy airplanes shot down in the whole Desert Storm conflict. With Aimee's approval, Eddie made that emotional, if not articulate, expression of gratitude to René Jr. for his marrow donation to Josh. René told Eddie that when a fellow *Tail Hook* member called about Josh's needs, and especially since he was the grandson of Eddie Parker, it became a high privilege. He couldn't move fast enough, and was even more ecstatic when he learned that he was a match. He went on to relate the race of many that wanted to be tested, and that another Navy Pilot actually did match, but René would have fought to the death for the honor. The Parker family couldn't believe René Jr. was in the hospital donating the marrow the very morning they were rushing around the two hospitals catching up with all three Parker men. He reminded Eddie that not many Distinguished Flying Crosses were passed out on the U.S.S. *America* during the Vietnam War. He went on to tell Eddie that his father's DFC and his own that he earned in Iraq hung side by side in his mother's home.

When he was old enough to understand, Aimee shared with René the friendship between his father and Mr. Parker. As he grew older and more curious, he became more and more impressed. He told

Eddie that it was his and his father's reputation that compelled him to apply for admission to the Naval Academy. Eddie could hardly believe that his escapades in the F-4 Phantom had become legendary. After his detailed debriefing of his landing of the damaged F-4, the skills and techniques he used filtered into part of the Navy Attack and Fighter jets training manual, called *Emergency Damaged Aircraft Control Protocol.*

With the visit being so short, Eddie and René Jr. managed to swap a few war stories only they could understand and appreciate. They could be seen gesturing with their hands as airplanes, the various moves and positions they must have remembered in their successful encounters. What a movie they could make. Aimee swelled with immense pride and could not believe how two families fit together so well. Eddie wanted more time with Aimee's husband, Jean, to learn about the charms of Paris and especially to pick his financial brain for smart investment choices.

Eddie became pen pals with René Jr. as he took pride in his adopted 'nephew', as René's rank went from Lieutenant Commander to Commander, and was a shoo in for at least Captain, more likely Admiral. Eddie couldn't help but think of how proud his late and dear friend René Senior would be of his son.

From the infusion of stem cells from

René's bone marrow, little Joshua's recovery was speedy and true; he was sure to grow tall and strong as Texas okra in August. The Parkers were finally whole, one and all!

Epilogue

July 1993

That next summer when Eddie had pretty much healed, he and Kathryn eloped to Barbados for a second honeymoon. They settled in at the familiar Sandpiper Inn, in Holetown, of St. James Parrish, enjoying unit number twenty-two right on the gentlest of Caribbean beaches. It was the same number of the hotel room at the Beachcomber in Corpus Christi where they first honeymooned. They walked two short blocks north to renew their vows at the St. James Anglican Church, the same church that ten years earlier had welcomed then President Reagan as he visited an old movie friend, Claudette Colbert. The owner of the local cab company and friend over the years, Mackie Thomas, who was a part time minister, did the honors. The Barbadian's smile that sparkled like porcelain veneers made a sharp contrast to his ebony skin, as he smiled the width of the Jolly Roger party boat when it was over.

After the exchange of vows, they took off their shoes and waded back down the beach a hundred yards or so to the Surfside Bar for a hamburger and bowl of pigeon peas. As they waded, they held hands as if they were dating and giggled for the first time in 20 years. After strolling back to the room, they popped a bottle of Brut champagne, courtesy of their friend and magical impresario of hospitality, manager Russell Croney, to toast the revitalized honeymoon.

Propped up on the inviting bed chamber, Eddie pulled Kathryn close and whispered, "Kathryn Whitmore, I love you, and I've loved you from the instant you bumped into me in 1961." She bounced on her knees a little closer. "And I really loved you the instant you served me that banana split at the A&W root beer drive-in. But Eddie, I love you mostly because I gave you the perfect right not to love me, but you loved me even more and embraced your son Michael all those years you didn't know he *was* your son. I will never forget you for that, Eddie William Parker. And by the way, you bumped into me at that Phi Tau mixer, you clod." As they snuggled more and more, stirring their senses with the tropical air and its heavenly orchid scents while anticipating a measured tumble in the sack, Kathryn asked Eddie. "When you were in the hospital last November, you vowed to take the time to learn more about me and to pay closer attention to me. I'm asking if you think you have done a good job with that promise?"

"Not only that one, and for both of us, every promise has been honored, as far as I can tell. Kathryn, sweetheart, between the two of us, I don't recall either of us ever violating our vows. When we dated you agreed to love me forever. Just before we were married in that little Kingsville Naval Chapel, you agreed to be faithful to me until the end. You have been aces on those and other vows not nearly so profound. Before I shoved off to Vietnam, I agreed to come back in one piece. I also promised, as you did, that I would never be unfaithful. I fulfilled both without fail. The Vietnam promise was hard, the other easy. Never tempted. I think some of the guys on the ship thought I was gay. Ha! So why do you ask?"

"Here's the deal, Big Boy. I will give you a test, and if you pass it, I will make this a night like you never could imagine. It will be so hot it will melt the wax in your ears."

"Hubba hubba, Baby, I'm your man, as 'Little Eddie' began to take notice. It didn't go unobserved by Kathryn, as she flipped her hair and Eddie her gave that 'gotcha smile.' "Go, ahead, give me a try. What's on your clever little mind?"

"Okay. Hush, and close your eyes real tight. No peeking. Now, after we returned from the beach and took our showers, I painted my toenails. It's only been a few minutes, but plenty of time to notice so tell me what color they are." Eddie paused way longer than he needed, leaving the impression that he didn't have a clue. "No, peeking."

"How could I? Besides, you have your

house shoes on. Then he leaned in real close, and after a long pause loudly whispered, "Passion Pink." "You rat. You guessed!"

"Nope. I just noticed the nail polish bottle on the bathroom counter." Kathryn, a little shocked, laughed out loud, and true to her promise, in the glow of the bedroom lit by seven candles, their lucky number, they snuggled up nice and close. As the veteran newlyweds undressed and lay on their scrumptiously soft bed, their bedroom mirror revealed a sun settling into the Caribbean Ocean for the night.

The room was flush with fresh thrusting anthuriums and smiling Hibiscus blossoms, floating lazily in water cradled in clear glass flasks shaped like fish bowls. At the instant the sun sizzled into the far away Caribbean waters, their lovemaking was instantly serenaded by the faithful chirping of the tree frogs. The tiny peepers signaled approval of this night of nights that would lead to days and days of shameless love between a banged up fabric salesman and an enchantingly beautiful woman on a world realigned to its authentic axis. Disney's Magic Mountain ride was tame compared to the one in room 22 at the Sandpiper Inn in St. James, Barbados, of the British West Indies in the crystal blue Caribbean Ocean that night in the summer of 1993.

"Jesus, Eddie, you make me feel so

naughty, and I love you for it." "You are nuts Kathryn Parker, it is you who makes me naughty. Here, let me show you...again." Kathryn rose up a little and said, "Oh phooey, I almost forgot." "What? Forgot what?" "It's a little surprise. Eddie sat up and became curious. They both put on their white terrycloth robes for the 'surprise.'

"What kind?" With a suggestive silly look, "another tumble in the hay." "Not that you old pervert." "Me? What about you? And I am not old!"

"Oh shush. Let me talk to you a minute." "Shoot, baby." "Edward, do you remember that phone call I got in the hospital just before you were discharged?" Eddie nodded. "Vaguely. It was the insurance guy, right?"

"Nope, it was the head honcho at Mooney in Kerrville. Now bear with me a minute Eddie." "I'll be bare with you anytime, anywhere."

"Eddie, you are just incorrigible. Now where was I?" I am kinda new at this 'surprise' stuff." She opened her nightstand and pulled out a large brown envelope and slipped out its contents. She pushed it to her puzzled husband. "Take a look at this brochure." It was the sales kit for a 1991 Mooney Bravo. The freshly shaven Eddie Parker took the heavy slick colorful brochure and held it like a holy relic. He read every page, outlining the new Bravo, a 270 horsepower dart designed to travel at cruising speeds of 250 miles an hour, significantly faster than the Mooney that Eddie plowed into the mountainside not that long ago. It could travel over 1600 miles before refueling and could make it coast to coast in 12 hours with one fuel stop. It was pressurized, quiet, and could travel in airliner traffic at 25,000 feet. He marveled at the engineering and technical details that made it the envy of every private pilot.

"Honey, look. It has a color weather radar display with storm tracking, top of the line moving map GPS navigation, back up alternator and fuel pumps. Wow, this sucker has everything." Eddie went back to his reverent reading. As his moistened eyes grew wide with wonder, Kathryn began to sob. Eddie reached out and put his hand on her shoulder. "Oh, Honey, what is the matter? Did I say anything? I hope I didn't hurt you. Today has been so perfect."

"No, dearest, I'm just happy. A foolish woman deeply in love." With a peck on the cheek, and a smile, he went back to the booklet. Kathryn knew she had done the right thing.

"Thanks for the brochure, Kath, it's fun to look back and dream. I knew Mooney was making real strides, but had no idea they were making such an upscale airplane, pressurized and everything."

"Look at the photo tucked in the back cover." Eddie found the glossy photograph of his old plane, Two Zero One Tango, restored completely, and parked next to it, a new M model Mooney Bravo, painted metallic military gray, with the top of the tail painted with three inch wide red, white, and blue stripes. In the center, a picture of a full moon, from a NASA photo made into a decal. There was writing underneath in Latin that read, *Lux Lucis of Vita*, or The Light of Life. Captain Duncan had told them both that his good fortune was due to the bright full moon that enabled the crew to spot his wreckage.

"Wow, that looks amazing. What's going on here, Kiddo. This brochure and a picture of my old plane, all like new now, next to a new Bravo. I don't get it."

"Lean back and let me get my notes." The bottomless Louie Vuitton had wisely been replaced with a simple straw clutch that had two small flashlights in the inside zippered pocket. She pulled out some notes she had scribbled, knowing the details would be important when the time came to share with Eddie. "As I said before, I'm not much of an airplane nut, until now, I think. Anyway, I talked to a Mr. Stringer at Mooney. He is the one who called at the hospital, and almost screwed up the surprise. He told me that after the insurance company sent us our check for the crashed airplane that the insurance people called him and when they offered to sell the wreckage to them, they were glad to buy it. Mooney probably got the airplane on the cheap is my guess. Your story was so compelling and popular, Mooney wanted to rebuild it and use it in their advertising, with our permission, of course. That was the reason for his call; to get our okay.

I thought about it and called him back. I told him we would okay the advertising, with one condition. That they either sell us your old airplane after it is refurbished at the same price they paid the insurance company, or to sell you the new customized Bravo at their cost and finance it to you at no interest for five years, then at the market price for bank cost interest rates, not to exceed five percent. Even though prime is nine and a half percent, he agreed to it and did one better. If you choose the new Bravo, they will discount the airplane by fifty percent from their cost of labor and materials.

The exposure of the Mooney brand, and the story of the signature steel tube canopy that saved your life, was so widespread; he confessed that new orders for the most expensive and profitable Bravo should keep them busy for a couple years and in the black for years to come. You can pick one, Eddie. Which is it? Either way, the insurance proceeds will almost pay for the new one, and for sure the restored one, whichever you choose." Now it was Eddie's turn to get emotional.

"Kathryn, no one's done anything like this for me. I am speechless and deeply humbled. I was just a pretend jock that did what needed to be done, and just happened to be good at my job. If I had to choose, it would be that new one, but . . ."

Kathryn, cut him off at the pass. "Eddie, over the years you have been the giver. You gave me a second chance, Michael a father, both kids a car and paid for their insurance when they didn't even know what insurance was. The wedding you gave Scarlett and Alex was so classy, it was talked about for ages in the Orange County Register's society section, getting more ink than Bob Hope when he dedicated the new wing of the Orange County Center for the Performing Arts. You gave up a perfectly good girlfriend for your best friend René, and gave my unpretentious parents a sincere respect they didn't even give themselves. In North Carolina when you dragged in from the road every week, you gave your factory a briefcase full of orders and us a comfortable home.

"You gave Scarlett's golden find in ancient Greece, a man without parents, self-respect, and love no one else would have given. To this old girl, your biggest gift was the one you made to me on the altar years ago, when you promised to be true to me in good times and in bad, in sickness and health all the days of your life.

"And finally, you gave your country five years of military service, and wouldn't even accept the Navy Cross because of a 'lucky shot'. By the way it's still being awarded, and like it or not, there will be a small ceremony at Miramar when we get back, with just family and a couple of newspaper reporters. When Captain Huddleson was at the little get-together at the hospital, he confessed, telling me he regretted not forcing the medal. They don't just give those away without reason, Sweetie. The Navy only gave just over a hundred during Vietnam, and many were Hospital Corpsmen and Chopper Rescue Pilots.

"He said your gun cameras confirmed the incident all right, one confirmed kill and another probable that was seen flaming straight down through the clouds. Also, there was a witness, an F-8 from the Kitty Hawk. You were jumped by a group of four MiG-21s. They had altitude and speed and came out of the sun. Somehow you still managed to shoot one down, probably another and you watched the other two scram out of there. Lucky shot my fanny. This at a time when you said you were emotionally gutted and had lost your zip. I say 'bull sugar' When you were in that Phantom, you were one with the machine and unbeatable, no matter what you say.

It's your time, Eddie. I want you to have it. The kids are all excited, especially Michael." Eddie sniffed. "Anyway, enough about your new airplane, except they will put *me* a cassette player into your intercom system so I can listen to music while you 'chat' with your buddies on the radio. I also made sure the airplane will have two safety items so we don't have a repeat of what happened last November, a rechargeable battery powered handheld VHF transceiver, built especially for you, and an Emergency Transponder positioned near the pilot's armrest within your reach."

Eddie kept staring at the photos, just sitting there; eyes glazed. "Honey, I realized that as unselfish as you promised not to fly anymore, I realized that flying is part of your fiber. I couldn't let that passion wither. I couldn't let you wither. Never. I have also come to the conclusion that the strength of our children, forged strong by your own example, is responsible for your physical and spiritual healing and has been the fulfillment of a promise from your children and their spouses, to never give up. A promise that holds us all together. All your promises to them were believed, not for just their hope of a promise that might come true, but because *you* gave them that promise."

Kathryn's flushed husband was very

still now. He just looked at Kathryn, gave her that boyish smile she enjoyed so much when they first fell in love, shook his head and scratched the top his ear. "Ya know Kathryn, if the poets had only first come to you, it would have saved them a lot of time and poetry would have enjoyed a much higher following." They both just smiled, then fell into an embrace and deep slumber, with the expectation of a warm sun, cool sand, and a future that had more wonder than the Parker's could ever imagine. The promises of their two souls were aligned flawlessly, and would be so forever.